PROLOGUE

In the silence of the snowstorm, the agonised scream jangled every last nerve in Fiona's body.

She twisted round to look over her shoulder. With the wind at her back and leading the group, it was the only direction the scream could have come from. She saw two red shapes behind her. The closest would be her friend, Donna, and next to Donna would be one of the other hikers who'd joined them for the descent.

The hike up to the knot of gathered people was a slog in these conditions, but Fiona gritted her teeth and followed Donna and the other red-jacketed hiker back uphill, to where they discovered the others:

Five where there should be six.

ONE

The view in front of Fiona MacLeish was more than worth the burning calves and chilly ears. Beinn Bhuidhe, one of Scotland's two hundred and eighty-two Munros. Situated at the head of Loch Fyne, on the western side, it topped out at just over three thousand one hundred feet. To reach Munro status a mountain has to be at least three thousand feet high, and while Beinn Bhuidhe wasn't the tallest, it was regarded by those who knew about such things to be a tough climb thanks to long flat approaches and untracked areas, where hikers could easily get lost in misty conditions. Fiona had climbed seventeen other Munros, and Beinn Bhuidhe would be the eighteenth she'd 'bag'.

From here, Fiona could see Loch Fyne and the Argyll highlands to the south-west, and looking north were the southern fringes of the Scottish Highlands, while to the east was Loch Lomond and the Trossachs.

It had been a slog to get here. Fiona had left her Lochgilphead home at six after defrosting her car. When dawn broke around quarter to eight, Fiona and her companions, Donna and Jack, were already trekking towards Beinn Bhuidhe's lower

THE
SHELTER

BOOKS BY G.N. SMITH

FIONA MACLEISH CRIME THRILLER SERIES

The Flood

The Island

THE
SHELTER

G.N. SMITH

bookouture

Published by Bookouture in 2023

An imprint of Storyfire Ltd.
Carmelite House
50 Victoria Embankment
London EC4Y 0DZ

www.bookouture.com

ISBN: 978-1-80314-906-6
eBook ISBN: 978-1-80314-905-9

For my son, no longer a boy, he's now a fine young man who makes his Old Man proud every day.

slopes, their way illuminated by head torches. At this time of year it was always better to get an early start and do the first leg in darkness, so there was time to bag the Munro and descend before darkness returned.

Donna and Jack had been childhood sweethearts who'd married young and grown together. They still held hands all the time and their complete devotion to each other was lighthouse obvious.

Along with Whitney and Olivia, Donna had been one of Fiona's closest school friends. Time and the vagaries of adulthood had pulled the four of them in different directions, but Fiona and Donna would always make the effort to meet up once or twice a year. Of her three friends, it had been Donna who'd had the courage to stand by Fiona through the darkest days of her life. Whitney and Olivia had shown face in those first terrible weeks, but it had been Donna who'd stuck by Fiona month after month. Donna's and Fiona's childhood homes had been at opposite ends of the same street in Gretna Green and she'd never known a time when Donna wasn't her friend.

'Look at that.' Jack's arm extended west to the clouds that were scudding over the hills. 'I think we'd best be getting back. I don't like the look of those clouds.'

Donna reached up and gave her husband a playful shove in the chest that barely moved him. 'Wheesht, man. You're always worrying about the day you'll never see.'

'He's got a point, Donna. The forecast said there's snow due tomorrow, but it looks like it could come early.'

'Coming too soon. Just what every woman doesn't want.' The comment was typical of Donna. Whatever the topic, she'd always find a way to make a smutty joke about it.

'You're terrible.' Fiona couldn't keep the smile from her face or tone.

'Oh yeah, I'm terrible, am I? Remind me, Fiona, who was it

bent my ear on the phone for an hour and a half about some Half Minute Harry she had the misfortune to date?'

'Donna!' Fiona turned to hide her burning cheeks from Jack. Donna was a good friend in all the ways that counted, but she had no sense of embarrassment for herself or others.

'Come on. Let's get going.' Jack's arm was still pointing west, and Fiona could see the clouds were coming their way at pace.

The hike back down would take only a third of the time it had taken to bag this Munro, but if those clouds closed in and wreathed Beinn Bhuidhe in mist, or the first of the snows started to fall, the return trip would be a miserable experience.

Another group of baggers was leaving the summit as Jack led the way to the track that snaked its way down the upper slopes like an alpine road. As was the custom, brief pleasantries were exchanged as the two groups set off downhill together.

There were six people in the other group and, as was his way, Jack struck up a conversation with them. No matter the company or occasion, Jack could always find someone to talk to, so Fiona led the way with Donna at her side and the others all following.

Fiona could overhear snippets of the conversation behind her.

'Is that how you all know each other, the hotel?'

'Aye. We all work there, although Neil moved on a few years ago.'

'I've seen the signs for it. We'll have to come for some scran there next time we're up.'

Despite the exertion and enough layers to repel the early December cold, Fiona could feel the temperature dipping as the clouds hid the sunlight that had warmed them all day. The wind was picking up too, and Fiona pulled her woolly hat down tight, making sure the lobes of her ears were covered.

As the person leading, Fiona set a brisk pace, although she

had to temper speed with caution when travelling down some of the steeper parts. Beside her Donna was doing her best to keep up as breaths of air were smeared across their cheeks by the increasing winds. The trek down should take around two hours, which would get them to Fiona's car around four p.m., when the sun would set.

The first snows came as a gentle flurry, but within five minutes the flurries morphed into a full-scale blizzard. Visibility was cut from miles to yards to feet. Worst of all, thanks to the recent dry weather, the snow lay where it fell.

The snow beneath Fiona's boots was no more than an inch deep, but she could see it was deepening all the time. Before long it would blanket everything. The contours of the land would show the track, but all the trip hazards that could be seen by the naked eye would be buried.

Fiona felt her pace was slowing and, as much as she wanted to press on, she knew to hurry in these conditions was to invite disaster. To their left the Munro sloped away at a steep angle, although the track they were on was wide enough for two to walk abreast. All the same, Fiona made sure she was on the summit side of the track lest she miss her footing at any point.

The world around Fiona had been vibrant and full of colours. Hues and shades decorating the landscape with a majestic beauty. All of that was now replaced with a dirty white shroud that billowed around them. The only noises Fiona could hear was the huffing of her breath and the crump of snow beneath her boots, and even they were faint sounds deadened by the snowfall.

In the silence of the snowstorm, the agonised scream jangled every last nerve in Fiona's body.

Fiona twisted round to look over her shoulder. With the wind at her back and leading the group, it was the only direction the scream could have come from. She saw two red shapes behind her. The closest would be her friend, Donna, and next to Donna would be one of the other hikers who'd joined them for the descent.

The hike up to the knot of gathered people was a slog in these conditions, but Fiona gritted her teeth and followed Donna and the other red-jacketed hiker back uphill, to where they discovered the others: five where there should be six.

The missing hiker wasn't lying on the ground at the feet of the five. Nor were they behind any of the others as the group all faced each other.

Fiona had three thoughts all of which arrived together. The first was to check if Jack was among the five; he was. Next she checked downhill from the side of the track, her head torch picking its way through the falling snow. Opposite the cluster of people was a scuffing of the snow that shouldn't have been there. Fiona's third thought was the one to pierce her psyche with the precision of a surgeon's scalpel; *not again.*

Twice in the past year Fiona had been trapped in a solitary location by freakish weather, and on both of those occasions a murderer had been among the people isolated alongside her. Fiona knew it was selfish of her to think that way, but there was no easy way to escape the ball of dread pinballing in her gut.

She took a breath and forced herself to be calm and to think with the rational part of her brain. Donna might be highly strung about such things, but Fiona always found a way to process rather than react. A psychologist she'd visited had suggested the foundation of this trait was the influence of Fiona's Aunt Mary. Indomitable in every way, Aunt Mary had repaired a broken teen and allowed Fiona to grow into the woman she was today.

The odds were the missing hiker had lost their way in the snow and tumbled down the steep side of Beinn Bhuidhe. That would by far be the best case scenario, but still not a desired outcome. All the darker thoughts assaulting Fiona's brain were just chatter and speculation that had to be silenced until she had more facts.

First of all, Fiona had to quickly determine who was missing, so she pulled on the arm of the hiker in the red coat, a tall woman with a pinched face and intelligent eyes. 'Who's not here?'

'Kevin. He must have wandered too close to the edge and fallen.'

Other voices echoed the tall woman's sentiments, and there was no mistaking the stress underlying everyone's tone.

A younger man, with a thin scraggly beard over a distraught face, was pointing down the slope. 'We have to find him.'

Jack aimed his head torch at the place where the snow was disturbed on the downhill part of the track. No matter how he moved his head, the torch's beam was always swallowed by the billowing snow as he tried to follow the path Kevin had taken.

As Fiona looked down the slope she felt a pressure at her back. Even before she had chance to tense against the pressure she heard Donna's voice in her ear. 'They're right, we'll have to find him. If he's fallen down there he could have broken his neck.'

Donna's opinion was one Fiona shared, although as much as she knew Kevin had to be found, she didn't relish the task of finding him. Not only would it be dangerous to follow the disturbed snow down the steep slope, but if the fey feeling in her gut was right and Kevin hadn't fallen of his own volition, there was every chance the person who'd caused Kevin to tumble down the hillside may harm anyone who went looking for the missing man. Fiona blamed the fey feeling on her training and years of policing experience. As a copper she'd grown used to expecting the worst of humans and always felt gladdened when she encountered a selfless act.

Fiona waited a moment to see who volunteered to search for

Kevin. If no one did, she would, but she wasn't going to lead the way.

The younger man stepped towards the top of the slope. 'I'm going to go down and see if I can find him. He could have fractured a limb, or knocked himself unconscious.'

A burly man eased in front of the tall woman. 'Good man, Steve. If he's hurt, shout up to us and Thomas and I will come down to help carry him. I know he'd do the same for us.'

Fiona cast her eyes across the group of strangers standing behind the volunteer. There were two men, and two women. The men were polar opposites. The one who'd spoken was in his late fifties, and he exuded a level of capability. Even in the falling snow with other things on her mind Fiona noticed that his jacket and boots were top quality. The other was mid-twenties, at most, and looked as if he'd put his back out picking up a pair of socks; he was the human embodiment of a runt and carried himself with a touch of the effeminate. As for the women, they were both in their forties, one tall with a straight back, the other short and dumpy with hypnotic green eyes. Like Fiona, Donna and Jack, the two men each sported a head torch, although the young guy's was incorporated into the woolly hat tucked down on his head.

As best as Fiona could judge, Steve the volunteer was late-twenties. His build looked average and other than the beard that was all wisp and no wealth, there was nothing to write home about his appearance.

While Fiona had no idea about the relationships the group of strangers had with each other, she'd noticed the stern faces and lack of chit chat between them as they stood on the summit of Beinn Bhuidhe. Whether they'd had words on the way up or were just a dysfunctional bunch was something to worry about later. Right now the foremost thought in her head was wondering whether the volunteer was a good guy looking out for another human who'd possibly hurt themselves, or a bad guy intent on finishing off his target.

'I'm Fiona, I'll come with you.' The words were out of Fiona's mouth before she realised she was speaking.

Donna's hands grasped Fiona's shoulders, and she leaned in to put her lips to Fiona's ears. 'Are you sure about this? We don't know who this Kevin is and it looks dangerous.'

Fiona made sure her voice was low as she answered. 'I'm a cop, Donna. I have to go. Keep your eyes on the others. It might not be an accident.'

Steve pointed at the slope. 'Let's get on with it before the snow gets any deeper.'

TWO

The first step Fiona took gave her more than enough warning about the dangers of looking for Kevin. As soon as her foot pressed on the snow covering the slope, the ground beneath her boot began to slide downhill. She reasoned it must be one of the many areas of scree they'd passed on the way up. They were impressive to look at, but fraught with dangers as a pathway.

Fiona planted the heel of her second foot into the snow first and then leaned back as she slid down the hill several inches before coming to a halt. Opposite her on the other side of the disturbed snow Fiona could see Steve was having the same issues. One of the two women had carried two hiking poles, and now she was on the slope, Fiona wished she'd borrowed one.

To combat the loose surface Fiona turned so she was side on to the mountain and used a series of small steps to half slide, half walk her way down the slope.

Down and down Fiona continued until she was enveloped by the falling snow. The only guides to her location, the pitch of the slope and the crumpled snow trail she and Steve were following.

Something caught Fiona's eye as she slipped down the

slope. A fist-sized rock had rolled part of the way down the hill and now sat on top of the snow. The rock wasn't close enough to the trail Kevin had left for it to have been disturbed by him. That jarred with Fiona. The falling snow wouldn't set off a landslide. Maybe when it melted it would, but as the snow was falling and coating everything, it was more likely to bind than propel. Fiona eased herself over until she could pick the rock up.

It was a typical rock with rough edges, flat planes and some rounded areas. Reddish grey in colour it looked just like any of the million others Fiona had seen on the scree slopes of Beinn Bhuidhe. Except this one had blood on it. Not dried old blood. But fresh, still moist blood.

Fiona clicked into a different gear. She was no longer a hiker taking in the beauty of Scotland. Now she had proof of foul play, she was PC Fiona MacLeish.

The sequence of events was obvious. The tension in the group of six had reached its peak and someone had grabbed a rock, clubbed Kevin with it, made sure Kevin fell down a steep slope and then tossed the rock away, further down the slope. No doubt Kevin's attacker had thought the rock would either create a snowball that would hide it, or would become lost among a million others when the snow thawed. It was nothing more than dumb luck that had caused it to end up where Fiona could see it.

A part of Fiona wanted to stuff the rock into her pocket in case it was needed as evidence. The idea was right, but she had no evidence bags in which she could keep the rock in a secure forensic condition. Even if she did take the rock and keep it forensically secure, it was a chilly December day and everyone was wearing gloves. There would be no fingerprints to identify Kevin's attacker and, while there may be fibres from a glove found on the rock, it was the longest of long shots.

On the off chance the rock might prove useful, Fiona pocketed it. As soon as it was in her pocket she felt the left side of her jacket weighed down by it.

Ever since the business on Luing, Fiona's left shoulder had given her problems. She'd trapped at least one nerve and while a series of agonising massages had released the trapped nerves, it didn't take a lot for her shoulder to protest against misuse or excessive burdens. X-rays had been taken at Oban Hospital and Fiona had been referred to a specialist at Glasgow. It was an appointment she wasn't looking forward to, as whenever doctors or nurses got her to move in certain ways so they could judge the extent of her injury, she felt shards of agony running her through like a vindictive lancer. Friends had advised her to take some time on the sick until she recovered, but that wasn't Fiona's way. In medical terms she was fit for work, the pain was a discomfort she'd rather not have, but so long as she could do her job, there was no way she was going to let her fellow officers down.

With the rock safe in a zipped pocket, Fiona resumed her journey downhill. Steve was ahead of her now, but Fiona was within sight of him, so she wasn't afraid of what he might do if he found Kevin first. All the same, she increased her pace so she was catching up with Steve.

The rock was proof Kevin's fall was no accident, and until she learned who'd attacked him, everyone except Donna was under suspicion. Including Jack. She'd known Jack for twenty-plus years, and while he was quick to chat with strangers, he was a marmite character and had a fiery temper. At school he'd been in constant trouble for fighting, and while Fiona was unaware of any recent fights he might have got himself into, Jack had always been one to hit first and think second. The chances of him being guilty of the assault on Kevin were slim, but although she didn't think he'd struck Kevin with the rock, until she had evidence to prove otherwise, she couldn't discount him as a suspect.

A glance at Steve saw him waving to her and pointing down the slope. She followed his aim and saw flashes of yellow among the white.

The more Fiona descended, the more the flashes became the solid shape of a body lying against a boulder that jutted out of the hillside.

Kevin's tumble downhill had been ungainly as he appeared to have collided with the boulder head first, as his legs still pointed up the slope. He was on his back and when Steve shone his torch at Kevin's face there was no reaction. Not a blink, nor a widening of the pupil. The right side of Kevin's face was bruised and bloodied above the ear. No doubt where the rock had impacted him, but there were other minor scrapes on his face too. So far as Fiona could work out, Kevin had either been knocked unconscious by the rock, or had been too dizzy to do anything to break his fall and halt his tumble down the slope. All Fiona could think as she approached Kevin was what may have started as assault may prove to be murder.

THREE

Fiona retrieved her mobile from the zipped inside pocket where she kept it and keyed in her passcode. The phone came to life, but as bright as its screen was, the signal bar was emptier than an upturned bucket.

Steve dropped to a knee and pulled his glove off as he reached for Kevin's throat. The way Steve twisted his hand to check for the pulse told Fiona he knew what he was doing. As did the fact he was looking at his watch as he checked for a pulse.

Most people look as if they're attempting to strangle someone when they check the carotid artery in the throat for a pulse. Fiona had been trained to check the nearside of the victim, but to rotate her hand so her thumb was pointing up or down the length of the body rather than across the windpipe. The thinking was that if the victim was aware of the check, they wouldn't feel panicked when a stranger put a hand across their throat.

All of this was a moot point. If Steve didn't find a pulse, she'd check anyway. It didn't matter how good Steve's first aid skills appeared to be; he, like the rest of the group, were under suspicion until she learned otherwise.

'Well?' Fiona made sure her voice was loud enough to be heard over the wind.

Steve looked up at her. 'He's got a pulse. It's weak, and I reckon it's barely above sixty BPM. I'd know better if I could hook him up to an ECG.'

'It's good that he's alive. You sound like you know what you're doing. Are you a doctor?'

'A nurse, but I work in A&E at Glasgow Royal Infirmary, so I'm used to undiagnosed trauma.'

Even as he was speaking, Steve was feeling over Kevin's arms and legs. Rather than touch the bloodied head wound with his bare fingers, he used the pinkie of his gloved hand to apply a tender examination of Kevin's injury.

Steve's face changed as he withdrew his hand. 'There's broken bone there. Lord knows what damage has been done to his brain. He needs to be medevacked at once. He's going to need scans and depending on what they show, he might have to have surgery. Possibly a stent.'

'Can he be moved?'

'Ideally not unless it's by paramedics with a spinal board; however, he'll die if he's left here.'

'I've no signal. Have you got one?'

Steve's face was rueful as he looked up at her. 'I left it in my car. I've been up here before and I know it's a blackspot.'

Fiona wasn't sure she believed Steve had left his mobile in the car. Beinn Bhuidhe might be a blackspot in terms of mobile signal, but the phone could still be used as a camera. Who didn't take pictures of such stunning scenery? She and Donna had taken loads. Even Jack, who didn't have even one social media profile, had pulled his phone out and taken a series of pictures and a couple of selfies.

Rather than tip her hand and start questioning Steve about

his lack of mobile, Fiona let it slide for now. Steve didn't know her, therefore he couldn't know she was a cop and the longer that continued, the more chance she'd have of hearing him say something unguarded.

After the business on Luing that summer Fiona had once again been thrust into the headlines by a Police Scotland eager for some positive press. She hadn't liked the attention then, and she disliked the expectations it still raised when members of the public realised who she was. So far she'd kept her hat pulled down over her forehead, and without a police uniform to help identify her, she would be just another Munro bagger so far as strangers were concerned.

Fiona had a decision to make. She and Steve wouldn't be able to carry Kevin by themselves. Not back up the slope, nor could the two of them guarantee him safe passage downhill until they bisected the next horizontal sweep of the track. If Kevin's jacket was anything to go by, he was a good few stone heavier than either Fiona or Steve. It could be fat, but more likely it would be muscle, as Kevin's face had a structure to it that spoke of a busy life rather than one spent chewing crisps in front of a TV screen. Like the other older guy in their group, Kevin's jacket and boots were top of the range.

To get Kevin back to the track would require help. It made sense one of them stayed with Kevin, not that there was much anyone could do for him. As a nurse, Steve was the logical choice to remain behind. He'd be better placed to monitor Kevin's wellbeing.

The problem with that, though, was Steve might be putting on a show of care for her benefit. As soon as Fiona disappeared out of sight, there was nothing to prevent Steve from sourcing another rock and delivering a second blow to Kevin's already damaged skull.

The flip side to this line of thought was if she stayed, Steve could easily spin a lie about them finding Kevin bruised but okay and Fiona had chosen to carry on with Kevin while he'd gone back up to inform the others. By the time the others realised they'd never caught up with Fiona and Kevin, the others would be too far away to identify the area where the fall had taken place. The snow was falling at a rapid pace and was already starting to obscure the tracks they'd made getting to this point. If she was left alone with Kevin, there would come a point where she would have to choose between abandoning Kevin to his fate, provided he survived much longer, or staying with him and risking her own life.

None of the options seemed good, so Fiona chose the one that put her in the least amount of danger. It was something her first sergeant, the indomitable Dave Lennox, had instilled in her. His choice of phrase had always been blunt and to the point, but he was right. 'You're nae good to ony bugger if you gan and get yoursel' killed.'

'Steve, can you stay here with Kevin while I go back up and get some of the others to help? Then we can carry him down to the track and meet up with everyone.'

'Of course.' He pointed at Kevin as he leaned towards Fiona and lowered his voice. 'Please be quick though. The sooner we get him to a hospital, the better his chances are.'

FOUR

The climb back up the slope had Fiona panting within twenty steps. She was doing her best to make the ascent as quickly as possible, but every time she planted a foot on the slope the scree beneath the snow slid her down three quarters of a step. To maximise her pace she leaned forward and used her hands to support her torso while splaying her feet wide to increase their footprint on the hillside. Even with this tactic, she was still finding herself struggling to get traction from the loose rocks and pebbles covered by the snow.

Fiona gritted her teeth and kept her legs pumping as ragged breaths blew from her mouth. No matter how the pain in her calves or shoulder intensified, Fiona never faltered. It was imperative Kevin get help as soon as possible.

Around Fiona the world had closed in to a sea of white, illuminated only by the head torch she wore. The ground was white, so was the sky and the very air around Fiona was nothing but a series of white flurries coming at her out of the darkness. Time had no meaning. Nor did distance, everything was about continuing up the hill.

Up and up Fiona clambered in her ungainly fashion. Legs

burning, lungs gasping and then it was over. She'd crested the top of the slope and was on the track.

Fiona rose from her hands and knees and looked left then right. She was alone on the track, which meant either she'd not come straight back up the way she'd gone down, or the others had moved on. Fiona knew in her heart there could only be one answer.

FIVE

Fiona knew there wasn't a universe ever created where Donna wouldn't wait for her to return. That was as unthinkable an idea as the Pope denouncing Christ and converting to Islam or Judaism.

Fiona dragged a foot along the track several times until she'd built a mound of snow bisecting the track. Next she dropped to her knees and used her hands to form the mound into a heaped bank. Her final act was to roll a couple of snowballs until they were the size of footballs and place them on the mound. As markers went, it wasn't the greatest, but it'd stand out for an hour or two until buried by the snow. Fiona didn't need an hour or two, all she needed was five or ten minutes to locate the others.

Downhill was the easy option, so Fiona followed the track as it descended. When she reckoned she'd gone at least a hundred yards without finding the others, Fiona turned back.

While Fiona was open to the possibility her ascent of the scree slope hadn't been as straight as her descent, she couldn't envision being a hundred yards off. The marker at her point of ascent was easily spotted and when Fiona stepped over it and trudged on, she started to count her steps.

Fiona's count was at fifteen when she saw a chink of light moving in the snow. By eighteen she could see vague shapes wreathed in gusts of snow. As she drew closer she could see the shapes were moving. Not walking or hiking, just stamping their feet, flapping their arms. Fiona got it. While she'd been slogging down and then back up the slope, they'd been standing on an exposed track with no shelter from the snowstorm. She'd had exercise to keep her blood pumping, while they'd had nothing and would all be frozen.

It was Jack and Donna who greeted her. Donna's smile was wide as she enveloped Fiona in a hug. 'Oh my god, I thought you were never coming back. I was picturing you having fallen and broken your neck or at the very least a leg.'

'I'm fine. But the guy who fell isn't.'

'Oh no.' A spark lit Donna's eyes, and Fiona recognised the macabre nature of her friend surfacing. 'He's not dead, is he?'

'No, he's not. But there's a good chance he will be soon if we can't get him to a hospital.'

Even as she was speaking, Fiona was weighing up how much to tell Donna. Her friend might be a bit of a ghoul and have a twisted and smutty sense of humour, but Donna wasn't the calmest person she knew by a long way. The flip side to this was Donna deserved to know what was going on if for no other reason than to keep herself safe, so Fiona maintained the hug and spoke directly into her friend's ear. 'I'm not sure the fall was an accident. Keep your eye on the others.'

When Fiona released Donna she could see her friend's eyes widening as she digested the news.

'Jack will look after me.'

'I'm sorry, Donna, but I'm going to need Jack to come with me to rescue the guy who fell.'

Donna's eyes narrowed and she gave a terse nod. 'Yeah. That makes sense.'

'I'm going to need help to rescue Kevin.' Fiona aimed a glove at the burly man. 'Will you come down the slope with me and Jack and help carry him down?'

'Of course I'll help.'

Donna stepped forward. 'What about the rest of us? Are we supposed to stay here and freeze our arses off?'

Fiona sent a warning glare at Donna. She had enough to think about without Donna throwing a strop. 'No, I want you to continue on down the track. Sooner or later it'll turn back and sweep round below where we are now. Count your steps and when you get to the part where it turns back on itself, stop and count a hundred fewer steps back. When you get to that point, I want you to drag your feet through the snow for at least two hundred paces so you're making a clear sign of where the track is. There's little enough visibility as it is and I'm afraid we might miss the track altogether if you don't help us out.'

Donna's mouth pressed shut, but Fiona could tell her friend was worried. For Jack, herself and Fiona.

Rather than continue the debate, she stepped to the edge of the track and began her descent. Behind her she could hear Jack's voice. 'Come on, Neil. Let's get on with this.'

How typical of Jack to have learned the man's name. Fiona planned to pay close attention to the faces of both Jack and Neil when they encountered Kevin. How they looked at him would be telling. Either of the two had more than enough physical power to have tossed Kevin down the slope with a sudden thrust, but that didn't mean they hadn't picked up the rock to make sure of the job they were doing.

Fiona didn't really think Jack had struck Kevin with the rock and shoved him down the slope, but she didn't dare discount it in case it was true. By the same token, she was experienced enough to have worked out that with the rock striking the blow it did, it could have been wielded by either of the two women, or even the skinny guy.

As she descended Fiona's mind played tricks on her. Would she find Kevin dead and Steve gone? Would she find neither of them, with Steve having moved Kevin's corpse to hide the evidence? Would they be able to even find them supposing Steve wasn't Kevin's attacker? The way the snow was coming down, it was impossible to follow any of the tracks that had been made earlier. All signs of the descent then ascent she'd earlier made were obliterated by the ever-thickening layer of snow quilting the ground.

As the worry they'd miss the boulder that had stopped Kevin's descent grew, Fiona heard a shout that was followed by a powerful man thumping into her.

SIX

Fiona slid down the slope with the man half under her, both hands balling into fists ready to defend herself if necessary. As she tumbled she picked out the red of Jack's fleece. Neil had been wearing a yellow jacket. While she doubted Jack intended her any harm, she wasn't taking any chances.

Something buried in the snow snagged at their legs, the sudden imbalance it caused enough to rotate them so they were tumbled down the slope in a barrel roll. Fiona's instinct was to protect her head, but even as she was drawing her arms up, a primal part of her brain made her reverse the movement and tuck her arms by her sides with her elbows bent and her fists level with her shoulders. By changing her position Fiona had transformed her body shape from a cylinder to an oval.

Twice Fiona tumbled downhill in this position before she came to a rest face down in the snow. Jack had separated from her and he cannoned past. Fiona eased her feet down the slope and resumed her descent. Jack's thumping into her could be nothing more than a pure accident after he'd lost his footing, or it could be something more sinister. Unlike Steve, Jack knew she was a cop.

As Fiona resumed her descent, she checked herself over for injuries. She was bruised all over from where she'd collided with various rocks, but as the scree slope was loose, there hadn't been any impacts hard enough to break a bone. Not that her shoulder could be persuaded otherwise. Right now it ached and throbbed with every movement, and if someone had told Fiona a devil was skewering her shoulder with white hot lances, she'd have believed them.

Ten paces down, Fiona spied the first sign of Jack. He'd managed to halt his tumble and was lying on his back with his feet buried ankle deep in a mound of snow.

'You okay?'

Jack nodded, his face as white as the snow he lay in. 'I'm sorry, Fiona. I slipped. Bloody stupid of me. Are you all right?'

'I'm fine.' There was nothing to be gained from laying a guilt trip on Jack for the pain in her shoulder. If he was innocent, he'd be aware of his failings. If guilty, he'd sense a weakness, and she didn't want that. Fiona gestured downhill. 'From now on, though, stay a few feet to the side of me. If nothing else, it'll make finding Kevin and Steve easier.'

As Fiona helped Jack regain his footing she caught sight of Neil coming down the hill. He was maybe five feet over and she fell into line between Jack and Neil as the three of them made their way down.

'There. They're over there.'

At Neil's yell Fiona traced the arm he was pointing and saw glimpses of light poking through the snowfall.

Fiona began crabbing that way. The light meant Steve had stayed with Kevin. Or did it? For a horrible moment Fiona imagined they'd passed Steve and Kevin and the light belonged to the others as they scoured the track for them. Other than the six strangers on the summit, Fiona hadn't seen any other baggers on Beinn Bhuidhe, and while she couldn't be one hundred per cent certain there was no one else on the

Munro, she knew the odds of them being halfway down this scree slope at the same time she was were too small to worry about.

The thought was only a fleeting one as she was soon close enough to determine it was in fact Steve, as he was waving his arms to attract their attention. Now was the moment of truth. Would Kevin be alive? Or had Steve finished the job he may have started on the track?

Kevin was alive. Better than that, when she made her way over to him and Steve, Kevin's eyes tracked her progress. His lips moved but there was no sound from them.

Fiona could see Steve hadn't been idle while waiting for her return. What looked like a red T-shirt was wrapped around Kevin's forehead, and Steve had pulled Kevin's hood up and fashioned its tie strings with their ends looped down so they were secured by the chest pockets on Kevin's coats.

As spinal boards went it was rudimentary at best, but the hood would prevent Kevin's head from lolling back as they carried him down the hill.

Fiona gestured at Kevin. 'How is he? Any change?'

'Still the same. We need to get him some meds and a proper assessment as soon as possible.'

Together they lifted Kevin, Steve controlling the lift with precise commands. Fiona had a leg as did Steve with the two stronger men supporting Kevin's torso.

To lift Kevin was the easy part. It was carrying him down the slope that was tricky. If one of them lost their footing, all five would end up cascading downhill. With a series of small and careful steps they descended to the track. It was easy to find as it had been scraped of snow by the others, and had Fiona been the religious type, she'd have offered up a prayer of thanks.

Fifty yards along the track they caught up with the others. The thin guy was at the rear of the group, kicking snow from the track like it was his life's mission.

Fiona did a rapid head count. There were four people on the track.

At Fiona's shout the thin guy whirled round and waved. A couple of seconds later he and the three women were coming back to join them, Donna making a beeline for Jack.

The thin guy came Fiona's way. She tensed ready for whatever might happen.

'I'll take a spell if you want. You look done in, love.'

If the guy had stopped short after telling her she looked done in, Fiona would have accepted his offer. That he'd ended the suggestion with a patronising 'love' meant she'd keep going until she dropped rather than allow his misogyny to flourish.

'I'm fine. If you want to make yourself useful, lead the way along the track.' Fiona twisted her head to look Donna's way. 'Can you get the other two women and follow him?'

'Why?'

'Because you'll trample something of a path for us.'

Donna squeezed Jack's arm and set off to do Fiona's bidding. Kevin's leg was a burden Fiona could have well done without. To make matters worse, she was carrying him with her left arm. Her shoulder was protesting every step she took as the dead weight of Kevin communicated itself back up her arm and into her shoulder.

As the party trudged on, Fiona's brain was going at a hundred miles an hour. From her previous experiences of bagging Munros, and the recent trek up Beinn Bhuidhe, she reckoned they were at least five miles from where they'd parked their cars near the Fyne Ales Brewery. This tallied with her memories of the online map she'd pored over before beginning the hike. Without the snow, it would be an hour and a half's walk. With the snow and the injured Kevin to carry, it was a trek that would take at least an hour longer, although she reckoned two was a more reasonable estimate. Did they all have the stamina to carry Kevin for so long? It wasn't as if they were trekking along a nice smooth road, or even a flatter surface like a field. They would come later, but for now, level ground was at least an hour and a half away. Daylight would be gone before that, and while there was little enough visibility as it was from the snowstorm, things wouldn't get any better when darkness fell.

Sooner or later one of them would stumble and they'd all go down. That wouldn't be as serious as when they were traversing the scree slope, but Kevin was in a bad enough way without being dropped.

Another concern was the way the snow was falling. Right from the start it had been coming down fast, but it seemed to have gathered pace since they'd started carrying Kevin. Despite the efforts of the thin guy and the three women to trample a path for them, the snow was still coming halfway up Fiona's calf. How much longer would it be before the snow was knee deep and slowing them even more?

There was another option, but it wasn't one Fiona wanted to take as it was sure to delay getting proper medical treatment for Kevin.

Somewhere along this element of the track there was a stone bothy. While once it may have been home to a shepherd, it had been outfitted as a place of shelter by the Mountain Bothies Association. It contained some first aid equipment, a wood-burning stove and emergency rations among other survival gear.

If they were to hole up there until the snowstorm blew itself out, or abated enough the morning light could illuminate a safe passage back to civilisation, they'd all be safer as a group.

That would work for eight of them. For the ninth it could be fatal.

Another option was they could use the shelter to protect Kevin from the elements while a couple of them braved the trek further downhill to summon help. That was a sound idea, but the help would be a long time coming. While a mountain rescue team would be able to hike up to the shelter and help them carry Kevin down, thanks to the lack of visibility and the infrequent gusts of wind buffeting them, there was no way a helicopter would risk hovering by the mountain and dropping a line with a stretcher.

When the grunts and curses from the three men sharing the burden with her became more frequent, Fiona cast an eye their way. A glance was all she needed. The gritted teeth, the narrowed eyes and the beads of sweat all told the same tale. There was nothing for it, they'd have to use the shelter. Sooner or later one of them was going to reach their limit. When that happened they'd stumble, most likely fall. Although the ever-deepening snow might cushion Kevin's fall, there was always the chance the rough treatment would inflict further injury to his already damaged head.

Another reason to use the shelter was the terrain ahead. There were parts where the track narrowed so tight it'd be impossible to walk abreast the way they currently were walking. Fiona could think of at least two slim wooden bridges over burns that only featured a handrail on the downhill side.

'Hey, Thomas.'

The shout from Steve was loud in Fiona's ear, but she was more interested in what he had to say. Thomas had to be the thin guy, as she already knew the burly man was called Neil.

Sure enough the thin guy came trotting back. 'What is it?'

'There's a shelter along here somewhere. By my reckoning it's not far away. Keep an eye out for it, will you? We can take a break there before heading on down to the bottom.'

Fiona kicked herself. Not once had she thought about using the shelter as a short-term refuge. Every consideration she'd had regarding the shelter had been focused on a longer term use of the structure. That wasn't good enough. She had to do better. One of the seven people with her had tried to murder Kevin;

the only person she was sure was innocent was the lifelong friend who'd been at her side when Kevin was attacked. Before she got off Beinn Bhuidhe, she'd have to identify the killer and possibly stop them from killing again.

The idea of using the shelter was a good one, but every minute they spent in it was another minute the snow had to deepen and the night to fall.

As she trudged on, Fiona had one question on her mind: was seeking temporary refuge in the shelter Steve's way of delaying treatment for Kevin? If they were to attempt to carry Kevin all the way down, they needed to do so as soon as possible.

They reached the shelter within ten minutes. When Thomas opened the door Fiona could see three strangers already inside. Except, from the way they greeted Thomas and the women he was with, they weren't strangers to them.

This was all Fiona needed: three more names to add to her suspect list.

SEVEN

The shelter had one window, bench seating around the walls, and a stove that was radiating a fabulous warmth into the room. With a fair amount of grunting and some un-muttered curses, they managed to lay Kevin onto the bench closest to the stove.

Fiona cast her eyes over the three new people. There was a couple in their thirties, him a shade under six foot and carrying a pumpkin-sized paunch, her around the same height but half the weight. The way the woman was sitting close enough to the man their thighs were touching, when there was plenty of space, was a clear sign they were in a relationship.

The third person in the shelter was a beefy guy who didn't speak when they all trooped in. He dropped nods of recognition to the other group, and Fiona heard someone call him Ivor.

Every person in both of the groups was watching as Kevin was laid down on a bench, an unspoken question hanging in their eyes. Fiona took a quick moment to run through the group of strangers in her mind. There was Steve the nurse, Thomas who was thin and the youngest of their group, Neil who was burly and around the sixty mark, the two women, one tall and the other short, the beefy Ivor and the as yet unidentified couple.

'Is... is he still alive?' The question came from the shorter woman, and it drew a glare from her taller companion.

Steve was checking Kevin's pulse again, his eyes on his watch as he did so. He nodded, but when he looked up, his face was grim. 'He is. Although how long he'll be able to hold on without the right meds and treatment is anyone's guess.'

Rather than stand around doing nothing, Fiona started to search the shelter. She'd been in a similar one while bagging Beinn Ime, some six or seven miles east. The shelter there had been well equipped. It had a substantial first aid box and a spinal board had been clipped to the wall. A cupboard had housed many packets of soup in a variety of flavours, mugs and a bowl with a couple of bottles of washing-up liquid. There had been a kettle which sat atop its wood stove.

This shelter may be larger than the one on Beinn Ime, and have another small room on the left, but it was nothing like as well stocked. There was no spinal board, the first aid box was largely empty save a few sticking plasters and a triangular bandage, and the doorless cupboard had just three tin mugs and six packets of soup. A tiny iron kettle stood at the far right of the cupboard and it was layered in dust. There were a couple of Tilley lamps and when shaken Fiona heard the sloshing of oil. Whether the sparseness of the supplies in this shelter was due to the public raiding them, or funds from the Mountain Bothies Association being too low to keep the former levels of supplies present in the bothies refreshed was unknown, and at this point immaterial. There was nothing to be gained from lamenting what they didn't have.

Fiona handed the first aid kit to Steve. 'Sorry, there's next to nowt left.'

Steve glanced inside and scowled. Whether it was at the idea someone had raided the cache, or those responsible for maintaining a supply had failed in their duty, Fiona didn't know, but she shared his dismay. 'I've got much the same in my backpack. I'm prepared for blisters or a sprain, but nothing more serious than that. The triangular bandages make a great sling for a broken arm, but other than using one to make a skull cap, they're bugger-all use.'

Fiona clicked on her head torch and examined the second room in case there was anything useful in there, but as soon as she cast her gaze around the room, she could see there was nothing more than a couple of benches.

Nobody seemed to be taking a lead in the shelter, and those who'd entered were largely pressed against each other as they circled the wood-burning stove to try and claim some of its heat.

From the corner of her eye, Fiona saw Donna round on her husband. 'What are we going to do, Jack? We can't stay here all night. What if the snow blocks us in? We'll starve.'

Donna was a lot of things, but subtle wasn't one of them. Sometimes Fiona wondered if her friend didn't care if she was overheard, or if she wanted everyone within earshot to hear her thoughts.

When setting out, Fiona as the more experienced Munro bagger had made sure they all had water bottles, and a good few protein or energy bars in their backpacks. She had one left, and knew Jack and Donna had devoured the last of theirs on the summit.

Jack didn't answer. Instead he pulled Donna in close and used his greater height to send a beseeching look Fiona's way.

Donna's words triggered a lot of minor conversations that were all taking place at the same time. Vehement voices filled the shelter, and Fiona recognised someone had to band the group together in a common purpose before factions were drawn.

Every head turned Fiona's way, so she stopped banging the tin mugs together. 'Okay, now I've got your attention, I need you all to listen up. We all have a choice.' Fiona gestured Kevin's way. 'Kevin is badly hurt and needs medical attention. There's enough of us we ought to be able to carry him down the hill to safety, if it was daylight and we didn't have to wade through the snow. Both the dark and the snow are factors that are against us carrying him out of here. I'm sure you all noticed how poor the visibility was, and it was getting worse as the sun was going down. By now it'll probably be pitch black. We also have no easy way of carrying Kevin down as there's no stretcher. On a certain level it makes sense we wait out the storm and see what the morning brings, as you don't need me to tell you any attempt to walk down the hill in these conditions is both dangerous and foolhardy. However, that doesn't help Kevin. Yes, we might not have a lot of food, but there's a stove to keep us warm and if we boil snow we can at least have a hot drink. I suggest we all pool our resources.' With that said, Fiona produced her precious last energy bar and put it in the cupboard beside the packets of soup.

Jack aimed a finger at the three people who'd been in the shelter when they arrived. 'No wonder there's no food. I bet them greedy buggers all had some soup before we got here.'

Protestations of innocence flew from the mouths of Ivor and the couple who'd been in the shelter first. The woman rose, her finger jabbing at Jack for the accusation he'd made.

The man whose shoulder the woman had been leaning on pulled her back. 'Sara, pack it in, will you? I'll deal with this.'

He looked up at Jack, who was at least three inches taller. 'You've got it all wrong, pal. You owe us an apology.'

As Fiona stepped between them she could see the tension in Jack's body, the setting of his feet and the balling of a fist. That's all they needed, a fight breaking out.

Fiona pushed the mug she held in her left hand forward until it touched Jack's face. 'Do you feel that? It's cold, isn't it?'

'Aye, what about it?'

'Do you think it'd be cold if it had just been used for soup?'

'Aye well, there's no knowing how long they've been here.'

'Yes, there is.' Fiona pointed at the stone floor by Ivor's feet. 'The ground there is damp. That means the stove hasn't been on long enough to dry the snow that came in on their boots. And before you try arguing it's really warm in here, that's an illusion because it's a good few degrees warmer than outside. They've been here the longest, but they're still wearing all their layers. If they'd been here long enough to light the stove, boil up enough snow to make themselves soup, drink the soup, and then let the mugs cool down, the stove would have this shelter like an oven.'

'Shit, Jack, she's right.' Donna nudged her husband's arm, the action speaking volumes.

'Okay, okay, I'm sorry. You haven't drunk the soup, and I was wrong to accuse you of doing so.'

Jack's apology was received with angry glares from the three people he'd accused. It was just what Fiona had been hoping wouldn't happen. They were all in a bad enough situation without turning on each other.

It was Neil who came to the rescue. 'I know you're aggrieved at what he said, but without him and the young lady there, we'd have never got Kevin off the hill and into here, so remember that. There's nothing to be gained by arguing.'

'That's all very well and good, but what do we do now?' It was the tall woman speaking and now there was decent light Fiona could see she had retained her pinched expression. It made Fiona wonder if it was her norm, or simply due to the situation they were in.

'We behave like rational adults.' Fiona shot a warning glance at Jack lest he start another argument. 'First of all, has everyone checked their mobiles to see if they have a signal?'

A cacophony of rustles broke out as the majority of the group retrieved their phones from whichever pocket they'd secreted them in and checked for a signal. As they rummaged an apple, a banana and a protein bar were added to the food in the cupboard.

Nobody made a positive noise and a couple of the men swore in disgust. Sara's husband swore the most, earning him a stern look from the tall woman.

'Don't you say a fucking word, Alice. You might go to church every Sunday, but we all know you're no saint.'

Alice's lips formed a thin line, but she kept them pressed together as she continued to glare at him.

Fiona seized the moment of silence to spell things out. 'Okay, we've no signal, so we've got to choose what to do next. As I see it, we have three options. We all stay here until it's safe to go back down the hill. We've next to no food, but so long as there's plenty of wood for the stove, we can drink boiled water.'

'There's lots of wood out the back, isn't there, Lewis?' Sara looked at the man she was with.

'Yeah, there's a great heap of it.'

'Our second option is to continue down. There's enough of us to carry Kevin in shifts, but doing that will be dangerous and there's no guarantee we won't get lost. Plus there's the risk of injury to consider.' What Fiona didn't say was one of the people in the shelter had attacked Kevin and caused his fall. For whatever reason, they'd chosen to attack him in a violent way that spoke of a desire to cause serious injury or death. Whether the attacker's reason had been deep-seated into them long before bagging Beinn Bhuidhe, or it had been an impulsive, heat-of-the-moment thing was a question for later. The more pertinent question right now was: would the attacker strike again? To either finish the job they'd started, or to silence anyone who started asking too many questions about how Kevin had fallen.

'I'm guessing the third option is that most of us stay here while three or four of us go down to get help for Kevin.'

'You're right.' Fiona gestured at the shorter woman who'd been in the group of six and let the unasked question hang.

'Frances.' The woman blushed a tad, but what caught Fiona's eye was the way young Thomas looked at her. What she saw in his eyes was definitely something to keep in mind as she tried to work out who Kevin's attacker was.

Fiona cast a look at Kevin, saw the gravity on Steve's face and prepared herself for an argument. 'I know this won't be a popular suggestion, but I think it would be too dangerous to Kevin to try carrying him down to safety. I also think it's too dangerous for anyone to try going down for help. The snow is getting deeper by the minute. I think we should stay here until it's safe for us to go down. We'll all be missed. I don't know about anyone else, but I've friends who know I'm up here and will no doubt raise the alarm when they don't hear from me tonight.' This was the last thing Fiona wanted to do, not with the appointments she had the day after tomorrow. After putting off the appointments for so long, she was loath to miss them, and regardless of the fact they could be rescheduled, she'd spent weeks preparing herself mentally for what was sure to be an arduous and painful experience. Even as she thought this, Fiona knew the appointments were the least of her concerns: to attend them, she first had to survive the night.

'She makes sense with what she's saying, but Kevin isn't in a good way.' Steve rose to his feet as he addressed everyone in the shelter. 'He's got a fractured skull, may have bleeding on the brain, and could have damaged his neck and, or, spinal column when he fell. If he's got a bleed on the brain he's at high risk of a stroke, and up here with no medical supplies, there's nothing I can do for him. I agree it's too dangerous to carry him down, but whatever anyone else thinks or does, there's no way I'm going to stand by and watch him die without trying to go for help.'

Ivor's voice carried across the shelter. 'He's your uncle.'

EIGHT

The three words from Ivor were the first he'd spoken since they entered the shelter, but the tone in which he said them jangled all kinds of alarm bells in Fiona. There was contempt, disinterest and apathy layered in his voice.

Fiona wanted to dig into the reasons he so obviously didn't care for Kevin, but that would have to wait. Right now, she was wondering if the group had been so strung out Ivor had been the attacker and had made his own way to the shelter. By the same logic, the hot-headed Lewis and his wife were also potential suspects. How they'd managed to single out Kevin and commit the assault without being spotted by any of the others was a mystery, but until she could rule them out, she had to consider them. The news Kevin and Steve were related was important, but at this stage Fiona had no idea how close the relationship between uncle and nephew was. It was time she started gathering more information, so she turned to Thomas. 'Are you all together, or do you just happen to know each other?'

'We all work at Inveraray House. Although Neil left a few years ago.'

So they'd set out as a group of nine and had presumably got split up at some point on the way up or down.

With Kevin being attacked the way he was, Fiona now had eight strangers and a friend of twenty years on her suspect list. A complete lack of backup would also hamper the investigation she knew must be conducted.

The two things Fiona had going for her were that only Donna and Jack knew she was a cop, and so far only she and the attacker knew for certain Kevin's fall was no accident. The longer it stayed that way, the more chance she'd have of hearing unguarded comments that would help her work out the attacker's identity. To try and protect her anonymity Fiona made sure her hat was pulled down over as much of her face as it could reasonably cover without blocking her vision.

'We should vote.'

'You vote all you want, Alice.' Steve's face was hard. 'If you vote to stay here, I'm going for help if I've to go by myself.'

'So much for democracy.' Neil shook his head as he tucked his hands into his armpits.

The vote wasn't something Fiona wanted as it could have deadly consequences for Kevin if the group decided to carry him. But, on the other hand, it would give her an opportunity to gauge the feelings of the group as a whole.

'Let's vote.' Alice aimed a finger at Steve. 'I presume you want someone to go for help?'

'I've just bloody said so, haven't I?'

'Sara, Lewis, what do you two think?'

Lewis gestured for Sara to cast her vote first.

'Stay put.'

'Go for help.'

Lewis's answer earned him a quizzical look from Sara as Alice's finger moved on to Ivor.

'Stay.'

The terse answer from Ivor was one Fiona expected.

Alice was in the centre of the shelter, her finger moving round the huddled figures.

'I think we ought to get help for poor Kevin.'

'Thank you, Frances. Neil?'

'Like you all, I'm sick of all the complaining he's done about the effort it took us to get up here, but that's no reason to not help the grumpy article.'

Thomas shot a pained look at Frances. 'Sorry, but I think it's best we stay.'

'I agree.' Donna clasped Jack's hand in hers. 'And so does Jack, Don't you, Jack?'

'I do.'

With Donna and Jack having voiced their opinion, there were two votes to be cast: Fiona's and Alice's.

Fiona had already stated her belief they ought to stay, and she did believe that, but if Alice voted to get help, it would give Fiona the casting vote. Not that it mattered what the final decision was if Steve was true to his word. It was clear Alice had a dominant personality, and while Fiona was comfortable with someone else being the focus of attention, as a cop she had a moral responsibility to make sure the group survived and Kevin's attacker was identified. To have the best chance of achieving those twin aims Fiona had to depose Alice as the de-facto leader.

'In light of what Steve said about Kevin's condition, I reckon we ought to try and get help. However' – Fiona raised a hand to stall any interruptions that might come – 'I believe it's best if those who go for help are volunteers. Steve, you want to go for help, I get that. But as a nurse, I think you're far more use to Kevin staying here, so I'll volunteer to go for help.'

'By my count, the vote is tied at five all between staying put and going for help.' Alice's mouth puckered into a cat's arsehole before she opened it to speak again. 'Like Neil, I grew weary of Kevin's complaints, but I don't believe that's enough of a reason to potentially condemn him to death. He's been good to us. All of us. I vote someone goes for help, and like Fiona, I'm also willing to volunteer.'

'Right, that's the votes cast and it's six to five in favour of going for help.' Fiona was speaking quickly as she duelled Alice for control. The older woman might have multicoloured laces in her boots, but there was no other hint of whimsy about her. 'We've two volunteers so far, do we have any more?'

Steve, Jack, Lewis and Neil all raised a hand.

Four more volunteers. That made six including Fiona. So far as Fiona was concerned, every one of the five was a suspect, as she expected Kevin's attacker would want to distance themselves from their crime as soon as they could. Although she was aware the attacker may be smart enough to use a double bluff and stay behind, which could make it every bit as dangerous to remain in the shelter as it would be to strike out for help. This applied even more if Kevin's attacker planned to remain in the shelter so they could finish the job they'd started. In turn, this thinking made everyone a suspect. Except Donna who'd been with Fiona when the attack happened. It was unlikely the woman in the red coat who'd been close behind Fiona and Donna had committed the attack, but not impossible, and until Fiona had evidence proving otherwise, the woman would remain on her suspect list.

NINE

Of all those in the shelter, only Donna and Jack knew she was a police officer. There was a chance either of them had told the first group while she was locating Kevin with Steve, but she didn't think it had happened. There was a time for telling strangers what you and your friends did for a living, but trudging through a snowstorm wasn't it. If they'd been at a cocktail party, or perhaps chatting across the table at a wedding, then it may have come up.

Fiona believed Kevin's attacker was among the volunteers and as such she automatically ranked them in order of probability. Alice and Steve were at the bottom of her list.

Some people might consider it sexist to think the attacker was male, but Fiona had studied the statistics. More than studied them: Fiona had interpreted the statistics and the likelihood of the stories behind them. Only seven per cent of killers in the UK were female. When it came to killing, women tended to fall into two main categories with a whole bunch of subcategories. Percentage wise, women used a sharp object as often as their male counterparts, but there was a reason for that. Many of the women who picked up a blade were defending themselves from a violent partner or a home invader. That trait skewed the statistics in the wrong direction. As did the times when a blunt object had been used to bludgeon someone.

In her first month as a trained officer, Fiona had been part of a domestic response unit called to a house after neighbours heard screaming. When they'd entered the house they'd been greeted by a woman holding a bloodied iron. They'd found the woman's husband in an unconscious heap on the kitchen floor, the back of his head stoved in. The man had survived the blow, although his motor functions were impaired to the point where doctors doubted he'd ever make a full recovery. Sergeant Dave Lennox had been there and upon seeing the gentle way he'd arrested the wife, an eager Fiona bombarded him with questions. Lennox explained how he'd attended multiple calls to the address and had twice arrested the man for violent conduct towards his wife.

Fiona would never forget the sombre tone Lennox had used to tell her this had been the day he'd dreaded. The day the worm had reached its breaking point and turned.

By and large Fiona's interpretation of the statistics had left her with an understanding of the nuances of murder, how it was committed, and the untold reasons that instigated the heinous act.

Women tended not to use violent methods to kill, and when they did it was in the heat of the moment, usually in self-defence. In pre-planned murders, women opted for less gory ways. Poison was a common method as was strangulation. Of the strangulations, most of these occurred when the victim was sleeping, often after having had a big drink. A rope or scarf would be wound around the neck and tightened. If the victim came to enough to fight back, they were already weakened by oxygen starvation.

A violent attack like the one on Kevin had all the hallmarks of a male perpetrator, and while Fiona would never discount a female attacker she would always keep the statistics in mind when assessing her suspects.

Steve was near the bottom of her suspect list due to the way he'd cared for his uncle, although had he not repeated an insistence on going for help so often he would be at the very bottom.

Above Steve, Fiona had Jack. She'd known him for twenty years, and while she couldn't for one second picture him as being dumb enough to commit such a violent attack when there were so many potential witnesses, he did have a temper that boiled over when he was pushed hard enough.

At the top of her suspect list were Lewis and Neil, with Neil as the favourite by a slim margin. She knew little to nothing about either of them. Neil had an outward appearance of capability, and with his burly physique he was more than powerful enough to deliver the debilitating blow that had left Kevin unconscious. His, or anyone else's, motive to attack Kevin wasn't known, but until Fiona knew more about him he was atop her list for no other reason than her belief the attacker wanted to get off Beinn Bhuidhe, and away from their victim at the earliest opportunity. The reasons for Lewis also topping the list were similar. Lewis might have a pumpkin-sized paunch, but he must be in decent enough shape otherwise, as nobody who didn't have a certain level of physical fitness would consider trekking up a Munro as isolated as Beinn Bhuidhe. Although the one thing he had in his favour was the fact he was in the third group. He'd been in the shelter when they'd arrived, so unless he'd committed the attack on Kevin and then trekked in a direct line down the hill instead of following the track, there was no way he could have made it to the shelter ahead of them. Both Ivor and Sara could have done the same thing, but while Ivor had the necessary physique, Sara had a slight build and may not have possessed the necessary strength to deliver a blow violent enough to have fractured Kevin's skull.

Ivor's physique put him on the suspect list, but his age

coupled with his slow and deliberate movements kept him near the bottom. For someone to have attacked Kevin and then trekked down the slope in time to join the others, they'd have had to have been quick and nimble, not words Fiona would use about either Lewis or Ivor.

'Right then, that's it settled.' Alice stood in the middle of the shelter, her eyes scanning the crowd. 'We've six volunteers. So half of us are leaving. That'll solve the food problem if nothing else.'

Fiona stepped to the door and faced the room with her arms folded across her chest. Alice seemed too keen to leave the shelter for her liking. And, she didn't care for the way the woman was taking control of the group. As a copper, Fiona had a duty to investigate the attack on Kevin, as well as a duty to preserve life. The trek down for help would be a dangerous undertaking. It should be easy to navigate their way downhill provided they could follow the track, but the trek along the track was fraught with potential dangers, not least the risk of veering too close to the steep edge and tumbling down a slope. Once they got off the slopes of Beinn Bhuidhe, with visibility the way it was now it was ten past four, and the sun would be fully set in a matter of minutes, it would be even easier to get lost trekking back to the road that led south through Glen Fyne. Once on the road they'd be able to summon the emergency services from a cottage along the way, but as simple as it sounded, there were a whole range of problems they could encounter. And that was before she factored the potential presence of a violent attacker into the mix.

'Steve ought to stay.' Fiona sent a nod his way. 'Unless one of you is a doctor, he's the most qualified of us to look after Kevin, so it doesn't make sense for him to leave.'

Frances was the first to respond. 'She's right, Steve, you should stay and look after Kevin.'

Most of those in the room nodded, and Fiona could see a

tinge of relief on Steve's face. It was too good an opportunity to waste, so she pressed home her advantage before anyone called Alice spoke again. 'I don't think so many people should go. Any number of things could happen on the journey down, so instead of five of us going, I think it should be four. Jack and I, and one from each of your groups.'

'You're saying two groups.' There was no sneer on Alice's face, but it layered her tone like a club sandwich. 'Apart from you and your two friends, we all know each other. We're one group.'

'You were in two groups when we met you so that's how I think of it. The group you're in we met near the summit. The other group were in the shelter when we arrived. Either you or Neil from your group, and Lewis from the group who were in the shelter. Now, can you decide who's coming so we can get cracking?'

Alice's nostrils flared. 'Surely a larger group makes more sense. You said before any number of things could happen. Surely having more people to help would be better.'

'In theory, yes. In practice, no. There are more people to get lost. More people to have an accident. You say you're all one group, but you got separated in daylight before the snows came. I believe a small group staying in close contact will have the best chance.' Fiona looked up to lock eyes with Alice. 'And one last thing, my name's Fiona, please don't call me Shirley.'

The reworking of Leslie Nielsen's famous line from *Airplane!* drew a few smiles, and a throaty chuckle from Neil. Fiona had intended the joke would lighten the antagonism radiating from Alice, but she'd misjudged the woman and received a fierce scowl for her trouble.

The spoof disaster movie had been a favourite of Fiona's parents and she had many fond memories of snuggling in between them to laugh at the rapid-fire sight gags, one liners and general absurdity of the film. In Fiona's mind her father was kissing the top of her head for the way she'd referenced the comedy movie.

Fiona turned her head. 'Steve, how's Kevin doing?'

Steve's face was grim as he looked back at Fiona. 'His breathing and pulse are stable, but I think he's slipped from unconscious to comatose. If there's a bleed on his brain from the head wound he could easily have a haemorrhagic stroke.' He gave a small shrug and somehow managed to look even grimmer. 'For all I can tell without a CT scan or MRI, he may have already had one. He's unconscious so not able to participate in the FAST test.'

Fiona knew about the Face, Arms, Speech way of checking for a possible stroke. It had been one of many lessons she'd received in first aid as part of her basic training. The T in FAST stood for Time, as in time to call 999, but that wasn't an option otherwise they'd have done it long ago.

From the corner of her eye Fiona saw Neil rise to his feet and head for the door. 'If he's had a stroke, the sooner we get help the better. I'll go down myself. No point in risking more folks getting injured.'

Everything Neil said made sense, both on a communal level, and as a way for him to slip off into the night and never be seen again. Perhaps he was just a good friend of Kevin's, but if he was the person who'd assaulted Kevin, then his insistence on leaving was nothing more than him engineering a way to escape.

Whatever Neil's motives for trying to bring help might be, Fiona knew she was duty bound to accompany him, regardless of the risk to herself.

'I'll go down with Neil and the big man over there.' Lewis pointed at Jack. 'You're right about it being dangerous. It's a job for men, not meaning any offence.'

Fiona's own anger at Lewis's casual misogyny was only a fraction of Alice's, as she rounded on Lewis.

'How dare you insinuate such a thing? And since when did you get off on playing the white knight? You can say what you like, Lewis, but either me or Fiona is going to be in the group that goes down the hill. Do you understand me?'

'Hang on a minute.' Fiona pushed herself in front of Alice and speared Lewis with a look. 'You can speak for your own group all you want, but you're not speaking for ours. It's up to us to decide, not you.'

Jack and Donna both nodded their approval at Fiona's statement, but she wasn't happy with what she'd said. It had been a mistake to show the presence of different groups. To highlight the factions among them. When she left there would be a certain underlying animosity towards Donna and Jack, as they'd end up being judged on the company they kept, namely her.

'I'll go, Fiona. Your legs are shorter than mine which means it'll be easier for me to wade through the snow.'

Jack made a good point. He had at least six inches on her and while Fiona's proportions gave her a long body, his furnished him with endless legs. Something Donna always complained about when trying to source jeans and trousers to fit him.

'You also have a wife. I'm single. If anything happens on the way down, it's better to happen to me than you.'

Donna's face paled at Fiona's grim reckoning. It might have been kinder to sugar coat things for Donna's benefit, but Fiona had a second agenda for making the attempt to summon help. In her mind, Neil was a strong candidate for the attacker. As a police officer she planned to keep a close eye on him in case he decided to try and make a move against others in the party, or simply tried to abandon the group once in the shrouding depths of the snowstorm.

Jack drew a long breath in. 'I'll be fine.'

Donna never uttered a word, but Fiona could see the apology in her friend's eyes as she reached out and took a firm hold of her husband's elbow and tried to draw him back to where she sat on a bench.

Jack slipped his elbow free of Donna's hand and sent her an instructive look.

As a way to end the debate, Fiona turned her back to Jack. 'Right, I'm going, who's coming with me?'

'I am.' Alice prodded her own sternum.

Lewis and Neil stepped forward, as did Steve.

'Here.' Steve gave Fiona a folded piece of paper. 'I've listed Kevin's symptoms for you to relay when you call Mountain Rescue. They'll make sure to either send a doctor or at least some meds so I can sedate Kevin. Alice, I understand your wanting to join a rescue party, but you struggled with the hike up. I think it's probably best if you leave this to the others. Kevin wouldn't want anything to happen to you.'

Alice let out a long harrumph and plonked herself down.

Ivor lifted his head and looked at Lewis and Jack. 'If you have to turn back, I'll make it easy for you to find the shelter.'

With a last look at the assembled faces, Fiona checked the compass was still in her pocket, opened the door and gestured for Lewis and Neil to lead; Jack could bring up the rear.

The way Steve had given the list to her rather than either of the men he knew made Fiona wonder if he had his own suspicions about Kevin's alleged accident.

TEN

Fiona had a strong reason for allowing the two strangers to lead. It meant she could monitor them both while also using Jack to prevent them from having an easy way of ambushing her from behind.

It was a great theory, stacked with common-sense practicalities. In the whirling maelstrom of the blizzard that was now blowing, the idea lasted less than a hundred paces. Neil had the lead, but she couldn't see him. Lewis was three paces ahead of Fiona, and she could barely keep him in sight thanks to the snow.

Fiona cursed her lack of foresight. There had been a length of rope under a bench in the shelter. Had she been thinking, they could have used a length of the rope as a safety line. With each of them holding the front, middle and end of the rope, they could have monitored each other's whereabouts at all times. It wasn't a failsafe system, as if anything happened to the person at the rear, their incident might go unnoticed by the other three.

However if the lead person were to try and slope off on their own, the dropped rope would inform those following him. The same would apply to the people in the middle provided the person in the rear could maintain a constant amount of tension in the rope to inform them of the rope no longer being supported in three places.

It was all moot now anyway, they didn't have the rope, and Neil either was or wasn't a couple of paces ahead of Lewis.

Fiona pushed herself that little bit harder until she was as close to Lewis as she could be without tripping his heels.

A new thought careered into Fiona's brain with enough force to sideswipe all previous ideas. What if there were more than one attacker? What if the hike up Beinn Bhuidhe was nothing more than a ruse to get Kevin to a remote location so he could have a convenient accident? That would mean two or more people working in cahoots to end the life of a human being – the police term was conspiracy to murder. It wasn't an unknown situation, but it tended not to happen with everyday people like those in the shelter. There was a real mix of ages and genders, but nothing about any of them had suggested criminal tendencies.

Conspiracy to murder was a charge almost always levelled at those involved in organised crime. On rare occasions it would be a couple of family members who decided to off a wealthy relative to speed up an inheritance coming their way, but those instances weren't commonplace.

As much as she knew all this, Fiona could feel her heart racing at the possibilities her latest idea suggested. So far nobody had admitted recognising her, but what if someone had? Neither Neil nor Lewis had said a word about her coming on this trek since she'd announced she was coming. Did that mean they were happy for her to come along, as they recognised her from one of the public relations posts she'd featured in after her success on Luing? If they had attacked Kevin, were they planning to make her their next victim? Were they planning to get a suitable distance from the shelter and then attack her? Would she be bludgeoned and left to die a cold lonely death?

As much as Fiona wanted to slow her pace so she could walk alongside Jack, she daren't let Lewis out of her sight.

The slog through the snow was sapping. It wasn't just the effort of trudging a path through shin-deep fresh snow. It was the consistent absence of any change to the experience. Everything was white and silent now the wind had dropped. Nothing showed that wasn't illuminated by the head torch she wore.

Not only was the sensory deprivation acute, but Fiona was also on high alert lest one or both of the men she was following decided to attack her. In her mind Fiona imagined Neil knocking off his head torch, taking up a position close enough to the track to see the light from her torch so he could ambush her. Now the idea was implanted she was more grateful than ever she had Jack behind her. He was big, capable and had a history of fighting.

Every step taken was a repetition of the previous step with nothing to indicate progress. It was like being on a gym's treadmill without the pulsing music to listen to and buff people to compare herself against.

As a way to combat the sense of not achieving any progress, Fiona cast her mind back to the trek up to think of possible markers that would prove to her they were moving towards their goal. The various curves of the track and its undulations meant nothing. Had she been able to see further than a few feet, Fiona might have spotted one of the stone benches someone had built as rest points for weary baggers.

The only marker Fiona could think of she'd be able to recognise in the current lack of visibility was one of the narrow bridges that crossed the burns which cascaded down the Munro. As best as she could remember from the trip up Beinn Bhuidhe there had been one about a quarter of a mile from the shelter. They hadn't encountered the bridge yet which showed just how little progress they'd made.

Fiona took a look at the watch on her left wrist: 4.55 p.m. It had been her father's watch and was neither expensive nor flash. A simple device with Roman numerals, two hands and a brown leather strap, she'd worn it since the day it had been released to her after the investigation into her parents' murders. The watch's face had scratches, the leather strap had been replaced four times and the battery eight. To Fiona it was one of her most precious belongings. As was the necklace she wore. It had been her mother's everyday necklace, and while her mother would put on something more elegant for special occasions, the twin interlocked hearts meant everything to Fiona.

By wearing the jewellery, Fiona kept her parents with her at all times. The imagined presence and companionship of her parents was a small comfort that provided a weak substitute for the reality Fiona had lost that fateful day when she'd been met leaving her History GSCE, escorted to the Head's office and informed of their murders.

Above all other cases, the murder of her parents was the one Fiona wanted to solve. She'd hired a retired detective who'd set himself up as a private investigator to look into their murders. He'd done no better than the cops who'd been handed the original case. She'd tried herself without joy, but she wasn't ever going to give up.

The one thing Fiona was sure of was that she had to somehow find a way to walk back into an exam room so she could sit her detective's exam. She'd had all the dispensations she could stomach to get as far as she had in the police. If she was to make detective and hone the skills she'd need to investigate her parents' murders, it had to be done properly. She would accept no cutting of corners, no special circumstances because of her phobias regarding exams. If those demons remained unconquered, she was the wrong person to find the closure she so badly desired.

Fiona wasn't naïve enough to think she'd be able to use police resources to run that particular case. If anything ever screamed conflict of interest it was a family member of the victims being part of the investigative team. She'd have to run the case in her own time, use her training, people assessment skills and deduction to follow a cold trail that would lead her to their killer's door.

Coming back to the present, ahead of Fiona, Lewis was wading through the snow in an upright position. And then he wasn't upright any more. Through the swirls of snow Fiona saw Lewis land in an untidy heap and then begin to slither off to one side.

On the fringes of the area illuminated by her head torch, Fiona saw the dark wood of a handrail.

Fiona dashed forward and tried to catch Lewis before he slid off the bridge and fell several feet into the burn below.

But as Fiona reached Lewis her feet went from under her and she too was on her back and slipping towards the drop.

ELEVEN

Rather than thrash around as Lewis had, Fiona forced herself to be calm and motionless to arrest her gradual slide towards the unguarded summit side of the narrow bridge.

It didn't work.

Fiona's next move was to roll herself over onto her front and then her back again until she could grab one of the posts supporting the handrail.

With something immovable to hold onto it only took a moment for Fiona to regain her footing on the slush-coated surface of the bridge.

A memory of the journey up Beinn Bhuidhe returned to Fiona as she crawled her way back towards the snowy track. The bridge had been dampened from spray kicking up from the burn. Its wooden decking slick and icy even on a crisp dry morning. To compound matters the metallic wire mesh that coated so many similar bridges to provide all-weather grip was absent. Worse still was the way the bridge had a slight lean towards the summit side. Had the bridge been constructed better and properly looked after, it wouldn't have been so treacherous to cross.

Even as Fiona directed her gaze, and the beam of her head torch, down into the small ravine into which the burn flowed, she was feeling guilty at not remembering this and warning Neil and Lewis. Neil was nowhere to be seen and from where she was positioned, the snow devoured her torch's beam long before it picked out Lewis.

Fiona cursed into her scarf as Jack appeared out of the snow and helped her pull herself upright. As soon as she was on her feet, she pointed to the edge of the ravine. 'Lewis slipped off the bridge.'

Together with Jack, Fiona inched forward, every step taken with a slow deliberation as she tested the ground beneath her feet. When Fiona was sure she was at the edge of the ravine, she sat down and probed the bank with her feet until she was sure she had found a stone or piece of earthen banking that would support her weight.

With Jack coming down beside her, Fiona used this method to descend the side of the ravine foot by careful foot until her torch picked out Lewis. At first she feared the worst, but then she saw him move.

Lewis was using the same technique as Fiona, except he was ascending the ravine. The closer Fiona got to Lewis the more information she could gather about his fall, and specifically his landing. He was using only his left leg to propel his journey, which told her his right must have been hurt in the fall.

Although Lewis was wearing a version of the light waterproofs Fiona and most baggers wore at this time of year, he appeared to be soaked. The woolly Celtic hat he'd worn earlier was missing, and his hair was slicked to his head in a way that suggested he'd fallen into a part of the burn deep enough to immerse him.

Without thinking, Fiona plucked her own hat off her head and handed it to Lewis. The human head is responsible for most of the body's heat loss and, after his ducking, Lewis would need every scrap of warmth he could either generate or preserve.

Even as they moved into a position at Lewis's side, Fiona was questioning where Neil was. He might have carried on downhill unaware of the accident that had befallen Lewis, or he could have thrown a few handfuls of snow onto the bridge to make it even more treacherous for those following him. It would be a simple tactic to buy him more time to disappear into the snowstorm.

Fiona didn't know if any of her musings were correct, but she could be sure there was no way Lewis had staged his fall as a way to lure her into the ravine. There was no need for such subterfuge when all he had to do was wait for her at the bridge, and under the guise of leaning in to make himself heard, give her a violent shove. Then Jack could be dealt with the same way. As it was Lewis was lucky to have escaped a far more serious injury from his fall, and she might not have shared his luck. Even if she had, it wouldn't take a lot of effort to finish the job that had been started.

A much more pressing concern was Neil's whereabouts. If he had orchestrated Lewis's fall in some way, he'd either be watching to see if it had worked or pressing on to make good his escape.

A new idea crept into the boundaries of Fiona's consciousness. It was one where forces other than the ones she'd already considered were at play. Maybe Neil had witnessed Lewis attacking Kevin. Maybe instead of calling him out on it, he'd bided his time and laid a trap as revenge. As theories went at best it was stretching things. Few people kept a violent attack to themselves when it was against someone they knew. Fewer still said nothing when the attacker was holed up with them and other friends.

It could be Neil was afraid of Lewis and feared he'd be the next victim, but even if this was the case, there had been eight others in the shelter to pitch in against Lewis if things had got violent.

There were so many scenarios at play in Fiona's head that when she saw a blaze of light above her she didn't know whether to be relieved or terrified.

TWELVE

Neil adopted a less refined way of entering the ravine and he slid two feet past them before halting. Fiona had just enough time to see the flash of light from his torch and lean out of the way before his arm crashed into her head.

Fiona was on high alert. The hand she had braced on the snowy bank was already burrowing down in search of a stone she could utilise should Neil make the wrong move.

Neil made a move.

A right move. Rather than waste time speaking he spent a few seconds watching Lewis push himself up a few inches on his one good leg, and then he clambered into a position where he could grip the back of Lewis's jacket and aid his progress up the side of the small ravine.

Fiona followed Neil's lead and moved to a point where she could lift Lewis's injured leg. Like a weird creation from the mind of Lovecraft the four of them bumped, grunted and strained together until they were out of the ravine.

All the time she was helping, Fiona kept a close watch on Neil. It would be too easy for him to fake helping and then shove Lewis into her and Jack. If that happened they'd all end up in the burn with who knew what injuries between them.

The most furtive thing Fiona saw Neil do was put a hand into his pocket as they sat gasping at the top of the ravine. Even as her heart raced faster, Neil's hand emerged with his asthma inhaler.

Asthma inhalers were an innocuous item. Somewhere around a tenth of the UK population had asthma, so the sight of someone putting an inhaler to their mouth and gasping down a puff of Salbutamol had become commonplace; so unremarkable a sight nobody commented on it.

Except in Fiona's eyes the inhaler could be a neon flashing arrow pointing to a violent attacker.

As she understood it, Neil's asthma was severe enough for him to carry the inhaler on his person. He needed it after perhaps three minutes of heavy exertion helping Lewis. That was fine, totally understandable. She'd have been more surprised if he hadn't needed the medical boost to his breathing.

What Fiona couldn't grasp was why Neil had decided to hike up Beinn Bhuidhe. The views, the sense of achievement all made very good reasons, as did the benefits of such exercise. What didn't add up was the risk factor. Fiona was twenty or so years Neil's junior, and the hike up Beinn Bhuidhe had taxed her muscles. After traversing some of the steeper slopes, she'd been out of breath and she kept herself in good physical condition with twice-weekly workouts and at least one four-mile run per week whenever her shift pattern allowed. With his asthma Neil would have struggled more than she did. Yet he'd reached the summit around the same time as she, Donna and Jack had. Therefore, unless the other group had set off even earlier than Fiona and her friends had, Neil must have trekked up at more or less the same pace she had.

Why would an asthma sufferer put themselves through such an arduous experience? The views were spectacular, but they weren't so good they were worth risking death for. It could be Neil's asthma was mild enough he could handle it, that he was determined not to let the asthma inhibit his life, or that as he aged he'd decided to have one last hike before he hung up his boots. Whatever the reasons he might claim, none were so strong as to shake the idea from Fiona's mind Neil had bagged Beinn Bhuidhe for one reason alone: opportunity.

Fiona knew it was wrong to create a single theory as to the identity of Kevin's attacker when there were so many unknown details about the other baggers she had yet to discover, but she couldn't help speculating based on the facts she had at her disposal. All she could do was keep a close eye on Neil from now on.

'Can you put weight on your right leg?'

It was Neil who asked the question, but it was one Fiona wanted the answer to. With Lewis as soaked as he was from his fall into the burn there was no way he could continue hiking downhill when the temperature was so low. Hypothermia or exposure would do for him long before they reached a place of warmth where they could summon help. If by some miracle he didn't succumb to either, pneumonia would rear its ugly head.

Lewis shrugged and reached a hand up for Neil to help him get upright. Fiona helped too, and when Lewis was perched on his one good leg he tried putting weight onto his injured one.

The tentative way Lewis's foot connected with the snow and the grimace on his face when his leg straightened said everything. When Lewis tried a small step, he roared in agony and hopped on his good leg.

Fiona watched as Jack looped one of Lewis's arms over his shoulder and waited until Neil had done the same. 'We have to go back to the shelter.'

'Really?'

There was enough scorn in Jack's voice to flay a rhino, but Fiona didn't care about that. She was an officer for Police Scot-

land, not a day went by when a member of the public didn't
throw an insult or sarcastic comment her way.

As much as what she was about to say would leave her at
risk, Fiona knew what must be done. 'I'll lead. See if I can
trample something of a path for you.'

As hard as the hike downhill to the bridge had been in the
blizzard, the trip back up to the shelter was worse. Not only was
their progress slowed by the gradient, but Jack and Neil had to
support Lewis as he hopped between them. Every few paces
Fiona looked back and she spied Neil's left hand rise to his
mouth with a greater and greater frequency. Kevin's attacker or
not, he appeared to be giving his all in the task of helping to get
Lewis back to the shelter.

Neil's asthma was a double-edged sword she was afraid may
eviscerate her and others.

If Neil suffered an asthma attack that left him gasping and
unable to continue, she'd have no choice but to leave him and
Jack with Lewis while she returned to the shelter to get help.
That in itself was fraught with risks, as the falling snow had all
but obliterated the tracks they'd made coming down. It would
be easy to miss the shelter's position, as it was set a dozen feet
back from the main track.

The idea Neil may be the attacker still wrapped its fingers
around Fiona's thought processes. Should he be the guilty party,
how long would it be before he realised a fake asthma attack
would give him an opportunity to abandon Jack and Lewis so he
could strike out by himself?

Fiona halted and took a step back towards the three men.
'Neil, swap with me.'

For a moment Fiona thought Neil was going to argue, but
he didn't.

The next half hour saw a slow and torturous advance back
towards the shelter.

Twice they fell when Lewis's standing leg lost its footing.

On both occasions the snow cushioned Fiona's landing, but each time she felt a jarring pain in her shoulder. No matter how she gritted her teeth against the agony, beads of sweat formed on her forehead as she used her pain-weakened shoulder to give Lewis support.

The appointments Fiona had for the day after tomorrow loomed over her. It would be an agonising experience, but after today's events, and the aftermath of what happened on Luing, the appointments were getting more necessary with every passing minute. No longer could Fiona soldier on, no more could she tolerate the dull ache creeping through her entire soul. One way or another the appointments would have a profound impact on her future. She'd either continue to live in pain, or she'd face the examinations with a firm jaw and tears she refused to shed. The odds of her getting off Beinn Bhuidhe in time for the appointments were lengthening with every passing hour, and she was resigning herself to the prospect of having to reschedule them if she made it off the Munro in one piece.

After ten minutes, Neil and Fiona swapped places again.

Fiona managed another dozen gruelling, trudged steps before she felt the weight of a human body slam into her from the uphill side of the track. The suddenness of the impact destroyed any chance Fiona had of maintaining her balance, and together with the mystery figure she cartwheeled over the edge of the track and began to tumble down the Munro.

THIRTEEN

Unlike the slide down the side of the Munro when Jack had lost his footing and cannoned into her, there was nothing controlled or graceful about the way Fiona rolled this time. To protect herself as much as possible, Fiona made her entire body into as much of a ball as she could.

Another way this tumble differed from the first was this time the snow was deeper. Not an inch or two deeper. Not twice as deep. A full two foot deeper than the three or four inches that had been present on the descent to find Kevin.

The snow acted as a buffer. Not against the rocks and packed earth of the landscape that jarred Fiona at every contact, but as a soft barrier that offered gentle resistance to her wild fall. Instead of barrelling down the slope until it either levelled off or Fiona collided with a boulder large enough to halt her progress, the tumble lost pace as the accumulative impediment of the viscous snow did its thing.

When she came to a stop Fiona was breathless and bruised. Her troublesome shoulder felt as if her arm had been pulled off by a gorilla and then reattached by a sadist with a nail gun loaded only with the longest nails available. That was a problem for later. There were other pressing concerns.

The first of which was the whereabouts of whomever had thundered into her. The second was more practical, but no less urgent. During the roll down the side of the Munro, Fiona had lost her head torch. Without it, she had no way of knowing where she was.

As wonderful as it was the snow had stopped her plunge down the slope, Fiona worked out she must have caused a minor avalanche, as whichever way she tried to reach or stretch out a limb, she felt icy snow. Worst of all, she had no way of knowing which way was up.

Everyone who knows anything about snowy conditions will have heard of people caught in an avalanche who, disoriented by the experience, had tunnelled sideways or down when trying to find the surface. Fiona didn't want to join their ranks. Didn't want to become a statistic.

As disgusting as the act may be, Fiona didn't hesitate in allowing a dribble of spittle to trace a path between her lips and across the flesh of her face.

The spittle cut a track towards Fiona's right ear, telling her she was more or less lying on her right side.

Fiona's jaw tightened as the agony from her left shoulder reached new heights when she extended her left arm straight up from her shoulder. She'd tucked her thumb into her palm to form as close to a spearhead with her hand as she could.

The fresh snow provided no barrier greater than the pain of her injury. By the time Fiona's arm was at full extension she'd broken the surface of the snow. As best Fiona could tell, the snow ended at her elbow.

After a moment widening the air hole, Fiona planted her right hand beneath her and pushed her body upwards.

Fiona's head broke the surface and she gasped in clean air.

As much as she wanted to ponder the identity of whomever had thumped into her, Fiona's immediate focus was on getting back to her feet.

Now her upper body was in a semi-upright position, Fiona wriggled her legs and feet until she was able to rear out of the snow. Although she was ready to stand, Fiona stayed where she was and shrank back down in the snow. Fiona wasn't ready to stand, not yet, not after what she'd just seen.

The snow she'd ended up lying on was compacted by her bodyweight, but Fiona had enough desperation in her movements for her probing hands to scour through it. Beneath the snow she felt the wispy fronds of mountain grass.

Fiona's hands increased the area of snow she'd moved aside to find earth until she'd found what she was looking for: the direction of the slope.

If Fiona rose to her feet now, she'd be facing a point midway between straight down and left along the Munro.

This meant the wisp of light she'd seen was off to her right, as it appeared to be at a similar height to her.

Inch by inch, Fiona worked her body around until she was facing uphill. That was a true constant, uphill lay the track, her friends and the shelter. Downhill lay disaster and, now she'd turned, the light was on her left. Yes, it was her weak side, but she knew the only direction she could travel was uphill.

As she adjusted her position Fiona caught flashes of the light as it swept over her head.

The questions Fiona could have no answer to were: was the light from Jack launching a rescue mission? Or was it coming from the person whose impact had thrust her from the track into deep snow?

Fiona tensed her legs, then thrust herself upright in a sudden movement. The light was no longer a number of feet away. It was right upon her and, now she was standing, it beamed into her eyes with blinding effect. Beyond the light, all Fiona could see was a shadowy figure standing two feet away.

What Fiona didn't see, couldn't see, was the hand reaching for her.

FOURTEEN

Fiona, felt a hand grasp her left forearm. Not hard, yet there was enough pressure in the grip for her to know shaking the hand off wouldn't be an easy task.

'Are you okay, Fiona? I'm so sorry for knocking into you like that.' The male voice wasn't one Fiona recognised at once, yet she knew she'd heard it before.

'I'm fine.' Until she put a face and name to the voice, Fiona wasn't prepared to concede an inch nor show even the merest hint of weakness. For all she knew the man in front of her was about to finish what he'd started.

The light dipped away from her face and down onto the hand gripping her arm. Fiona didn't follow the light; instead she looked at the man who was wearing the head torch. It was Thomas. The slight man who she couldn't help but think of as runtish.

Thomas made a gesture up the slope. 'Come on, I'll help you get back up to the track.'

'Like hell I need your help. Go on, you lead, I'll follow.'

Fiona let Thomas set off before she fell in behind him. She had no idea why he'd done what he did, and beyond his initial apology he didn't seem too sorry. There must be a good reason for him to leave the shelter, but until she was back with Jack and Neil instead of being left here alone with Thomas, she could wait for answers; although she was on her guard in case Thomas had left the shelter as he was the killer and when he'd seen them returning had decided attack was the best form of defence.

As much as Fiona wanted to leave some distance between her and Thomas, there was no way she was prepared to let him out of her sight. He may try attacking her again, and also, Thomas had the only light between them. Without a torch of some kind, it would be near impossible to follow the track back up to the shelter without risking another downhill plunge.

All the same, Fiona kept a good couple of feet behind Thomas as well as placing herself the same distance to the side. It wasn't the best defence, but she was out of reach and would have a chance of reacting to any move he might make.

The only moves Thomas made were trudging uphill as he forged a path towards the track. Every few steps Thomas would twist his head to check Fiona was still following him. It was at these moments Fiona's heart beat a little bit harder. His checks might be a genuine thing, but every time he looked round, the head torch he wore dazzled Fiona and whenever she couldn't determine Thomas's body language, she felt vulnerable.

Should Thomas be Kevin's attacker, and had he recognised her as a cop from the PR pieces she'd featured in, it made sense for him to try and eliminate the threat she carried as a police officer. Yet when he'd found her after their tumble, there had been no aggression in his body language. Fiona knew the time she'd taken freeing herself from the snow created the best chance Thomas was likely to get to finish the job he'd started.

Fiona got that Thomas might not have fancied taking her on in unarmed combat. It's no secret police officers are trained in how to defend themselves, and are taught a variety of holds designed to subdue attackers. Had the slight Thomas not dared engage her in a one-to-one battle?

It made sense he'd baulked at the idea. Their joint tumble down the slope could be explained away as a mishap, but if he'd returned to the group sporting wounds synonymous with a fight there would be little doubt as to what had happened. If Thomas was Kevin's attacker, it meant Jack wasn't, and Fiona knew Jack wouldn't give up searching until he found her. Not just because he was a decent guy, but because there was no way Donna would accept anything less from him.

Another consideration was Thomas had perhaps seen something when Kevin was attacked. Something he'd kept to himself. If that was the case, had he then come after the attacker and picked on her by mistake?

Should this new theory be correct, it put Jack and Neil squarely in the frame. At this realisation Fiona began to dread what she might find when they did reach the track. Would she find either Jack or Neil with their head caved in? Or would one of them simply be missing?

The trip back up to the track was a purgatory hell, as however much Fiona thought she had a good surface to push off, her foot slid back at least half a step every time she moved upwards.

Fiona bent her mind to what might have inspired Thomas to barrel into her. Good old misogyny would have a lot of men thinking that, in a procession, the woman would be in the centre protected by a man in front and behind. If that idea was correct, there was still the question of who Thomas thought he was targeting. She understood that in the conditions it was difficult to distinguish one human shape from another, but there were some major differences between her physique and that of Thomas's potential target. Jack and Lewis were both a good six inches taller, and while Neil was much the same height as Fiona, he was far bulkier across the torso.

It wasn't easy for anyone to mistake Fiona for either of the three men who'd been with her.

For all Thomas was in the same party as Neil, they hadn't seemed too close. And if Jack had been the one to attack Kevin, it didn't tally Thomas had kept his mouth shut for so long. Fear for his own safety was an obvious reason for him not to tell everyone the truth of what happened, but that didn't stack up as a credible excuse. Discounting Kevin, when they first met, Thomas was in a group of five along with another two uninjured men who'd be able to prevent Jack from attacking his accuser.

When they'd arrived at the shelter, the odds had shifted even further in Thomas's favour as the burly Lewis and Ivor were there. With so many people to prevent Jack from harming him, Thomas hadn't a good reason to stay silent. Or had he?

Fiona allowed the back of her brain to nibble a morsel of a developing idea. Perhaps Thomas had kept his silence for a reason other than self-preservation. If Kevin died and Thomas knew the identity of his attacker, had he planned to blackmail the attacker once they got off Beinn Bhuidhe and he'd had a chance to create an insurance policy against something happening to him? Had a crisis of confidence seen him reverse his plan and decide to give Kevin's attacker a taste of his own medicine?

A light ahead twinkled rainbows from the deluge of snow-drops passing through its beam. It wasn't coming from Thomas's head torch; it was someone else. A tall figure.

The rangy figure of Jack was soon displayed by Thomas's torch. Jack stayed in place as Thomas trudge-slipped his way past, but as soon as Fiona was within reach, he wrapped a long arm around her and hugged her tight, the embrace pouring a generous amount of petrol onto the fire in Fiona's shoulder.

'I thought you were deid for a moment there. Donna would kill me had owt happened to you.'

'I'm fine.'

'What happened?'

'I don't really know. He came out of nowhere, crashed into me and we went tumbling. By the time I'd picked myself up, he'd come looking for me.'

'I see.'

Jack released Fiona and gestured for her to continue her passage uphill.

A minute later Fiona was standing on the track beside Neil and Thomas, watching as Jack clambered to his feet.

Jack didn't speak, didn't show any hint of what he was about to do, as he thundered a huge punch into Thomas's face, sending him flying into the uphill slope.

FIFTEEN

The one positive Fiona could find about Jack's assault on Thomas was he seemed to be content with only throwing the one punch, as he made no move to follow up with further blows.

Neil was of a different mind, and he squared up to Jack with his fists bunched. 'What the blazes do you think you're doing, you fool? Why did you punch him? For goodness' sakes man, he's no more than half your size.'

Jack pulled a face and remained otherwise still, his expression a blatant dare for Neil to try throwing a punch at him. Before either man could strike the other, Fiona pushed her way between them. 'That's enough. We're in enough trouble as it is without fighting each other.'

'You tell that to him, he's the one who just clocked poor Thomas.'

'That's enough, Neil. Instead of acting the macho hero, why don't you check Thomas out?'

When Neil pulled away, Fiona jabbed a finger into Jack's chest, as she leaned in to hiss in his ear. 'Are you mad? You assaulted someone right in front of me. An unprovoked assault at that. You do know I should be arresting you for that, don't

you? What do you think will happen when we return to the
shelter and the rest of them learn what you did? As soon as they
find out I'm a copper they'll either insist I arrest you, kick you,
me and Donna out of the shelter, or a couple of them will try
and get revenge. Why, Jack? Why did you hit him?'

'Because he tried to kill you.'

Fiona had to give Jack some credit; after she'd spelled out
the consequences of his violence, he looked ashamed of himself.
It wasn't a lot of credit though.

'I heard you scream and when I whirled around I caught
sight of the two of you tumbling down the hill.' Jack's arm
pointed up the Munro. 'For some reason he tried to send you
crashing down. Not me, Neil or Lewis. You. I reckon it's
because he knows you're a copper. Donna said you didn't trust
the others, and that made me wonder if you think there's more
to Kevin's accident than you're letting on. Don't kid yourself,
Fiona, you were targeted. You said yourself he came looking for
you after the fall. I'll bet when he saw you were all right and
hadn't been hurt, he daren't take you on without the element of
surprise. If you had been hurt, I reckon he'd have covered you
with snow and left you to die.'

As Fiona cast her eyes to where a dazed Thomas lay in the
snow, Jack's thought's jibed with her darkest suspicions about
the way Thomas slammed into her. Whichever way she stood it
up, Thomas had knocked her flying, not any of the three men.
Jack was right: she was a threat to someone on Beinn Bhuidhe.

Other than what she'd said to Donna, Fiona had been
keeping her suspicions to herself. She'd played dumb about
Kevin's fall, not once had she made even a suggestion it was
anything other than an accident. It was the same with Lewis's
slip on the wooden bridge. She'd kept her thoughts on that quiet
too, as she wasn't sure whether Neil had set a trap, or if it had
been a genuine accident. After this incident with Thomas,

Fiona was now thinking others among the group shared her suspicions about Kevin's accident.

Now Thomas had shown an act of aggression by slamming into her, Fiona couldn't help but wonder if he was in cahoots with Neil. The motive for the attack on Kevin was still unclear, but for two people working together, it would have been easy for one of them to halt and speak to Kevin, while the other used the cloaking effect of the snow and the distraction of conversation to launch a sneak attack. That all spoke of planning, though, and the snow hadn't been due to arrive until the early hours of the morning, by which time they'd all have safely made their descent off Beinn Bhuidhe. The same applied to this situation. Neil could have agreed to lead a rescue attempt and then created a reason to turn back, by which time Thomas could have joined him and together they could have disposed of those making up the rescue party and then made their escape.

From the corner of her eye, Fiona saw Thomas had regained his feet with Neil's help and was looking their way. Thomas's free hand was held up in surrender, his left eye already swollen enough it was slitting.

'I don't know why you hit me, but I'd guess you think I tried to hurt Fiona. You got it wrong, you great ape. I was chosen to come after you to stop you risking your lives going for help. There's no point now. Kevin passed shortly after you left the shelter. I was cutting a corner so I could catch you up. I lost my footing and came down at speed. If Fiona hadn't been there, I'd have probably gone right over the track and ended up a lot further down the hill. Believe it or not, crashing into Fiona probably saved my life.'

Fiona held an arm across Jack's chest as a way to stop him launching a second assault on Thomas. There was no way the arm was strong enough to hold him back – it was more the message it sent.

'I'm sorry, Thomas. I got it wrong. I thought you were attacking Fiona.'

The first thought in Fiona's mind, after sorrow at learning of Kevin's death, was assault had become murder. As Dave Lennox had taught her to, she probed at what she'd just heard from as many perspectives as she could. If Thomas was telling the truth, he'd risked his own wellbeing to save them from endangering their lives. That was a positive act.

Yet if Thomas had concocted a lie to cover up his reasons to attack Fiona, the lie would be disproven upon their return to the shelter. Therefore, logic suggested there was more truth in Thomas's statement than falsehood. Thomas's voice had dropped when he'd broken the news of Kevin's death, but that wasn't hard to fake. Neil, on the other hand, had pulled a face as his eyes misted. Not so easy to fake without fair warning.

There was another alternative, a less than palatable one. If Neil and Thomas were working together, and Thomas was lying about Kevin's death, Fiona, Lewis and Jack couldn't be allowed to return to the shelter.

The only way they could be prevented from getting back to the shelter was for Neil and Thomas to either lead them on the wrong path, or kill them.

If this were a typical Friday night shout, as emergency services referred to a 999 call, to the White Oak, Fiona would back herself against either of the two men when fully fit. With her shoulder aching the way it was, and none of the usual police arsenal at her disposal, she knew she'd struggle to best either the scrawny Thomas or the asthmatic Neil.

Fiona was clear about what she must do. It was the only course of action open to her that didn't involve risking her life slogging through snowdrifts for hours. She pushed Jack towards the uphill slope. 'Come on then, let's get back up to the shelter. It'll be a damn sight warmer than standing around here like spare parts at a wedding. You guys can lead, we'll follow.'

Thomas raised a hand and helped Neil pick up Lewis. As soon as they were two paces ahead, Fiona and Jack started after them. The only light Fiona had to guide her came from Jack's head torch so she had to stick close to him.

It wasn't just the thought of warmth that had Fiona eager to get back to the shelter. It was the friend she'd left there, alone in a room full of strangers. She'd thought there had been safety in numbers, but now, thanks in no small part to Jack's quick temper, it was looking more and more like they were being outnumbered. Not a position anyone wanted when there was a murderer among them.

SIXTEEN

Fiona got why Jack had lashed out, she just wished he hadn't. Not only would it create a level of distrust between them and the others, but it was also a perfect example of his quick temper. If Steve or anyone else had suspicions about Kevin's fall, the fact Jack had felled Thomas would make him a potential suspect in everyone's mind.

With the act of violence, Jack had painted himself as the villain of the piece. While Fiona could believe he'd lashed out at Thomas for the right reasons, there was no getting away from the fact Jack was wont to hit first and think later. That's why she couldn't discount him as a suspect for Kevin's murder. And until it was proven otherwise, Fiona was working on the principle Thomas had told the truth about Kevin.

As much as she could, Fiona tried to convince herself that if it was Jack who'd murdered Kevin, he wouldn't do her any harm. Not when she was one of his wife's oldest and best friends. Donna may forgive Jack for lashing out and killing a stranger, if a conviction for manslaughter was how it ended. Yet, Fiona knew her friend well enough to know Donna would never stand by Jack if he killed someone she cared about. Fiona also knew how much Jack doted on his wife. It was obvious in his every glance and embrace of her. So far as Fiona was concerned, Jack's love of Donna was a potential reason deterring him from attacking her.

By the same token, Jack's punching Thomas hadn't been a sudden lashing out. He'd waited until Fiona had regained the track. There had been a minute or two where he'd had an opportunity to strike and hadn't. Instead he'd picked his moment. That meant he'd had time to consider his actions. To think of the consequences. And he'd still thrown the punch.

Some women might feel flattered by a man riding into battle for them. But when Fiona had ever felt flattered by a man, it came when they listened to her thoughts on a topic and then had an intelligent conversation.

On and on they trudged. As much as they were following the path, they also trampled in the snow on the tracks left behind from their attempted descent, so the challenges of trekking uphill negated any advantages they'd earned.

The more distance they covered, the harder the going became for Fiona. Not just on a physical level, but also a mental one. On top of all her theorising about everything that had so far happened, she was worried about any number of things.

As much as Fiona was close enough to keep the three strangers in sight, she was also far enough away to react if they tried anything. Her eyes were flitting up and down between the snowy path she walked on and the men in front of her. Every muscle she possessed was ready to react at a moment's notice if either of them moved in a way that made her feel threatened.

Even though the complete lack of visibility created by the blizzard made it impossible to gauge distance with anything close to a degree of accuracy, Fiona was convinced they ought to be nearing the part of the track where it curled back on itself and ran along the section where the shelter was located. Neil and Thomas were leading, and if they were planning to harm her and Jack, one of the best ways to do so would be to carry on past the turn in the track and then abandon them to wander on the side of the Munro. That would be a risky strategy as they'd need to ensure their own return, but now the thought was in her head, Fiona couldn't help but worry about it as a prospect.

There was also what might greet them at the shelter. Fiona didn't believe any real harm had come to Donna yet, but she knew her beliefs guaranteed nothing. As much as she feared one or two of the other group might have worked together to attack Kevin, all eight of them being in collusion didn't make sense. Two or three, yes. Four to five, not impossible, but improbable. All eight, no.

None of this hypothesising meant the killer hadn't sown seeds of doubt and dissent. If it had been surmised Kevin's fall wasn't an accident, fingers would be pointed and what better suspect was there than a stranger?

If any of those in the shelter had remembered the order they were in when Kevin fell, they'd recall she and Donna were leading the group. A fact she knew Donna would remind them of. Jack had been among the other group, though. It was him the finger of suspicion would be aimed at. His name that would be associated with the attack.

Were all Fiona's musings about Neil's and Thomas's role in Kevin's murder to prove groundless and they made it back to the shelter, Fiona could only see a hostile environment awaiting them.

Whether Kevin was anything more than a liked colleague was unknown. But it was certain he would be mourned by Steve, and there was no telling how Steve would react when cooped up for hours with a person he believed had killed his uncle.

Fiona tensed. Ahead of her Neil had reached across Lewis's back and touched Thomas's arm. Was this a signal? Were they about to attack? To dash off and leave her and Jack behind to founder in the blizzard?

Neil's arm moved in front of Thomas and, together with Lewis, the two men changed direction. Fiona upped her pace as much as the snow gripping her legs allowed. Neil's head turned their way, and he smiled at her.

There was no urgency in the body language of any of the men in front. They did nothing more than continue to trudge onwards. In a different direction. At the same laboured pace.

Fiona realised her error. This wasn't the point in their trek where they were ambushed. It was the point where the track curled back towards the shelter.

Now as Fiona trudged forward, the biggest worry she had was that they'd carry on right past the shelter as the footprints they left on their way down were now all buried by the snow.

It was the wrong thing to worry about. A fact Fiona realised when she saw Neil's legs fold beneath him as he crumpled to the ground, pulling Lewis with him, although Thomas managed to release Lewis before he was dragged down too.

SEVENTEEN

As Fiona dashed forward to get to the men, she was keeping a close eye on Thomas and Neil in case the collapse was nothing more than a ruse to get her and Jack in close so they could be attacked.

Jack was on her heel and he barged Thomas out of the way then stood guard while she checked out the fallen Neil.

To see what she was doing, Fiona whipped Neil's torch from his head, jammed it over her head, and shone it into his face at an oblique angle so as not to dazzle him.

Fiona saw blue lips, and confusion on Neil's face. His breaths were nothing more than panicked gasps. Everything Neil was displaying were symptoms of an asthma attack. That would also explain the collapse.

Except it was cold enough for Neil's lips to be blue. And confusion wasn't the hardest thing to fake. As for the panting, that took no doing at all; she was panting herself from the exertion of the climb and she was younger and fitter than Neil, plus Neil was half carrying Lewis. Had she not been so suspicious of Thomas and Neil, she'd have continued to take her turn at Lewis's side.

As a police officer, Fiona encountered fake confusion almost every time she questioned someone about a crime they were alleged to have committed. Fiona's radar was attuned to the various tricks people used when trying to lie to her. She knew all the signs and how best to counteract the attempts to deceive.

Instead of asking questions Fiona chose to make a statement. 'You're having an asthma attack. Stay still and try to be calm. If you tell me where your inhaler is, I'll get it for you.'

Neil pointed a hand back the way they'd come. If he'd lost the device during their trek, it wasn't good for him; however, Fiona didn't believe Neil had dropped it without his knowledge. The inhaler was something he'd used at frequent intervals during their treks through the snow. Therefore, it was something he'd take great care of. It wasn't a few pennies falling from his pocket to hide themselves between the cushions of his sofa; the inhaler was something that helped him breathe.

As Lewis rolled himself clear, Fiona bent until she was on her knees beside Neil. To protect herself from a sudden attack Fiona made sure his arm was trapped between her knees and his body, and she planted a hand on Neil's shoulder as she patted the pocket she'd seen him use to store the inhaler. If he tried to rise, she'd put more weight on the shoulder to pin him down.

Through the padding of Neil's jacket Fiona felt something hard and square. It could be the fob of his car keys or any number of other items, but when she pushed her fingers into the pocket and retrieved the square shape it was the inhaler she was holding.

Rather than administer the dose herself, Fiona took Neil's hand, planted the device in his palm and moved his hand to his mouth, then looked at Thomas and Jack.

'You two, help me sit him up.'

Neil depressed the canister and sucked in a breath of the atomised drug. A minute later he was sitting up in the snow, his back braced against Thomas's legs and his feet pointed down the track.

'What happened? Where am I?'

The questions were answered by Jack, but Fiona wasn't convinced they weren't a ploy to reinforce the confusion element of the supposed asthma attack. Neil was on her suspect list for a reason, and this episode had yet to play out to its conclusion. If this was a ruse, their move would come any moment.

'We'll have to carry him.'

The words came from Jack, and not for the first time since leaving the shelter Fiona wished he'd use his brain more. Where before Jack had been so suspicious of Thomas he'd clobbered him, he was now accepting at face value the supposed asthma attack. Fiona put Jack's about face down to the fact he believed Thomas's story about coming to save them and felt guilt for punching the younger man. Whatever his reasoning, his statement showed he was taking Neil's condition at face value.

Jack's naivety burned at Fiona. Either he was wrong to be so trusting, or she was wrong to have so many doubts.

Thomas made sure Neil could sit without support and positioned himself at Neil's right side. 'Jack, you get the other side. Fiona, can you manage his feet?'

'I could, but what about Lewis? We can't just leave him.' Fiona gestured at Thomas. 'I'll take over from you, and you can help Lewis.' While Fiona believed Lewis to be innocent, she still didn't want to be one-on-one with anyone in the other group until she'd contented herself they weren't the murderer. As both Lewis and Neil were large men compared to her and Thomas, it made sense Fiona and Thomas helped Neil while the stronger Jack assisted Lewis, but that would leave her in a potential two-on-one situation, and if any attack was to be made, Jack would be far more able to repel it.

The place where Thomas had stationed himself made

Fiona doubt herself even more. When they lifted Neil, they'd all be facing down the track. To return to the shelter they'd have to rotate themselves through a hundred and eighty degrees.

Fiona managed to wriggle her way into a position that allowed her to support Neil as Thomas withdrew his aid. The weight of Neil's body on Fiona's left side had her arm and shoulder screaming for mercy, but there was nothing she could do about the pain except grit her teeth against it.

They'd gone less than a dozen lumbering steps when it struck Fiona they were close to the shelter. Instead of them struggling to haul Neil and Lewis back between the three of them, it would make a lot more sense to let Neil rest and get his breathing back under control while one of them went to the shelter to get reinforcements. Now Kevin was dead, Steve would be able to come and help; the quiet guy, Ivor, was built like a steam locomotive and would be a damn sight fresher than any of them.

Fiona was on the point of suggesting this when the snow before her sloped away. She had no memory of this slope, but when Fiona descended the incline the head torch picked out a bank of snow boulders forming a wall at the other side of a rudimentary trench.

'This is the shelter. Ivor said he'd make it easy for us to spot when we came back.'

It was a clever touch, but until she saw the actual shelter Fiona was on high alert for any sudden movement from Neil or Thomas.

None came.

Five paces after discovering the trench, Fiona saw the shelter.

Few sights had ever looked as good to Fiona as the former shepherd's house. It had never been an architect's special project; its purpose was to provide function over form, and shrouded as it was by billowing snow, its rough stone construction was uglier than ever. To Fiona, in this moment in time, the shelter was the most beautiful building in the world. Prettier by far than the Basilica de la Sagrada Familia in Barcelona or the Notre-Dame Cathedral. Even the stunning Taj Mahal didn't get a look in.

Two kicks on the door saw it opened and the rugged face of Ivor staring at her, a walking pole held out in front of him like a spear. Its tip had been blunted by use, but was still sharp enough to pierce flesh if thrust by a man as powerful as Ivor.

EIGHTEEN

When they entered the shelter they were greeted with surprised looks from everyone as Ivor sprang to help them with Lewis. But Fiona's eyes sought a different view. She found it in the shelter's second room. On the bench closest to the door, Kevin lay still with his jacket draped over his head and torso. It wasn't the greatest mark of respect for someone who'd passed, but Fiona could find no fault with it as there was nothing else anyone could do.

It made sense they'd moved him away from the stove, but Fiona could only imagine how traumatic the act would have been for Steve.

The urge to pull the jacket from Kevin's face and check for further foul play was strong, but Fiona resisted it for the time being. The longer the other group didn't know she was a copper, the more they might reveal.

Ten minutes later Fiona, Jack, Thomas and Neil joined Lewis by the stove. Lewis had been stripped of all clothes bar his underwear and redressed in a variety of garments sourced from most everyone.

As part of the stripping process, Steve examined Lewis's

leg. As soon as he could, he fed Lewis's hiking boot back onto his afflicted limb and tied the laces tight.

'Lewis, your ankle appears to be sprained. You need to keep your weight off it, okay?'

'Will he be all right?'

The question came from Sara, Lewis's wife. Fiona had watched her with care as soon as the door was opened. By clinging onto Jack's arm earlier, Donna had shown her feelings about him risking his life on a rescue attempt. Sara had done no such thing.

'He'll be fine. He'll be dancing with you afore you know it. I'll strap him up. Can you make him an ice pack from the snow outside to help the swelling?'

Instead of rushing to her injured husband upon their return, Sara had remained in her seat, what could almost be described as a look of disappointment on her face. It could be she was used to Lewis being a clumsy lump, or she was dejected help wasn't on its way, but whatever emotion she was wrestling with, it wasn't spousal concern. Even her question to Steve seemed to be for form's sake rather than a genuine interest in Lewis's wellbeing.

This information was stored away with a dozen other tiny details Fiona had picked up when they'd re-entered the shelter. Now it was time to see what else she could learn about this group of strangers.

Fiona gazed at the mug of hot water Alice had given her. Now the wood stove had been going for a while, the shelter had enough heat for the occupants to shed their jackets. Someone, Fiona guessed at the domineering Alice, had got the old-fashioned kettle and boiled up some snow to give everyone a hot drink. Perhaps one of them had sought out a water source, after all, there must be one near the shelter for the shepherd to use when he lived here. Fiona couldn't recall one, but there were many small rivulets that had been piped beneath the track up Beinn Bhuidhe.

Fiona took care to blow on the liquid before touching it to her lips. It had to cool, and she had to warm up otherwise she'd be scalded, or at the very least would end up with chilblains on her lips. A fine look to have when she went to Glasgow for her appointments.

When Fiona took a sip the water tasted better than any of the fancy coffees Aunt Mary had sent as a birthday gift. Better than her favourite meal, chicken Caesar salad with garlic croutons, at the Harbour View restaurant in Oban.

Thoughts of that delicious salad brought back memories for Fiona. The last time she'd eaten there, she'd been treating Edwin Hamilton. Edwin was a guy she'd met on Luing. At first a suspect, he'd ended up providing invaluable help, and she credited him with saving a life. There had been nothing romantic between them and never would be. Edwin was a kind man with a good heart, but he was nothing more than a friend. Like his mind, Edwin's tastes were uncomplicated, and he'd demolished the double burger eating challenge then rounded off the dinner with a bowl of ice cream he'd slurped from his spoon with an expression of rapturous delight.

Across the shelter from her, Neil and Lewis were cradling mugs of soup Alice had made from one of the packets.

Jack sat beside Fiona, his head bowed as Donna clung to him. Suspicious glances had met them all when Thomas's blackening eye was seen by the occupants of the shelter.

'Come on then, Thomas, tell us what happened out there. And don't you be giving me any of your usual nonsense, I want the truth of it.' Alice stood with hands on hips like a headmistress admonishing a naughty child.

Fiona didn't care how Alice stood or what her body language said. It was the words from her mouth she was focusing on. There was history between her and Thomas, and for the time being, the best way to learn more about the other group was to sit back and observe.

'I hit him.' Jack held up both hands in apology as Donna pushed herself away from him. 'He came down a slope and crashed into Fiona. The two of them went tumbling down the hill. I thought he'd deliberately tried to hurt Fiona so I clocked him one. It was a mistake, I got it wrong, but you've no idea what it's like out there. When you're cocooned by the snow like that, you can only see four or five feet in any direction. Your minds starts playing tricks on you. You find yourself imagining all kinds of weird things. It's not just that, but the snow was getting deeper and deeper and it was hard work taking even a single step. I shouldn't have hit Thomas. He was coming to save us making an unnecessary trip. I'm man enough to admit I was wrong. If it makes anyone feel better, Thomas is welcome to take a swing at me to even things out.'

There was a rustle at Fiona's side as Donna nestled back into her husband.

'Thomas is half your size, you great bully. If anyone gets to even things out, it should be someone who can hurt you as much as you hurt poor Thomas.' Frances rose to stand in front of Jack, her face grim as she pointed at Ivor. 'He's closer to your size. He should be the one to pay back what you did to Thomas.'

'Not happening.' Ivor folded his arms, his face set into the kind of grimace that forbade argument. 'Fighting solves nowt.'

Frances's nostrils flared. 'He hit your friend, someone you've worked with for years and you're going to sit there and do nothing? I thought you were better than that, Ivor. They're not locals, their accents tell me as much. We don't know them any better than they know us. We've all worked at Inveraray House for years. You've known poor Thomas for years and you're going to let an outsider thump him without doing anything? And to think I thought you were a good man.'

'Oh do be quiet, you silly woman.' Alice gestured at

Thomas then Jack. 'Jack getting punched won't help anyone. It won't make Thomas's face hurt any less, and what Jack said makes sense. In his shoes I would have skelped Thomas too.'

'He should be punished.' Frances's lip stuck out like she was a chastised kid. 'It's not right that he hit Thomas.'

'No, it's not. But it is understandable. If you could think with more than one brain cell at a time, you'd realise that. Jack made a mistake, but at least he has the decency to admit it. We're stuck on a Munro in the middle of a blizzard, and he was out there risking his life trying to get help for Kevin. Yes, he got it wrong when he punched Thomas, but are you really so stupid as to not see the big picture here?'

At Alice's brutal comment, Frances backed off and wedged herself on the bench between Ivor and Lewis's wife, Sara, her face a picture of distressed fury.

Steve's yell silenced everyone.

When Fiona cast her eyes to where Steve was pointing, she saw Neil was now clutching his throat.

'What's wrong with him?' The question came from several voices.

Steve was bent in front of Neil, his face a mask of concern. 'He's gone into anaphylactic shock. Does anyone know if he's brought his epi-pen?'

NINETEEN

While the others rooted in Neil's backpack and pockets looking for an epi-pen, and argued about what they knew about him being allergic, Fiona stayed back and paid attention to as many of the conversations as she could while also thinking deep thoughts.

Alice had been the one to provide the soup, but when she'd reached for the packet she'd taken a long look at it before handing it to Frances with a few words. Frances had then moved the packet back and forth until she no longer had to squint as she examined it. This told Fiona both women had been checking the listed allergy information.

Nobody at the time had mentioned allergies, so both women must have known to be careful.

Neil was gasping for breath as Steve knelt in front of him and pulled Neil's sleeves up in what Fiona presumed was a search for an allergy identifying bracelet. Both arms were bare save for a battered watch.

Alice tapped Steve on the shoulder. 'We haven't found an epi-pen. Sorry.'

'It says here it may contain wheat.' Thomas waved a packet of soup as if it was a winning lottery ticket.

'That's good. Does it mention nuts? He's allergic to nuts.'

Fiona got why Steve was asking about nuts. Nut allergies were often the most dangerous as one of their symptoms was a closing of the oesophagus. People with nut allergies tended to let those in their orbit know, however, as the allergy could be so strident as to be triggered by airborne particles from someone who'd eaten nuts.

There'd been a shout she'd been called out to one time because a drunk guy had eaten peanuts and then visited their peanut allergic neighbour. The airborne particles on their breath had been enough to trigger a reaction. That hadn't been the reason for her attendance; she'd been there to arrest the woman's sons for beating the peanut-breathing neighbour unconscious.

'No.'

Lewis snapped his fingers. 'What else does it contain? He's allergic to celery as well.'

'You're wasting your time.' Alice snatched the packet from Thomas with a snarl on her face. 'We gave Neil tomato soup. Like the eejit he is, Thomas is giving you the allergy information from oxtail soup. Frances and I checked the ingredients for nuts or traces of nuts, as it's no secret he's allergic to them.'

'Where's the packet for the tomato soup then?'

'Frances threw it in the stove.'

The shelter fell quiet enough to hear a wasp fart as they all looked at one another. Thomas had been right to try reading off another packet, though it was unfortunate there was more than one flavour. Frances had no doubt thought she was reducing litter by burning the empty packet. Fiona was sure that in Frances's mind she'd assumed nobody could think what she'd done was in any way sinister.

Fiona could. Both Alice and Frances had examined the

packet for information regarding allergens – she already worked that out. By passing the packet to Frances, Alice had shifted, or at least shared, the blame. Frances's burning the packet could be viewed as good housekeeping or destroying evidence depending on how you looked at things.

An idea came to Fiona so she acted upon it. 'Can someone pass me those two packets of soup over, please?'

The packets were handed over without comment by Thomas, although Fiona could feel every eye in the room watching her as she looked at the back of the packets. 'Steve, I don't know if this will help you any, but the allergy information is pretty much the same for both the oxtail and chicken broth. They both contain soya, celery and eggs. The oxtail warns it may contain wheat, and the chicken broth may contain wheat and milk.'

'Right.' Steve's head tilted as he considered what she'd just said. 'Of those allergens, the ones that can cause anaphylaxis are milk, soya and celery. Neil had tomato soup, which was likely to be cream of tomato. Which will probably have milk and soya in it. I'd guess at celery too as it's used in a lot of dishes. I don't think it's the milk or soya. Anaphylaxis is a rare symptom for those allergies, and when you look at how much has splashed over his leg and onto the floor, I think it's fair to say Neil didn't drink a lot of the soup, but he's probably had enough to trigger an anaphylactic shock.'

Lewis cradled his mug to his chest. 'He's right, celery's great for adding flavour. Kevin and me never made soup without it. Will Neil be okay?'

Steve answered without turning his head. 'If he can stay calm, I think he will. I'd sooner give him a jab with an epi-pen though. After this and with his asthma to contend with, he cannot exert himself at all. He'll have to be airlifted, or carried down.'

'What about his inhaler? I've seen you giving him puffs from it. Won't it make him better?'

'No. The Salbutamol in his inhaler will help ease symptoms such as the anaphylaxis, but it won't treat the root cause. Untreated, he could suffer from anaphylaxis for hours.'

Once again silence enveloped the shelter. It was obvious what was needed, but nobody wanted to be the one to say it. Fiona didn't let her mind go that way, as she had other things to think of.

The negligence of Alice and Frances in giving the allergen-laden soup to Neil could be nothing more than ignorance. If they hadn't known of Neil's second allergy, they couldn't be held accountable. If they had known and had claimed not to have seen it, there was something else afoot. That made Frances burning the packet all the more sinister.

If either Frances or Alice had meant Neil to suffer an allergic reaction, Fiona wanted to know why. Both women had been in the first group she, Jack and Donna had encountered. The members of that group were all suspects in Kevin's murder. They were also potential witnesses.

Fiona couldn't help but wonder if one of the women had seen Neil attack Kevin and had fed him the soup as a way to exact revenge. It was a leap to imagine either woman behaving in such a manner. Alice's caustic nature meant she wouldn't have been able to keep her mouth shut. She'd have called the killer out as soon as she dared. With a room full of people, there were more than enough bodies present to make sure there could be no violent retribution against her. The same logic applied less so for the mousy Frances, but Fiona couldn't see her keeping quiet either.

Frances had been furious with Jack for punching Thomas, and it was Frances above all others who'd campaigned for Jack to be punished for his crime. Those kinds of moralistic traits weren't picked up and put down at will; they coloured a person's thinking throughout every interaction. While Frances was perhaps not confident enough to point the finger herself, Fiona could see the woman confiding in someone as to what she'd witnessed. From what Fiona could tell, in the short time she'd been in the group's company, Frances had something of a soft spot for Thomas and found comfort and protection from either Ivor or Sara, or both of them.

To carry on that logic, Neil and Thomas seemed close so it didn't seem probable it would be Thomas in whom Frances confided.

With so many relationships to assess and keep track of, Fiona didn't realise Jack had stood up and was reaching for his jacket until she heard the rasp of his zip being fastened.

'Neil needs an epi-pen, or at the very least a fresh inhaler. I'm going to go get one and raise the alarm. No need for anyone to come with me, I'll go by myself.'

As Donna yelled at her husband not to go, the shelter descended into chaos as everyone voiced their opinions by shouting down others.

It was just as Fiona had feared it would be. Fractious. Everyone was scared, tired, hungry and worried about their companions. Each person in the shelter had someone with them they cared about. Some wanted Jack to go and get help and medical supplies, others – Donna most of all – thought all he would achieve was the throwing away of his life.

Fiona's opinion was that a murder suspect, albeit one who was low on her list, might be making a bid for freedom. Were Jack not possessed with his fiery temper and tendency to lash out first and think later, he might drop off the list altogether, but Fiona knew of too many instances when Jack had got himself into fights he had no business starting. The one saving grace about him was that to her knowledge he'd never once been that way with Donna.

TWENTY

The uproar at Jack's declaration of intent was loud and fierce. Of the eleven people in the room, only three were silent: Neil who was still fighting for breath, Ivor because he never seemed to speak unless directly spoken to, and Fiona.

One of the many lessons Fiona had been given by Dave Lennox when the wise sergeant had taken her under his wing, was the value of observation at a time of strife. Instead of getting into the middle of group arguments and adding her voice to all the others, he'd taught her it was best to stay calm and look for the little tells which told a truer story about the relationships each protagonist had with the others.

He'd likened his theory to a game of chess with the king rarely being used for offence or defence. Instead the king was the piece others revolved around, leaving the king to observe and assess every square on the board while others were sent into battle and oftentimes sacrificed for the greater good.

As a naïve young woman, Fiona had pointed out the most powerful piece on the board was the queen. Instead of arguing Lennox agreed the queen was far more dangerous than the king. He then pointed out the realities of the situation. The most dangerous and powerful piece was also the one most prized as a trophy.

Fiona would never forget how he'd explained the next part of his theory. 'Think of it this way. If there's a bunch of eejits going at it, the sooner you can identify the various chess pieces among them, the sooner you can neutralise them all. Sometimes the big guy doing all the mouthing off is nothing more than a pawn or bishop who will be sacrificed by others. You need to work out who the king and queen are, and they may not fit the gender roles so don't assume the queen is always a woman. Find the true source of the group's power and either neutralise them, or get them to get everyone else to stand down.'

Lennox's theory had seemed like a wind up until the two of them had attended a shout where they'd encountered two street gangs facing off against each other. Other officers were between the gangs and while no violence was actually happening, the threat of it hung in the air like an autumnal mist.

Instead of getting between the gangs with the other attending officers and adding his voice to the din, Lennox stood on the sidelines for thirty seconds then pointed out a tall lad decked out in a faded St Mirren away strip. 'Go and arrest him for breach of the peace and get him in the van.'

Three minutes later the St Mirren fan and another lad from the opposing gang were locked in the caged rear of the van. As they drove away, Lennox explained to them both they'd be taken to the station and charged. This would happen every time there was an incident involving their gangs. Nobody else would be charged. Just them. It was then up to each of them to control the others because sooner or later, one of the charges would see them do serious time.

It had been an eye opener. With his tactic Lennox was beheading the snake, or at the very least defanging it.

So now Fiona sat and observed what was going on. Alice was raging away as expected, a bishop at most. Sara had come full circle and was demanding Jack be allowed to go for help as her husband was injured. She was a rook, deadly in straight yet obvious lines.

Steve was with Jack on the need for help, but Fiona saw him as a pawn. Someone who gets used as bait for the opening skirmishes. That didn't mean he couldn't play a major role, but the odds were against it happening.

Thomas and Lewis were the second row of pawns to advance; nothing more than backup to protect those in front of them. Their words merely echoing the arguments others put forward with more eloquence.

It was the near mute Ivor that Fiona gave highest stature to; he was the king, with Neil in the role of queen. As the chief instigator of this heated debate, Ivor was exercising a large amount of power while also adding levels of threat. If someone went with him, they'd be at risk, but the need to get Neil proper assistance off Beinn Bhuidhe was a counterbalance to the dangerous undertaking Jack was volunteering for.

Frances was a pawn, happy to follow others' directives even if they put her at risk.

That left Donna and Jack. Donna was screeching her thoughts into the argument with increasing fervour. Fiona ranked her as a knight, not because Donna wasn't a higher-ranking piece, more because her friend had that quality of being underestimated. That made her a wildcard piece who could attack in unimagined ways.

Jack was a rook or bishop. Straight lines were his thing, and when Donna's influence over him was exerted, he'd become a pawn, manipulated for the benefit of a higher-ranking piece.

It was Frances walking across the shelter who silenced everyone. Jabbing fingers drooped and faces contorted with anger settled into a more normal look as she eased her way between people.

She was walking towards Fiona. Her face carrying an expression of puzzled uncertainty.

Every eye in the shelter was on Frances as she looked at Fiona from a distance of two feet. 'Forgive me if I'm wrong, but aren't you the copper who was involved in that business on Luing in the summer? The murders in the Borders last year?'

Never underestimate the danger of a pawn. No matter they are the least mobile of all the playing pieces, they can still determine the outcome of a game.

Fiona had two choices. Admit Frances was right and deal with not only the expectations of the innocents in the shelter, but also the attacker knowing she was a threat to their liberty, or lie.

After both recent incidents, Police Scotland had publicised her success. She'd been photographed in dress uniform and the picture had been sent to all major news outlets along with a press release that overlooked the mistakes she'd made and celebrated her achievements. The resultant press attention and clamouring for interviews wasn't something Fiona liked or wanted. She'd refused all and when a relentless reporter had dug up the murder of her parents and asked for her comments, she'd threatened to ram her pepper spray up his arse and then release it.

The reporter had backed off, but the clamour hadn't yet died. Both Donna and DC Heather Andrews, Fiona's closest friend in Lochgilphead – where she worked and lived – had alerted Fiona to an online petition calling for her to be given detective status.

Both flattered but furious at the public's interference in her private business, Fiona had resisted the urgings of friends to try and use public opinion to get her the detective status she so craved. None of them understood her reality, nor her reasonings. If Fiona ever became a detective, it would be down to the fact she'd been able to leave her demons at the exam room door and sit the exam the same way every other detective had.

The picture of her in dress uniform made Fiona look a lot different to how she looked now. The picture had been taken on a bright day and she'd been parade-ground smart. Now she was bedraggled, cold, wet and wrapped up in a collection of layers. It would be easy to laugh off Frances's query, except for one thing. The reporter she'd threatened had taken a parting shot some weeks after. He'd snapped her and other officers responding to a fight outside a pub in Inveraray. It was a warm night, but there had been a sudden downpour and she'd been drenched as she wrestled with a drunk woman on the pavement.

The piece had been written out of spite. Instead of writing about the way Fiona and others had defused a violent altercation, the narrative of the article centred on the topic of how the mighty had fallen. The smiling press release images of Fiona were contrasted with ones of her hard-faced as she gave no quarter to a drunk and stoned woman who two minutes earlier had tried to bite Fiona's arm. Instead of praise for someone doing a thankless task, the reporter had questioned Police Scotland and Fiona's ambition, asking if both parties were content for the hero of two extraordinary cases to 'deal with things a teuchter with a big stick could sort'.

Fiona and Police Scotland had taken great exception to the comment. Not least because the term *teuchter* was a commonly used insult for those who lived north of the Glasgow-Edinburgh line.

More piercing than anything for Fiona was the accuracy of the accusation. She wasn't precious about her appearance, and anyone with live cells between their ears would be able to read between the lines of the picture. What got under Fiona's skin most was she possessed the ambition the reporter accused her of lacking. She had it far more than he'd ever understand. But, with her ambition came responsibility. No matter the corners that might be cut to aid her journey to detective, she was going to do it right, or not at all.

The Inveraray picture, as Fiona thought of it, was a game-changer. It had shown her day-to-day self, and she imagined that right now she looked every bit as bedraggled as she did in that damned picture. A few members of the public had recognised her from the PR pieces, but a lot more had identified her from the Inveraray photo.

This all left Fiona with a dilemma, now. If she lied, then Kevin's attacker might not believe her. In his place, she wouldn't. By lying, and getting caught in the lie, or even disbelieved, she'd be telling the attacker she was trying to hide her cop identity. To do that would then make them question why. She'd been heavily involved in the search for Kevin. The attacker would know as much. They'd also know she hadn't exposed the attack on Kevin for what it was. At least not to the group as a whole. Paranoia about what Fiona knew or suspected was sure to take root in their mind. If they then worked out Fiona was trying to catch them, the only way to protect their liberty was to strike again. At Fiona.

The one good thing about the weight of expectation that came with Fiona's unwanted celebrity was that it put every eye on her. She'd experienced it a few times and while it had been a burden then, in this situation, it could provide her with some safety. Or it would if she didn't have so many reservations about allowing Jack to make a solo attempt to raise the alarm.

Fiona looked at Frances's hypnotic eyes for a moment then lifted her gaze over the shorter woman's head so she was addressing everyone in the shelter. 'Yes, that was me.' Fiona paused as murmurs rumbled among the strangers. Most were of the 'I knew it' or 'I don't watch the news' variety.

It was Alice – who else? – who had the most to say on the subject. 'If you're a copper, why didn't you arrest that great ape for punching Thomas? Surely you saw what happened, or were you conveniently looking the other way?'

There was nothing Fiona could do to save herself, or Jack. She had many flaws, she knew she did, but lying wasn't one of them.

'I saw Jack punch Thomas, but I'm off duty, so I don't have handcuffs should I decide to arrest him. Down there' – Fiona pointed out the door – 'I didn't know if I could trust Thomas. Jack is married to one of my oldest friends. I've known him for more than twenty years. In short, I trust him. If Thomas wants to make a complaint against Jack when we get out of here, I'll listen to it and take the appropriate action, but for now I'm doing nothing. Not because Jack is my friend, but because there's not a whole lot I can do that won't cause us more problems than we're already facing.'

Every eye looked at Thomas. He looked round the room, as if assessing who may or not back him. It was Frances whose eye he held. She nodded.

'I won't be making a complaint. Not now, not when we get down.'

A clamour rose as Frances, Lewis and Sara disputed Thomas's decision, while Donna and Jack thanked him for his graciousness.

Alice wasn't finished, though. 'I trust you're not thinking this is going to be another one of those instances where you get your photo in the paper?'

'Of course not.' Fiona aimed a hand at Jack. 'As for you going for help by yourself, Jack, that's a non-starter. It was tough enough when there were three of us to help Lewis. If anything happened to you when you were on your own, you'd freeze to death before anyone even realised you were in trouble. With the snow as deep as it is, it's at least a four-hour trip to get help. It'll also be fully dark by now, so the visibility will be even worse. By the time you raised the alarm and a rescue party made their way back here, those four hours would become at least ten, probably twelve. If you had an accident like Lewis did, say an hour after leaving here, it'd be eleven hours before we'd even start wondering if you'd made it down safely. If you were hurt, there's a chance you wouldn't be able to stop the snow covering you. Then when the snow eases enough that someone else tries venturing out, or those who are expecting us back raise the alarm and send a search party to look for us, there's every chance they'll walk right by you if you're buried by snow.'

Jack didn't speak. But nor did he sit down. All he did was gesture towards the other room where Kevin's body lay, Neil and then Lewis. The action said everything. But everything was too much. If they waited until morning or at least for the snow to stop falling, Lewis wouldn't be able to hike down with them, and it was too far for him to be carried without a stretcher. That meant Lewis and at least one other person, probably his wife, Sara, would have to remain in the shelter with very little food to see him through until rescuers arrived. What Fiona didn't care for was the unspoken insinuation Lewis would die. Humans can survive three weeks without food, and there was no way Lewis would have to wait that long.

Fiona had already worked all of this out in her head and divined a solution of sorts. Under no circumstance was she going to allow Jack to strike out by himself. Not just for the reasons she'd stated, but also the possibility of him being Kevin's attacker and therefore desperate to abandon the group to its fate.

'You're not going alone, but I do believe an attempt to summon help ought to be made. As I've already said, I'll go along with you.' Rather than take another stranger along, Fiona wanted someone she knew well. Jack may be on her suspect list for the attack on Kevin, but he was near the bottom and it was better to have someone she didn't much trust than someone she didn't trust at all.

'You might think that's okay, Fiona, but it's not okay by me.'
Donna was on her feet, her face a mask of restrained fury.
'What was it you said earlier? You're single whereas Jack has
me? In case you think we might have split up since you said
that, let me set you straight. We haven't.' Donna's arm flashed a
counter-clockwise sweep of the shelter. 'Let one of them other
buggers go. Why should my Jack risk his life for a stranger? It's
different for you, you're a copper. It's your job.'

Trust Donna to get the wrong end of the stick and use it to
beat the wrong target. A fabulous friend, Donna was someone
who thought nuances were a kind of pasta sauce. She'd never
been able to read between the lines, and whenever she heard
something she didn't like, she'd always speak long before she
thought about what she was saying.

'Donna, listen up a minute.' Jack took his wife's hands and
looked straight into her face. 'No, don't look at Fiona, look at
me. Neil needs an epi-pen as soon as possible; Lewis is in no fit
state to hike down either. If it was good weather, as a group, we
might be able to carry one of them down, but it's awful weather
and we can't carry them both. You have to trust me. Trust I'll be
okay. Trust I'll make sure Fiona is okay too. And you have to
trust Fiona to not let me do anything stupid. Can you do that for
me and Fiona?'

'Bastard.' Donna slumped back onto her seat and glared
their way. The insult was her way of conceding defeat and
letting them know how she felt about it. 'See if you don't come
back, I'll be on Tinder and Plenty of Fish as soon as I have a
signal.'

Fiona saw Jack wink at Donna. 'No worries. I'm already on
both anyway. Shouldn't be hard to find you.'

'I'd swipe left if I saw your ugly mug.' Donna leaned
forward to give Jack a kiss. When she broke contact she retained
her grip of his head with both hands. 'Seriously, you better
come back unhurt. Both of you.'

Fiona nodded her thanks at Jack and wished she didn't have to leave the shelter. As well as the trip being a dangerous one, what she really wanted to do was learn more about the group of strangers. Beyond their names and the fact they all worked together, she knew nothing about them, and to solve the murder, she'd have to learn a lot more about them all.

TWENTY-ONE

Donna pushed past Fiona and squared up to her husband. 'I can't risk losing you. I won't risk losing you. If you think you're going without me, you've another think coming. If you're going, so am I.'

Fiona wedged herself between her friends. 'That's enough. This is all getting far too *Spartacus*. Donna, I think the world of you, but you're not leaving this shelter. Trust me, I've been out there, it's too much for you. Everything Jack said about thinking all kinds of crazy ideas happened to me too. Jack and I will go. If there's another volunteer to come with us, then fine, otherwise we'll go alone.'

Donna's top lip curled as she plonked her backside onto the bench. She knew she was prone to histrionics, it was something Fiona and Jack often teased her about. Whether saying she was going with Jack was something said only to prevent him from going, or she intended to accompany him on the trek for help, didn't matter to Fiona. What mattered was Jack now accepted her company.

Since her own hat was still on Lewis's head, Fiona reached

over and rested her hand next to where Donna had laid hers. 'May I?'

'Of course.' There was truculence and fear in Donna's tone.

'I volunteer to go with you. We can't let your group hog all the glory.'

Fiona had been half expecting Alice to chip in. The point about glory was a stupid one, but Fiona let it fly past without comment. There was a bigger reason why she didn't want Alice along. For all the woman seemed to be in good physical shape, journeying through the snow required more than stamina and determination. To be successful the attempt had to be co-ordinated between the various people present. Alice's nature was to take charge; she'd want to lead, and as the leader, Fiona expected Alice would get so far and then come up with an idea of her own to try and shorten the trek. To get safely down, there was only one way, and that was the track and then when it reached the glen floor, hike across the fields to the bridge crossing the River Fyne.

Another reason she didn't want Alice to join them was Alice was the self-appointed leader of the other group. As such she'd keep them more or less in check. Alice would be the one to organise people to get wood from the pile at the back of the shelter. She'd make sure the stove was kept warm and everyone got their turn to have a warm drink. That more than anything else is what Fiona wanted Alice to be doing.

'Thanks, Alice. You're very welcome to tag along. Who do you think we should nominate as leader of the shelter if you're away? Sara? Frances, or maybe Ivor?'

Alice's mouth opened and closed as she looked at the people Fiona had named. Fiona had selected each the three for different reasons: Other than her insistence Jack be punished in kind for punching Thomas, Frances appeared to be a caring soul who'd make sure everyone was looked after, but there was no authority about the woman. So far as Fiona could judge, Sara would have enough about her to do everything Alice would, but Fiona had spied a certain coolness between the two women and guessed ceding power to Sara would burn at Alice's sensibilities. As for Ivor, the taciturn man exuded capability, but the idea of him being centre stage was laughable, as he was as far as anyone could get from being one of life's communicators.

By highlighting how she saw Alice as the leader of the group, Fiona was hoping that being allowed to 'tag' along with them would make Alice realise that if she was to join them, she'd be giving up power to adopt the role of a minion. If Alice accepted those terms, Fiona would admit she'd misjudged the woman.

'I'll come too.' Thomas eyed Jack with caution. 'Unless you still don't trust me?'

Fiona saw Jack give a nod but she wasn't sure about whether Thomas's presence would be a good or bad thing. He could prove to be either an asset, or if he was the killer looking to find a way to escape, a dangerous liability.

'Then it's settled, Alice. I'd say you're needed here more than I am.'

Fiona turned to face Thomas. Over his shoulder she could see relief on the faces of Frances and Ivor, but disappointment on Sara's. 'You sure?'

'Yeah.'

'Don't be a fool, Thomas. You can hardly see out of one eye.'

'You got any steaks with you, Alice?' Thomas gave a lopsided grin as Alice shook her head. 'So if you haven't got a steak for my eye, the next best thing will be a cold compress. Being out there will be better for my eye than being in here.'

Fiona felt no amusement at Thomas's destruction of Alice's argument. All she could think of was the fact she'd be going out into the blizzard with two men who'd already clashed. Large parts of Thomas's story had so far checked out. Kevin was dead, and therefore Thomas's reason for coming after them to save them the trip was indisputable. However, the way he'd cannoned into her still rang alarm bells in her mind.

As she prepared to exit into the snowstorm once more, Fiona tried to consider everything they may need on the way. Snow shoes were the obvious thing they'd most benefit from having, but wishing wouldn't make them appear. Her thoughts turned to what they already had a supply of. 'Does anyone have a torch, or spare batteries, heat warmers for our hands and feet? What about dry socks or clothes?' Fiona would have asked for walking poles, but the three she'd seen were traditional walking poles without the snow baskets a couple of inches up from their tips. They'd be more of a hindrance than a help.

'I have a spare head torch.' Lewis fished it from the pocket of his jacket as Ivor opened a camouflage backpack and handed over a small torch.

Ivor said nothing as he passed his torch to Jack, but there was enough mistrust in his eyes for Fiona to feel relief at the fact the two men were about to be separated. She knew from bitter experience the longer people were cooped up together in a perilous situation, the more they fell out with each other. For all Thomas seemed accepting of Jack's apology, it didn't mean Jack hadn't made other enemies when he'd lashed out.

There were a few mumbles from the others about how they'd either passed spare clothing to Lewis, or had used their dry socks on themselves.

Donna rose from her seat and wrapped her arms around Jack. 'You two better look after each other. If anything happens to either of you, I'll hold you both responsible.'

'Ignore her, Fiona. If owt happens to me, she'll be on Tinder before she calls the undertaker, and if anything happens to you I'll be looking at a fortnight in the spare bedroom. Three weeks tops, she'll miss the tickly game too much to keep punishing me.'

Fiona could see from Donna's expression Jack's teasing assessment had missed its intended mark. Instead of triggering Donna's habit of sexualising non-sexual situations or phrases, and drawing a smile from his wife, all Jack got was the kind of stern look that was more familiar on Alice's face than Donna's.

TWENTY-TWO

Fiona hadn't travelled more than a dozen steps from the shelter before she realised something was different about the blizzard.

On her previous attempts to trek downhill the snow had swirled at her from every angle at once as if she herself was the eye of the storm. Now it was coming from a uniform direction, but with less of a driving force behind it. In its own way, that could be a good thing, or it would be if the new conditions weren't more likely to create track-obscuring drifts.

Another difference in the snow was the size of the flakes. Earlier they were the size of a ten pence piece; now they were at least as large as a two-pound coin. Not good. The smaller flakes had soon built up a sizeable depth, but these larger flakes would only create deeper drifts in a shorter time.

Before leaving the shelter a second time, Fiona had sourced a length of rope. It was perhaps a dozen feet long and that was perfect for her purpose. She gave a quick demonstration of how she wanted the rope held. Thomas was to lead then Jack in the centre of the group and her at the rear. Between the two men the rope was to be allowed to droop a little. Should anything happen to Thomas, the dropped rope would soon alert Jack.

However, the rope between her and Jack would be kept under a gentle tension. Should anything happen to either of them a change in the tension would inform the other. Fiona had considered keeping the whole rope taut, but doing so wouldn't inform her if anything happened to Thomas. Or if he decided to strike out on his own.

Not for one moment did Fiona believe Jack would abandon Donna. That among other factors, including her knowledge of the man, made him the least likely of all her suspects. It didn't mean she could discount him, though. Not with his temper and the way he was so quick to raise his fists when challenged. She'd always thought he'd grow out of it as he aged, but an incident a couple of years ago had taught her that if anything, his penchant for settling matters with his fists had got worse.

She'd stopped in to see Donna and Jack on one of her trips down south to see Aunt Mary. Jack had dropped her and Donna off at a pub near Gretna, where they could have a bite to eat, a few glasses of wine and a good catch-up. It had been a great evening filled with laughter and gossip until Jack came to collect them.

Throughout the evening Donna and Fiona had noticed the sidelong looks coming towards them from a couple of guys at the next table. From what she'd overheard of the guys' conversation Fiona had deduced they were staying in the area for a couple of nights due to work, as they kept talking about some project or other.

Fiona hadn't been under any illusions as to who the guys were looking at: Donna had always been the pretty one. It was she who got hit on, not Fiona. That suited Fiona, who had no interest in forming a relationship with any man. When she felt the need she could find someone to sate her biological urges for a week or two and then she'd end things. Fiona knew losing her parents in such an abrupt manner was the reason she never let herself fall for anyone. She accepted that as her lot in life. So far as Fiona was concerned, it was better to feel lonely from time to time than to risk loving someone and losing them. With Aunt Mary's help, she'd overcome one debilitating tragedy in her life, but it didn't mean she felt strong enough to do it again. Not when avoiding the pain was so easy to do.

Just as Jack walked into the pub to join them for a quick drink before driving them back, the two guys were standing by their table in the middle of chancing their arm. One was passing Fiona and Donna each a glass of wine, while the other carried two pints.

Fiona was telling the guys they weren't interested, but they weren't taking no for an answer. When Jack moved close enough to overhear one of the guys call them frigid lesbians, things went belly up. Fast.

Neither of the men saw Jack coming. The one closest to him got a shove in the back that sent him sprawling over the next table, both the pints he carried spilling to the floor amid the tinkle of broken glass.

The second guy didn't get off so lightly. He'd barely released the wine glasses as he put them down before Jack had spun him round and slammed him into the wall, his hefty forearm pressing into the guy's throat.

It had taken both Donna and Fiona to pull Jack off the man. As soon as they'd got Jack to release the guy, Donna ushered her wild-eyed husband out the door, while Fiona apologised to the two guys and the woman behind the bar who was shouting for them to get out or she'd call the police.

On the drive back to Donna and Jack's Gretna home, Donna had raged at Jack for not trusting her. Jack had tried to protest, his temper waning as every defence he mounted got shot down.

Donna had been right. Jack had behaved like an animal. He had acted without thinking. His temper would one day be his downfall.

Was today that day? He'd already lashed out at Thomas. Would he punch him again? Or maybe goad him about their altercation? These were questions Fiona couldn't yet answer. She wanted the answer to be no. Not just a no, a resounding no. But not for Jack's sake, for Donna's.

Regardless of Jack's temper, Donna loved the bones of him. In all other ways he was a wonderful husband. Jack was attentive, sympathetic to Donna's needs, he didn't drink too much, didn't gamble and never once had Donna confided in Fiona she thought Jack had a wandering eye. But he did have a fearsome temper when something he cared about was jeopardised in a real or imagined way.

They hadn't gone any more than a hundred paces before Fiona realised how much deeper the snow was. Where before it had come up to the middle of her shins, it now reached her knees.

Every step was close to becoming an endurance feat. It would be worst for Thomas at the front of their line, as he didn't have the luxury of treading in someone else's footsteps. Fiona could tell from the fresh tracks Jack was using Thomas's path to ease his own, and it was a move she aped. Even so, it was hard going.

Doubts about the wisdom of their attempt started to plague Fiona. As the representative of the emergency services among the group, ought she have made an executive decision and forbade this excursion? How sensible was it to endanger three lives? Would the next time she featured in the press be her obituary? Earlier Steve had insisted on getting his uncle help, and it was Kevin needing urgent medical care that had prevented Fiona from discouraging the first attempt to get down to the glen and raise the alarm. If she had pulled rank then and decreed there should be no attempt to strike out for help, she could have been putting her head in a noose should Kevin die before help arrived. But that was then and this was now. Kevin was dead. And here they were, risking three lives to hopefully save one.

Fiona balled her left fist and thumped it against the outside of her right thigh, the action hurting both her shoulder and leg. The pain was a distraction she needed.

The die had been cast and they were trying, come what may; now they'd started, there could be no changing a decision that had already been made.

As Fiona huffed and panted with the exertion a new thought came to her. It wasn't a welcome one. The trek was taxing her, she was fit, she made sure of that. Never a sprinter, Fiona had always been better at distance running. She had a good core stamina and even though she might be a little breathless, she knew she could continue on like this for a good few hours before she was in any real danger of her strength giving out. Jack was big and strong and fit, but Thomas's slight body made him appear puny and runtish, and while he might have a wiry strength about him, how much stamina he had was anyone's guess.

It was with this realisation Fiona made a decision. When they got to the bridge she'd insist Jack and Thomas swapped places. Jack's long legs would forge the best path through the snow, and the rope would give her fair warning should Thomas decide to try anything underhand.

After twenty minutes of that order she could take a turn leading with Jack behind her. Then Thomas could have another shift at the front. To share the burden of leading among them all would be to third it. It was a nice theory, one that had all kinds of merit, or would have if Fiona had factored in one alarming point: the snow was no longer reaching her knees; now it was covering them.

Short of walking like a stork crossed with an Irish River-dancer, the only way to keep progressing forward was to lift each leg as high as she could and then kick her foot through the top few inches of snow.

It was easier to wade through chest deep water than it was to walk forward. Still Fiona pressed on, until two hard jerks of the line halted her.

Jack was sending her a message. The message was unknown but there were no more pulls on the line. Rather than remain tight it went slack, so she forged her way through an area of snow that came to the middle of her thigh.

She didn't know what to expect when she caught up the three-pace lead she'd given Jack, but it wasn't the presence of Thomas at his side.

Thomas's head shook side to side as she approached him.

'The snow's near up to my you-know-whats, and it's getting worse the further we get from the shelter. We need to decide if we keep going or turn back while we still have a chance of making it back to the shelter.'

Fiona realised all her worries about their endurance levels had been a subconscious trick of the mind. By fixating on this, rather than the reality of their situation, Fiona had distracted herself from thinking what Thomas had just voiced as the snow deepened.

A glance at Jack saw him looking back at her. Jack wasn't one of life's natural leaders. He was a follower, and other than the occasions where his temper got the better of him, never put himself in a decision-making position.

Whether Jack felt they should go on, or return to the shelter, he'd take his lead from her, that much was clear from his face.

Fiona looked at her watch for two reasons. The first being she wanted to see what time had passed since they'd left the shelter. The second being it was her dad's watch, not hers. By looking at the watch, she could perhaps divine what her dad wanted her to do.

Half an hour had passed since they'd closed the shelter door behind them. The first attempt had seen them reach the bridge in twenty minutes. Twenty minutes to cover a quarter of a mile meant they'd been travelling at a mile every eighty minutes. At that pace they'd have reached their cars just over six hours after setting off.

Now their pace was slowed even further and after a half hour they hadn't yet reached the bridge. The six hours she'd calculated for the previous attempt had just become eight or nine for this one. She and Jack and Thomas might be able to keep going for that long, but there was no telling how deep the snow might get the longer they kept going. They were still a good way off it yet, but once they got a certain distance from the shelter, it'd be harder to turn back than continue forging forwards.

At some point it would get to a zero sum game. They'd only sink so deep into the snow before the compressed snow underneath their feet acted as a support. The problem was if that happened to be crotch deep, it would be a torturously slow journey.

By every common-sense metric the decision to turn back and return to the shelter was a no-brainer.

Equipped with show shoes and so forth, a rescue team would make far quicker progress up Beinn Bhuidhe than they were making down it. An additional point to this was the fact that, alerted to Lewis's and Neil's conditions, the rescue team would bring with them the appropriate equipment.

Fiona reasoned with herself about those at home who were expecting any one of the twelve of them to return having raised the alarm. She couldn't speak for the others, but nobody was awaiting her. She was next on shift in three days. The dreaded appointments were in two days' time, but how much fuss would be made if she didn't show for them? She was due to call Aunt Mary for one of their twice-weekly catch-ups tomorrow night, which in real terms was a long time away.

One of the others would have a partner or family member of some sort who called it in. There were too many of them not to. Likewise, a concerned citizen such as a worker at the Fyne Ales Brewery where they'd left her car might have raised the alarm after they didn't return.

The question was, how would the emergency services react? It was a job for Mountain Rescue, of that there was no doubt. However, with a capricious wind and zero visibility, no helicopter pilot would be fool enough to try searching for them. Even if someone was brave enough to take a helicopter up, the best they could do would be to fly at a height where they'd be safely above all the Munros and try searching for them using thermal imaging.

Fiona had no idea at what distance thermal imaging cameras worked up to, but she assumed the ones used by Mountain Rescue helicopters would be among the best on the market and would therefore work at a respectable distance. However, even if the helicopter was directly above them and picked up their presence, there would be no way the pilot would be foolish enough to attempt to land on the side of the Munro, or even hover above the shelter and drop a rescue line, regardless of how much he trusted the instruments in his cockpit.

The way Fiona was thinking, if a pilot was courageous enough to risk flying in these conditions, their equipment would pick up the heat signal from the shelter first. The Mountain Rescue team would know about the shelter and would assume any stranded baggers had holed up there to wait out the snowstorm. Once the pilot knew the shelter was in use, there was every chance the heat signals given off by the three of them were likely to be dismissed as belonging to sheep.

All of these musings left Fiona undecided. A man's life could hang in the balance. It would be a dereliction of duty to not do everything in her power to get Neil the medical assistance he needed. But, there was nothing to be gained by the potential sacrifice of herself and two others. To press on was a near-suicidal mission.

Fiona looked at Thomas. 'We can't go on. With the snow as deep as it is, it'll take us hours to get down and there's every chance we'll either freeze to death, get lost, or have an accident like Lewis did. I know Neil is your friend and seeing him lying on the bench without any dignity upsets you, but we have to face facts: it's too dangerous to go on.'

Thomas' face tightened as he gave a tiny nod and set off back up the track.

When Jack followed him, Fiona fell into her position at the rear of their expeditionary party. She'd hadn't gone five paces before she felt the weight of guilt settle onto her shoulders.

TWENTY-THREE

The head torch Fiona wore illuminated no more than four feet in front of her as she trudged uphill after Thomas. Jack was leading and she was content to bring up the rear.

As expected the going was slow and laborious as they trekked along the track. Even before they got to the first switch-back, Fiona was breathing hard and had developed a sheen of sweat on her torso.

As she felt trickles of perspiration trickling down her back, Fiona's fingers, nose and toes were numbed from the cold, and no matter how much she sniffed, she couldn't prevent her nose from running.

The one benefit of being so isolated in the snow was it gave her the chance to think without interruption. Although Fiona had to stay alert to her footing, and the tension on the rope they each held, the going was so slow and measured she could do that on auto-pilot.

Fiona's mind was focused on the people in the shelter. If she'd had more time with them and the conversation wasn't so dominated by either attempts to summon help or recriminations about individual actions, Fiona knew she'd have made a point of

making innocuous enquiries about the group to give her a better
handle on their various relationships and what any of them may
have had to gain by murdering Kevin.

Rather than rehash what she'd already considered about
some of the shelter's occupants, Fiona bent her mind towards
those she'd yet to shine the spotlight of suspicion on. She knew
little about any of them, but the taciturn Ivor was someone who
intrigued her. None of the other group, not even the forthright
Alice, had challenged Ivor on not having much to say which
indicated his wasn't a voice they were used to hearing a lot of.
Therefore his silent behaviour was the norm.

Ivor was old enough for others to look his way for guidance,
yet that hadn't happened. With everyone in hiking gear there
wasn't too much to gauge about anyone's social status from the
way they dressed, but Fiona had spent enough time researching
her own hiking gear to recognise that both Neil's and Kevin's
equipment was almost as good as money could buy while
Thomas's seemed to come from the bargain basement bin. Ivor's
salt-and-pepper haircut gave him the look of a businessman
rather than someone whose hands provided his income, but that
didn't mean a lot. None of the three women wore makeup, but
then again, she didn't herself, and Donna had applied nothing
more than a quick smear of lipstick.

From previous experience in dealing with the public, Fiona
had learned when a taciturn person spoke, they were worth
listening to. That had been the case so far with Ivor, but to
Fiona the way the others didn't ask his opinion sat with the
slump of an untrained puppy.

The only way Fiona could get her thinking aligned with the
others' ignoring Ivor's opinion was to assume she was mistaken
about him. Yes, he might have made a couple of wise utterances
and have a businessman's haircut, but that didn't mean he was
who she guessed him to be. For all she knew he could be
anything from the hotel manager to a pot washer with a vain

streak. It was wrong to assume that if he did have what some might view as a lowly occupation he could be of any less help, or his opinion didn't count, but other than the vote, none of his group had turned to him for advice. That told Fiona Ivor's opinion wasn't valued; yet it had been him who Frances had urged to punch Jack. Did Frances's haranguing of Ivor suggest he was handy with his fists? If so, was it the biggest clue yet as to the identity of Kevin's killer?

Were it the case Ivor was disliked by the group at large, if he'd been considered to be intelligent, someone would have said something to bring Ivor into the conversation, even if it had taken the form of a sarcastic comment.

All of these thoughts reverberated around Fiona's brain like a hyperactive pinball, but each thought always bounced off the same bumpers. Ivor's eyes held wisdom. Ivor's beefy physique seemed ideal for the physical demands of a trek for help.

Yet Ivor had voted to stay in the shelter and wait for help to come, or at the least morning and the end of the snowstorm. Ivor hadn't volunteered, which in some ways made him less of a suspect; however, if he had struck the blow that led to Kevin's death, he was perhaps playing a huge bluffing game.

The lack of challenges to Ivor from the others also had a variety of potential sources. It could be the others knew he was hopeless at directions and didn't trust him not to get a rescue party lost, or that Ivor had an illness or recent surgery making him a poor choice for the taxing endeavour going for help was sure to be. It was here Frances's entreaties for him to punch Jack again reared into Fiona's perspective.

The list of potential reasons nobody pushed Ivor to get involved with either opinions or physical help was long, but the one Fiona wondered about the most was if Ivor wasn't asked because for one reason or another, the others were afraid of him. It was the reason which made the most sense, and sat with her copper's way of thinking.

Assume nothing, believe nobody and challenge everything were the foundation of police training. The ABC mnemonic was something Fiona reminded herself of every time she put her uniform on.

As much as she could, Fiona had to challenge her own thought processes. Had to make sure she was forming theories from her observations and suspicions rather than creating a theory and shoe-horning facts into her thinking to make her theory work.

Ivor and the other group's interactions with him were something to think about, but not something she could use to point a finger without a lot more evidence.

Fiona moved on, Ivor wasn't the only person she hadn't given a lot of thought to. There was also Sara to consider. Sara had been somewhat vocal when her opinion had been asked, but had otherwise left the speaking to Alice. The way Alice dominated the conversation wasn't something that made assessing a group easier, but Fiona had long ago learned how to listen to one person while observing others. She wouldn't have lasted five minutes in uniform if she'd not been able to do so.

Sara and Lewis were married. Fiona knew that much about her. She also knew the marriage was in trouble. When Lewis, Jack, her and Neil had left on the first attempt, Sara had neither sent her man off with a hug, nor told him to take care. Fiona understood everyone was different and while Donna and Jack were very public with their affection of each other, another couple might not be. That was normal, everyone had their limits and like-minded people tended to find each other.

For a wife not to offer any hint of affection or even tell her husband to take care when he was about to risk his life spoke volumes about the condition of their relationship.

Likewise, when Lewis had returned with an injured ankle, Sara had shown little more than a perfunctory concern. To

Fiona it was almost as if Sara was doing just enough to not draw attention to herself. A trait common among guilty people.

As Ivor did when the vote had been taken, Sara voted to not risk an attempt to get help. Yet despite not thinking it safe, she hadn't protested Lewis's involvement in the first attempt.

All of this indicated to Fiona Sara no longer cared for Lewis in any meaningful way. So why were they still together? What had gone wrong for them?

The answers to these questions were in their dozens and not something Fiona wanted to waste time considering. As a couple they'd chosen to bag Beinn Bhuidhe together with colleagues. Whatever the source of strife in their marriage, and whatever reason they had for sticking it out, that was their business and would only become Fiona's if she found either of them in the frame for Kevin's murder.

Another thing Fiona had noticed was all the time Steve had been examining Lewis's injured ankle, Lewis had kept his other leg well away. This was something he continued to do long after a spare pair of socks had been sourced and Lewis's good ankle was covered.

Fiona was aware of the risks of jumping at shadows and figured this was nothing more than an attempt from Lewis to protect his injured ankle from collision. All the same it hadn't escaped her attention that as soon as the rudimentary ice pack had begun to melt, Lewis had reached for the other sock and boot.

Ahead of Fiona, Thomas's back seemed to disappear into a swirling white gloom. Fiona's brow furrowed, the tension on their lead rope hadn't changed and the distance between them seemed the same as it had been since adopting their formation.

Realisation struck Fiona a cold blow. From her pocket she produced the small torch Ivor had given Jack. No longer than the width of her hand it seemed feeble compared to the heavy police torches she was familiar with.

Fiona's thumb depressed the button and the torch flared into life, its beam a bright whorl that dimmed within seconds. Ivor's torch gave off more light than her own, but not by much.

Not good.

They'd passed the first switchback on the track, but they still had a long way to go and many hours before daylight even thought about trying to slink its way through the blizzard. How long the torch would last was unknown. For now it illuminated the trench made by Jack's and Thomas's footsteps just fine, but if the initial flare was its usual output, it was now operating at no more than half of its capacity.

Jack and Thomas each had a torch, and Thomas had the spare given to him by Lewis. That left them one spare between three of them. They'd manage with two torches, but how long the remaining two might last was anyone's guess.

Cold sapped batteries. That was something Fiona had learned the hard way. She'd bought her first car during a cold snap. Overeager to get her own transport, she'd ignored the fact the car had struggled to start when she'd taken it for a test drive and believed the salesman's line about it 'just needing a decent run out to put a good charge on the battery'. A fortnight after handing over payment for the car, Fiona had to fork out for a new battery as no matter how far she drove, the old battery was incapable of maintaining a charge overnight if the temperature dropped below zero.

When given Ivor's torch by Jack, Fiona had looked it over. There was a port where a charger would be plugged in. Therefore, even at a full charge, it was unlikely the battery would be as good as a new one. To try and preserve the battery life Fiona encased as much of the torch in her gloved hand as she could. There was little chance the action would have a significant effect, but if it prolonged the battery by even a quarter of an hour, it would help.

As Fiona trudged after Thomas she was trying not to think

about Ivor knowing the torch wasn't at its best. Trying not to think he'd passed it over without any hint of a warning about it. Maybe he didn't know. Perhaps he'd used the torch often enough to know it would last for hours.

Or maybe he'd known it would only last long enough to get them too far away from the shelter to safely navigate their way back in the dark.

TWENTY-FOUR

Time lost all meaning for Fiona. It would be easy to pull back her sleeve and look at Dad's watch; to take comfort from whatever its hands indicated. It would be a pointless act. Whether it was now midnight or March was of no consequence. All that mattered was distance. And depth.

Fiona had no way of knowing how far they'd travelled, but she was sure they'd soon encounter the final switchback in the track. So far as she was concerned, it couldn't come soon enough as the snow was now up to her hip and every step was a fight to wade forward.

Ahead of her, Fiona noticed Thomas slowing. She tensed, her every instinct warning her of looming trouble. Past Thomas's shoulder, Fiona could make out flashes of red from Jack's coat. That hadn't happened before so she reasoned Jack had found a reason to halt.

Thomas pulled off to one side, and the three of them clustered together so they could talk.

Fiona looked at her friend's husband, but made sure to also keep Thomas in sight. 'What's up, Jack?'

'Nothing much.' Jack pointed over his shoulder at the track.

'I'm pretty sure we're at the switchback, but rather than lead you round it, I wanted you both to check it out in case I'm wrong. It's one thing going in a straight line, but picking out turns is a nightmare when the blizzard is so disorientating.'

The sheen of sweat on Jack's face and his shortness of breath didn't escape Fiona's notice. His leading the way uphill through the snow was taking a hard physical toll on him. He wasn't complaining, but she planned to suggest she or Thomas lead for a while to give Jack a breather. Jack might well be the tallest and strongest of them, but that didn't mean his endurance could be taken for granted.

Both Fiona and Thomas took a look at the area Jack thought was the switchback and they agreed he was right.

Moving forward again with Jack still leading, Fiona knew they weren't far from the shelter, but the distance was relative. They had to get back before their torches gave out. Before their physical reserves gave out. However, if Thomas was planning to make any kind of move against them, it would have to happen soon.

Already holding tight to cosset the device's battery, Fiona's grip on Ivor's little torch increased. As a defensive weapon, it was little better than a paperclip, but it was all she had so she clung to it, more to comfort herself than anything else.

No police officer ever wants to see a murder suspect walk away from them. But as Jack and Thomas vanished once more into the blizzard, Fiona wasn't thinking like a police officer. She was thinking like a human being. A human being who'd just been left alone on a hillside. In an unprecedented snowstorm, with only a fading torch to light her way.

The rear of Thomas's jacket showed itself between snowy flurries, then faded from vision. The fact he might be a killer did nothing to lessen the sense of abandonment Fiona was feeling after the brief moment of comradeship she'd felt while checking if Jack was right about the switchback.

Both men were now out of her sight, her sphere of influence. Was this a moment one would use to prey on the other?

A minute after rounding the switchback Fiona again found the two men were waiting; Jack reeling the rope in so it maintained a tension and Thomas trampling a small area for them to stand. Both of their faces were grim, and it took Fiona's brain a few seconds to interpret the reason for this.

Jack's head torch was dimmer than it had been at the bridge a couple of minutes ago, and even as Thomas was creating a level area, his hands were fumbling with Lewis' spare head torch.

No matter how Thomas prodded at the head torch he couldn't get it to switch on. Fiona's mind flashed back over the evening's events. After the fall, Lewis's head torch had been missing. She'd presumed he'd lost it in the fall, and the one he'd given to Thomas had been a spare he'd carried with him. If that was the case then unless his pocket had a waterproof zip it stood to reason the spare torch had suffered the same immersion in the burn that Lewis had.

If not, it was the one he'd been wearing and he'd retrieved it after it had been knocked from his head.

Head torches are designed to be used in wet conditions, and no sane hiker would tackle one of Scotland's Munros with one that wasn't designed to work in all weathers. The one Fiona owned had cost less than twenty quid online, and it was advertised as waterproof.

However much any electrical device may purport to be waterproof, they're designed to be protected from falling water. What the vast majority of head torches aren't designed for is violent immersion. Whether the one in Thomas's hands was Lewis's spare or his original one, it had been knocked around and then dunked in the waters of the burn. One tiny crack in its casing would be enough to allow water in. And if it was a rechargeable one like Fiona's, the charging connection would act as a welcoming committee for the burn's waters.

Thomas thrust it at Jack. 'Here, you try and get it going before I launch the bloody thing away.'

Jack took his turn at fumbling with the device. The longer he probed at it, the more his face mirrored Thomas's frustration.

Fiona watched with disinterest as Jack tried to get it going. She was already thinking several steps ahead.

Jack was a practical man, Fiona knew that. Donna was always getting Jack to do various projects around their home and posting pictures online to show his handiwork. Just yesterday, while she and Donna were chatting with a cuppa, Jack had busied himself fixing a kitchen unit with a sticking drawer, and had assembled a flat pack wardrobe Fiona had never got around to putting together.

When Fiona tried to pay Jack for his efforts, Donna, in typical bawdy fashion, had told Fiona to buy her a bottle of wine as it was her who had to deliver Jack's bedtime reward. As Jack and Donna laughed, Fiona had felt a tinge of colour rising to her face. Not at the comment, that was just Donna being Donna. The blush was fuelled by something else.

Jealousy.

So far as human psyche and the English language were concerned, jealousy was one of the ugliest words anyone could use. As an emotion, it ate at the soul, devouring insecurities with a side order of unfair comparisons. As a word, it was malignant. An accusation that could never be taken back. It implied dissatisfaction, a grass-is-always-greener mindset belittling those accused of it.

Yet it had been jealousy Fiona had felt. Not jealousy of Donna getting to bed Jack – he wasn't her type – but jealousy of their intimacy and affection for each other. Fiona wanted someone in her life who made her feel the way Jack made Donna feel. Except Fiona daren't allow that. Jack and Donna knew love. That was great, she was happy her friends had each other.

Fiona knew loss.

Soul-crushing, debilitating loss.

The loss Fiona knew hurt every part of her. Mind, body and soul all suffered the same crushing pain. Yes, she could get up in the morning and function as a human being, but Fiona knew she'd never ever be able to achieve a sense she'd fully healed until she'd identified her parents' killer and brought them to justice.

Every idea she'd had about the reason her parents were killed had either been disproven, or worse, left hanging as a possibility a lack of evidence could neither confirm nor deny.

Jack's voice cut into Fiona's mind. 'It's goosed. Come on, let's get cracking. Thomas, do you want to lead for a while? If I stay close to your heel, I can do without a torch.'

Thomas nodded, and his head torch went out. By the time Fiona had swung her torch up at his head, he'd already raised a hand and was prodding at the switch.

The torch flickered back into life and then back into slumber. Five more times he got it back on only for it to refuse to work. It was clear Thomas's nod had dislodged something and the torch was as goosed as the one Lewis had loaned them.

'Shite.' Fiona didn't like swearing as she felt it was a loss of control, but there were times only bad language would do. 'I'll lead.'

She'd only gone two steps when she felt a hand rest on her shoulder. With a twist of her head she saw the red cuff of Jack's coat. As for Thomas, Fiona had to trust he'd fallen in close behind Jack.

Fiona was content to take the lead for several reasons. She could set the pace, and she made it as rapid as she could without risking anyone overexerting themselves. With Jack between her and Thomas, she had a level of protection. The hand Jack had placed on her shoulder would give her warning should anything happen behind her.

More than once Fiona felt a nudge at her calves or ankles as the close proximity of Jack's long legs caused issues. She let the collisions pass without comment. Jack had nothing to gain by tripping her. If he was going to move against her, and she couldn't see him doing so, he'd do far more than bump the back of her legs.

Even though all three of them had forged a trail leading through the drifting snow, the going uphill was almost as hard as the trek downhill through virgin snow had been. Fiona's lungs ached for respite and clean dry air, while the muscles in her legs felt punch-drunk with the effort of keeping going.

Fiona made no complaint. Nor did she plan to. All her focus was on getting back to the shelter as soon as she could. Fiona knew it might be her mind playing tricks, but Ivor's torch no longer seemed to shine with the brightness it had earlier.

There was no point in stopping to inform the other two, doing so would waste precious battery life. Fiona had a torch app on her mobile, but it was an absolute last resort as she wanted to preserve her mobile battery as long as she could. As soon as it was possible to get a signal, she'd be onto Lochgilphead police station demanding help and assistance.

No matter how much Fiona's logical brain told her she was doing the right thing, the burden of guilt was growing with every hard-fought step. The decision to turn back to the shelter was one that could have dire consequences for Neil if he went into another, worse anaphylactic shock. Common sense told Fiona it could still happen at any point from them leaving the shelter to help arriving, but if they'd managed to summon help, at least her conscience would be unburdened.

The battery on Ivor's torch died. In some ways it was good as it reinforced their decision to return to the shelter. Fiona didn't see it that way as she pocketed the torch and retrieved her mobile. The first thing she did was put it onto power-saving mode and only when the screen darkened did she activate the torch.

Upon reaching the shelter Fiona was greeted by seven pairs of expectant eyes. There should have been eight.

Alice was missing, and nobody looked too concerned about the fact.

TWENTY-FIVE

'Where's Alice?' Even as Fiona asked the question she was forming her own theories. Alice appeared headstrong enough to try going for help herself. That fit with her nature, but if that was the case, then why were Frances's eyes red, and why did both Sara and Steve look so sheepish?

The sole positive Fiona could find was Neil was now sitting up and sipping from a mug.

It was Donna who met Fiona's eye. 'There was a falling out about the soup and how it affected poor Neil. Alice stomped out saying she was going to use the toilet at the back and come back with some firewood.'

Fiona slid next to her friend and appreciated Jack positioning himself on Donna's other side. When Fiona spoke she made sure to keep her voice low. 'Tell me everything. Who said what to whom, their tone, their body language? Everything you can think of. But first, how long has Alice been out there?'

Even before Donna began to speak a fey feeling was creeping over Fiona. It was expected tempers would fray as time passed and the level of discomfort grew. Fiona herself was battling cold, frustration, hunger and exhaustion, but getting into arguments with the shelter's other occupants wasn't a good idea for anyone.

'Only about five or ten minutes. She's probably giving herself some time to cool off.' Donna's eyes dipped towards Frances then back. 'Alice said a lot of nasty things. The kind of stuff which can't be easily taken back. After she'd said them, Sara and Steve gave her a taste of her own medicine.'

Not good. Downright bad if Fiona was honest. 'Okay. Give me the whole story from the start, please.'

Fiona listened without interrupting Donna once as her friend laid out the whole sorry mess. The stramash had started when Neil had a coughing fit that left him gasping for air. Sara had rounded on both Frances and Alice, calling them idiots for not checking the packet properly or asking someone with better eyesight to check it for them. She'd claimed they all knew about Neil's allergy and their stupidity might just kill him.

Alice had defended herself by saying she'd done as much as she could, and if anyone was to blame, it was Frances. Steve had got involved as a peacemaker, only to be shot down by a series of acerbic comments from Alice.

After Alice's broadside, Steve had left the three women to argue it out between them. Things settled down for a period and then Sara had started sniping at Alice and Frances with sly barbs.

Frances had cried and apologised to everyone, and that's when Alice had lost her cool and really laid into her. Sara had sprung to Frances's defence and started poking Alice in the chest, telling her she was out of order.

In the end, it had taken Ivor, Lewis and Steve to separate the two women.

With everything laid out by Donna, Fiona had enough of the information she needed.

Sara had been the one to react to Neil's condition with a strong emotion. Therefore, she cared about Neil. That made sense as the group must have known and liked each other to have bagged Beinn Bhuidhe together. What also made sense was Sara might have seen the allergy thing as a way to get a dig into Alice's ribs. When Alice had passed the blame to Frances, Sara had switched from prosecution to defence. That told Fiona whatever Sara's motive for pointing the finger at Alice and Frances, it was really Alice she was gunning for.

While it seemed Frances was caught in the crossfire, it could be there was more to any of it than met the eye. People who worked together often ended up hooking up or forming relationships. If Fiona's judgement of their respective ages was to be trusted, both Frances and Alice were older than Sara and Lewis. But, not so much older a secret fling or a one-time dalliance could be discounted. If that was the case, it could be Sara had found out and was using the soup and Neil's allergy as an excuse to have a go at them without it becoming public knowledge about Lewis's infidelity. That would allow Sara to save face while also giving her a chance to belittle a woman who'd been intimate with her husband.

Sara had defended Frances, though, which she wouldn't have done had she turned Lewis's head. Therefore, Fiona reasoned, it must have been Alice.

What led one person to be attracted to another was a mystery as old as time itself, and while Fiona couldn't imagine anyone fancying someone as domineering as Alice, she knew that kind of thinking was wrong on every imaginable level. Over the years she'd seen as many odd couples as ones who seemed perfect for each other. Eights with fours, pairs of sixes. Sometimes the guy would be punching above his weight, and sometimes it would be the girl.

Whoever had slept with whom, infidelity was a good candidate when it came to the underlying anger fuelling the argument.

As with everything else about this case, there were too many imponderables. Too many unknowns to make assumptions or formulate theories.

Fiona put her lips to Donna's ear. 'When the guys had to split the women up, was Lewis hopping or limping?'

Donna's brow creased. 'No, now you ask, he seemed to be walking normally. Don't quote me, though. It was chaos for a while and I may have it wrong.'

The disclaimer at the end wasn't something Fiona wanted to hear, but she had to go with Donna's version of events. If Lewis was faking the severity of his injury there were several reasons that could be behind it. He was guilty of Kevin's murder and was using sympathy as a smokescreen. He might be hoping his injury would invoke a softer side from Sara and their relationship troubles could be fixed. Or maybe he'd had a bad fright when he fell and didn't have the courage to try going for help again. The sprained ankle would be the perfect excuse to keep him safe and, if not toasty warm in the shelter, then not freezing.

Fiona stood. 'Right, we need to go and find Alice. I don't give a monkey's about what happened while we were away, or how any of you feel about her; Alice can't be left out there to freeze to death.'

Jack and Thomas also rose, but the two of them weren't enough for Fiona. She wanted some of the others to get a taste of what it was like being outside in the blizzard.

'Donna, you and Frances stay here to look after Neil and Lewis. The rest of us will be in pairs for our own safety. Steve, you can pair with Thomas. Ivor, you go with Sara. If Alice isn't in the toilet or getting wood, she'll be gathering her thoughts somewhere. It's imperative we find her and get her back in here. She will die out there if we don't bring her back. All the torches are dead so use the torch app on your mobiles. When we've got her, we'll all bring a big armful of logs from the rear of the shelter so nobody will have to go out in the snow again. She can't have gone far.'

That last line was a falsehood and as soon as it fell from her lips Fiona regretted saying it.

TWENTY-SIX

Working by the light of their mobile torch apps, Fiona led Jack and the other pairs around the shelter. There was something of a depressed track in the snow and Fiona guessed it was from trips made to collect wood or use the toilet.

What she hoped to find more than anything was Alice standing behind the shelter. If the woman was crying, or furious with the others, that could be fixed. What Fiona didn't want was for Alice to be elsewhere.

At the rear of the shelter Fiona's light picked out the shape of the outhouse. It was the size of a portaloo and she gave a shudder at the idea of having to use it. Public toilets were never up to her standards of sanitation and this one would at best have a chemical toilet. Still, even this outhouse and whatever horrors it may contain would be preferable to a spade and a roll of toilet paper. In the angle between the outhouse and the shelter, a stack of wood lay beneath a tin roof layered with snow.

Fiona aimed her mobile so its torch displayed the outhouse door. There was a handle on the left and hinges to the right. Therefore, the door must open outwards.

The snow wasn't as deep in front of the outhouse as it was

everywhere else. Rather than a full quarter circle in the snow being scraped back, there was only enough of an area for it to be obvious Alice had opened the door just enough to squeeze her way in.

Fiona thumped on the door and shouted Alice's name.

There was no answer so Fiona gripped the handle and teased the door open a crack. When she saw what was inside, she gasped.

Alice wasn't in the outhouse. And Fiona couldn't blame the older woman if she'd chosen to relieve herself in the blizzard. That's what Fiona would have done. The chemical toilet in the outhouse was piled high and stank worse than rotting fish. Only someone with a cast-iron stomach could have even considered using the outhouse.

So Alice wasn't here. The question was, where had she gone?

Fiona knew Alice hadn't left the shelter and struck out down the track, as if she had, they'd have met her upon their return when their torches had failed. Even if they'd somehow passed Alice by without noticing, at some point they'd have seen the tracks she left in the snow.

That left three basic directions for Alice to take: back up the track towards the summit, straight uphill, or downhill.

None of them made sense. No possible good could come from leaving the track. That was a sure-fire way to get lost, and to lose your way in these conditions was to invite death. Yet it didn't make sense for Alice to have gone up the track either. Yes, it might afford her some solitude so she could gather her thoughts, but she could get the same peace huddled into the leeside of the shelter. What shelter by the wall wouldn't give, though, was privacy if she did want to relieve herself. When Fiona factored in the only light Alice would have would be the torch app on her mobile, it seemed even less probable Alice had tried to make her own way down the Munro.

Fiona turned ready to issue suggestions as to where each pairing ought to search next. The only person she found was Jack.

'Where are the others?'

'When you slammed the toilet door shut you were shaking your head. Sara said there was no point all six of us looking in the same place, so they went off looking for her.'

'Where did they go?'

A shrug. 'They all just grabbed an armful of logs and went off.'

Fiona hurried to the shelter door as fast as the snow allowed. Piled to the left was a small heap of firewood. A look inside revealed none of her fellow searchers had returned, so she closed the door to keep the heat in, and thought about what to do next.

The light from Fiona's mobile was strong enough to reach a couple of feet in every direction before the heavy snowfall devoured it. Above the rustle of her waterproof leggings, Fiona could hear the wind whistle as it swirled around the contours of Beinn Bhuidhe. When Fiona cast her torch around in the area outside the shelter it displayed fresh tracks leading in several directions but no searchers.

Fiona sucked a breath through her nose and moved towards the leeside of the shelter. Tracks went before her, but there was nothing to be seen along the side of the shelter except undisturbed snow.

'Quick everyone, over here.'

The shout came loud and the urgency of its words were matched by the panicked tone of the shouter. It had come from behind Fiona, so she turned and with as much pace as the snow allowed forged a path up the track. As she powered onwards, Fiona wondered what it was Thomas had found.

Instead of following the track uphill, the disturbed snow took a sharp left turn and went straight up the incline.

This part of the slope wasn't as steep as others, but Fiona's breaths still rasped from between bluing lips as she fought her way uphill.

A cynical part of Fiona's psyche filled her heart with dread as she imagined the shout was a setup. Nothing more than a ruse to lure her to a point where the killer could attack her, and nullify the threat to their liberty she presented. She eased her pace, and dropped a rapid glance over her shoulder. Jack was at her heel, but she kept her pace slow until he reached her side.

'Take care. We don't know what we're facing here.'

When figures emerged from the darkness, Fiona could see four people. Thomas's arm was extended and when Fiona followed what his mobile was illuminating, she saw a flattened area of the snow. It was like someone had trampled enough snow to give them a place where they could stand with a surety of footing.

From the area, a set of tracks set off left along the slope.

Fiona assessed what she saw with a rapid calculation. Although it seemed like they'd travelled a long way, Fiona reckoned they were still within thirty yards of the shelter. The trudge uphill had been laborious, where progress had been a case of sliding back eight inches for every foot gained.

The way Fiona saw it, Alice had veered away from the track to buy herself more thinking time and had created herself a safe space to gather her thoughts. Alice had stayed close because at first she was planning to return to the shelter when she and those she'd clashed with had some time to calm down.

Except Alice's plan had changed. In Fiona's mind, by cutting to the left behind and above the shelter, Alice had planned to bypass the shelter and join the track somewhere downhill before continuing down the track.

It was a crazy plan and Fiona could only imagine the thoughts compelling Alice to so endanger her life. She was bound to run out of battery life on her mobile long before she got anywhere near the bottom.

There was no time to waste, they'd have to find Alice before she got too far away from the shelter and put the lives of the search party at risk.

Fiona didn't know which way to go. The quickest way to find Alice would be to go down the track until they picked up her trail through the snow. Yet if they trailed Alice's tracks in the snow, there was far less chance of missing her.

With her decision made, Fiona set off. She knew Jack would follow her, what the others did was up to them, but for now she had something to follow, and who knew whether it would lead her to a killer?

TWENTY-SEVEN

Fiona pushed on, time once again her enemy. No matter how hard she tried to make good speed, she was hampered by the deep snow and the slope of the ground beneath her feet. Time and again she slid down the slope and had to scramble back up to stay on Alice's trail.

The burning of her calves was offset by a deadness throughout her legs Fiona knew was a combination of the initial trek up Beinn Bhuidhe, the time spent slogging through near waist-high snow, and a lack of food to replace the calories she'd burned throughout the day. Instead of complaining or worrying about her depleted reserves, Fiona set her jaw firm and kept going.

At a point some ten yards past where Fiona judged the shelter to be, there was a significant disturbance in the snow on the ground. Everywhere virgin snow lay, the contours of its surface were a series of gentle undulations as it smoothed out the uneven surfaces beneath its depths.

Yet in this area there were unexpected ridges, deeper troughs and a different look altogether. To Fiona's eye it looked very much like there had been a fight where different parts of the ground had been trampled while others were left untouched.

Fiona would have slowed her pace, but such was the struggle to move forward, any decrease in momentum would have brought her to a halt. Instead of slowing she cast her mobile's torch around the edges of the disturbed area.

The light picked out a trail leading downhill at a forty-five degree angle. By Fiona's reckoning, this trail would intersect the track leading down Beinn Bhuidhe well past the shelter.

Possibilities for the disturbance in the snow ran through Fiona's mind at warp speed. The first was the obvious one. There had been a fight and Alice had continued her journey. Initially that didn't stack up because none of the others had shown any sign of injury at the flattened area where they'd surmised Alice had stood to gather her thoughts. Of course, it could be the fight had been nothing more than pushing and shoving, but there was no reason for whomever had fought Alice to not mention they'd seen her. Unless, the fight had a more sinister edge to it. If that were the case, Alice may have come into contact with Kevin's killer. The questions were, had she been attacked? Made her escape?

The trail veering off at forty-five degrees suggested someone had taken the route Fiona surmised Alice planned to take, but there was no quick way of learning if the trail was made by Alice after escaping the killer, or by the killer leaving a red herring after dealing with Alice.

It wouldn't be hard to follow the trail until it came into contact with the track and then see if it led downhill, but if it didn't, then it stood to reason Alice had encountered the killer and then disappeared. The deep snow offered an easy way to hide a body.

Fiona halted and cast her torch over the disturbed area in a considered sweep. She didn't know quite what she was looking for until she found it. All the time she was carrying out this search, a ball of dread was growing in her stomach. Whatever the outcome of the altercation that had taken place here, it wasn't good. Alice was either embarking on a suicidal mission to get off the Munro, lying injured somewhere, or already dead.

When Fiona's torch beam crept over a part of the suspicious area, the ball of dread in her gut bounced. Not a series of bounces decreasing in height, but a single one that fell downwards with the thudding menace of a medicine ball.

Fiona half waded, half swam her way through the snow until she was at the point which her sixth sense had told her she ought to examine. She knew the sixth sense was nothing more than a subconscious examination of minute pieces of information gathered by the other senses and compared to past experiences. Fey feelings and psychic powers weren't something she believed in, but as she began to thrust her hands deep into the disturbed snow, she was expecting to find a dead person.

A bump at Fiona's shoulder signalled Jack had dropped down to join her quest. At the other side of her, a figure in a red jacket was also burrowing away with feverish intent.

Fiona didn't know whether those aiding her were actively trying to help, or just humouring her.

Their intentions didn't matter to Fiona, all she cared about was finding Alice as soon as possible.

Fiona's hands felt something hard impede her attempts to scoop the snow away. The medicine ball gave another malevolent bounce. No way was Fiona deep enough for the solid thing her hands had encountered to be a rock. Fiona traced round the object and leaned to one side so the light someone was shining from behind her could illuminate the hole.

There wasn't a rock in the snow. Nor was there a tree stump, or any other part of nature that could have given her a false sense of dread. Instead there was a boot, a hiking boot with multicoloured laces. Just like the ones Alice had.

TWENTY-EIGHT

Every instinct and sense Fiona possessed was heightened. There were five people with her. Logic dictated one of them had attacked Alice, as both Neil and Lewis were still in the shelter with Frances and Donna. She'd found Alice. Therefore there was now a massive target on her back, and there was no telling how the killer would react to Alice's discovery. After all, they had tried to hide her body.

Fiona nudged Jack's elbow with hers. 'Stand up and watch over the others. This was no accident.'

As Jack rose to his feet, Fiona's mind was working with the same feverish intensity as her hands and arms as she traced her way up Alice's body. The person to her right had moved over and was now scooping snow off an area where Alice's head and torso ought to be.

Jack had to be innocent of the attack on Alice. Fiona knew this because he'd been with her since they returned to the shelter. There had been a moment or two when he'd been out of sight, but there was no way he'd had the time to commit this attack and then return to her side with his absence unnoticed. Whether he was innocent of the attack on Kevin remained to be determined, but for now he was the only person she could trust. That, as well as fears for her own safety, was the reason she'd asked him to stand guard.

In an ideal world, Fiona would have liked to have been standing guard so she could observe the faces of the strangers when they learned of Alice's fate, but as important as the investigation may be, getting Alice dug out of the snow while she may still be alive had to be her priority.

Fiona uncovered another boot and Alice's legs.

'Shit.'

At the exclamation Fiona looked to her right. It was Ivor who was digging at Alice's upper body. He'd removed enough snow that Fiona could see Alice had an arm over her face. The snow surrounding Alice's arm was tinged red.

Ivor laid hold of Alice's arm and teased it away from her face revealing a bloody pulp. On the areas of Alice's face not wounded or untouched by the flow of blood, the skin was mottled a pale blue.

Steve's hand pushed Ivor aside and a bare hand was touched to Alice's throat. Fiona's gaze was on Steve's face as he sought the information they all craved.

A terse nod from Steve was followed by a slumping of his shoulders as the tension left his body.

Alice was alive. Big picture, it was great news, and Fiona would have punched the air were it not for one glaring fact. The attack on Kevin couldn't be proven as suspicious, unless some DNA could be found from the rock in her pocket. Likewise, the feeding of the soup containing celery to Neil may have been nothing more than an unfortunate error, or a sinister attempt to cause harm.

The attack on Alice wasn't something anyone could pass over as either an accident or a mistake. Alice's nose resembled a burst tomato and both of her eyes were swollen. Her lips were a mass of cuts and her cheeks bore grazes that spoke of contact with an abrasive object.

'What the hell happened to her?' Sara's face was as white as the snowstorm around them.

Steve twisted his head until he was looking at her. 'She's been battered, you daft cow. Now stop asking stupid questions and let's get her back to the shelter.'

Fiona gestured for Steve to take the lead. He was a nurse so he'd best know how to lift Alice in a way that caused the least amount of damage to her already injured body.

While Fiona held one of Alice's legs as they carried her back to the shelter, she allowed her mind to start examining her four suspects for the attack on Alice.

TWENTY-NINE

By the time they had returned to the shelter and laid the unconscious Alice on a bench, Fiona was still none the wiser as to the identity of Alice's attacker.

Thomas was a good candidate after the way he'd barrelled into her earlier; and Alice had berated and insulted him which could provide a motive. The opportunity had arisen when they'd gone looking for Alice, but as with the three other suspects, for the opportunity to have presented itself, he'd have had to separate from his search partner.

The same stood for the other three suspects. As did the means. Alice's injuries spoke of something far harder than a gloved fist connecting with soft flesh. The obvious answer was another rock, but the snow had buried all of them. Another weapon easy to source was one of the logs from behind the shelter. Stacked as firewood, they were available in plentiful supply, hard enough to inflict grievous injury, yet small enough to conceal inside a jacket until opportunity arose.

Fiona's theory about a log being used as a weapon made logical sense to her, but she'd only arrived at the conclusion a few minutes after getting Alice settled on the shelter's bench.

By then each of them had carried in the pile of logs they'd previously dumped by the shelter's door. It would have been easy to
secrete the offending log in with the others, if it hadn't been
launched away once used to batter Alice into unconsciousness.

As she sat working things through in her mind, Fiona
gripped her leg above the knee. At the realisation of her mistake
in not carrying out an immediate search for a weapon, Fiona put
some strength into her fingers until she felt her nails digging
into the flesh of her lower thigh. It wasn't a deliberate attempt to
punish herself, more an involuntary reaction borne of self-
recrimination. She had to do better as there was no knowing
how many other people may be harmed by the killer nestled in
their midst.

Fiona returned her mind to her four suspects. The taciturn
Ivor had more than enough physical strength to inflict Alice's
injuries without using a log, but he was the one member of the
group who didn't appear to have any gloves. A glance at his
hands showed no impact lesions, and while his bulbous
knuckles would have no trouble bursting Alice's face apart, they
weren't likely to be coarse enough to graze Alice's cheeks.
Therefore, if Ivor was guilty of the attack, he'd used a log. What
motive he might have was unknown at this time, but she
planned to learn a lot more about him, as well as all the others.

Steve was low on Fiona's suspect list, but he was on it. Left
alone, as he had been with Kevin, there had been plenty of
opportunity for him to press on the wound to Kevin's head
causing further damage. He'd stood back and allowed her and
Ivor to unearth Alice, and this made Fiona question his feelings
towards the woman. It could be he was keeping back rather
than getting in the way, and soon sprang into action when
Alice's face had been revealed, but that could have been an
attempt to show willing rather than an actual desire to help.

Fiona planned to keep a close watch on Steve and his efforts
to treat Alice. So far, he was doing the right things, but she was

on high alert for any little ambiguity in his care for the injured woman.

Sara's behaviour jarred all kinds of nerve endings in Fiona. For a vocal woman, she'd been quiet the whole time they'd been out searching, barring the inane question about what happened to Alice, which seemed out of character.

Everything Fiona knew contradicted a known fact, or was undermined by a lack of knowledge. Fiona huffed out a breath and rose to her feet, clapping her hands together as she did so. Things had spiralled out of control, and it was now time for her to take a firm grasp of the situation, to take the lead and prevent any more attacks or murders before they happened. What Fiona planned to do would paint an unmissable target on her back, but provided she kept her back covered, she ought to come to no harm.

'Listen up, everyone. I'm formally declaring this shelter as a crime scene in a murder investigation. Everyone in this hut with the exception of Donna is under suspicion of murder.'

THIRTY

As Fiona expected would happen, the occupants of the shelter all voiced their thoughts on her placing them under suspicion. There were too many people speaking at the same time for her to digest what any one person was saying, but she caught enough comments such as 'crazy bitch' and 'fucking amateur' to know her statement had caught them off guard.

Fiona raised her hands to silence the crowd then pointed a finger at Frances, inviting her to speak.

'How can you say it's a murder investigation? It's obvious Alice has been attacked, but she's alive, look.' Frances jabbed a finger in Alice's direction. 'Her chest's going up and down, therefore she's breathing.'

Fiona was ready for this comment, although she had to fight to not roll her eyes at Frances's poor grasp of events. 'Alice was found beaten and buried in the snow. Yet there wasn't enough time for the snow to have buried her. Therefore, whomever attacked her, covered her unconscious body with snow and left her to freeze to death. I'm classing what happened to Alice as attempted murder.'

Frances's brow puckered. 'Then who's been murdered?'

'Kevin, he's the only person who's dead, you eejit.' Sara's tone was laced with scorn, and her face twisted even further as she turned to Fiona. 'Come on then, Little Miss Smartypants, explain to us all why you think he was murdered.'

Fiona took a step back so she could see as many faces as possible. 'Because I found the rock that had been used to bash his skull in.'

Once again the shelter erupted as everyone spoke at once. It took Ivor banging one of the tin cups on the cast-iron wood burner to silence the room.

'Let the lass explain.'

Fiona dropped a grateful nod his way, although she was thinking he might be trying to seem sympathetic as a way to throw her off his scent. Instead of keeping her gaze on Ivor she pointed at Thomas. 'Go on, say what you have to say.'

Thomas cleared his throat as if preparing to address a court. 'You said everyone except Donna is under suspicion. Why is she different? Is it because she's your mate?'

Expectant eyes turned Fiona's way, but this question was easy to answer. 'In a way, yes. Because we're friends, she was walking beside me when Kevin was attacked; therefore, she couldn't have attacked him. That's why I didn't include her. As with Donna, I admit I've known her husband, Jack, for the best part of twenty years, but he is under suspicion because I can't vouch for his whereabouts at the time of the attack.'

A ripple of murmurs came from the strangers, but Donna was on her feet, eyes blazing as she stepped in front of Fiona.

'You're counting my Jack as a suspect? Are you out of your bloody mind? He stayed in your house last night. Fixed that cupboard drawer for you, and you treat him like he's some common criminal. You just said yourself you've known him for twenty years. Can't you see he'd never kill someone?'

'It's a murder investigation, Donna. I can't rule anyone out until I have either evidence or witness statements to prove or disprove any suspect's level of guilt.'

'I hope you're a better copper than you are a friend. And considering how you've never solved the murder of your parents, I reckon you'll never work out who killed Kevin.'

Fiona bit back the retort that bounded up from her heart. She unclenched her fists and let the breath she'd held trickle from her nose. Under no circumstances was she going to rise to the line-crossing bait Donna was dangling under her nose. The only reaction she gave to Donna's incendiary accusation was a diamond-hard stare that bore deep into Donna's blue eyes. Fiona wanted the stare to be something Donna would take to her grave. Their friendship was now over in Fiona's mind. Not even Aunt Mary knew as much as Donna did about the efforts Fiona had made to catch her parents' killer. It had been Donna who'd provided a listening ear, a shoulder to cry on when Fiona had encountered dead end after dead end. Except the ear had been a deaf one, the shoulder cold. Everything Donna had provided was now revealed as lip service. No doubt there was some ghoulish entertainment for Donna in Fiona's pain. That's what the worst part of Fiona's life was to Donna, a novelty distraction.

Throughout her police career, Fiona had been insulted by drunks, grieving relatives, domestic violence victims and gangs of street-roaming neds, and never once had she felt the anger she now felt at Donna.

A hand went to Donna's mouth as she recoiled under the intensity of Fiona's stare. 'I'm so sorry, Fiona. I don't know where that came from. I didn't mean it.' Jack was pulling at Donna's shoulders, but his hands were shrugged off. 'Please, Fiona. I didn't mean it.'

Fiona didn't look her former friend's way. 'Sit down, Donna. We'll talk later.' The chill Fiona put into her voice was enough to make Donna do as she'd told her to do. She directed her eyes towards the strangers. 'Does anyone else have any questions?'

'I do.' Steve had his hand raised like a kid trying to get their teacher's attention. 'How can you know Kevin was murdered? So you found a rock with blood on it, so what? That proves nothing. He'll like as not have tripped and banged his head on the rock. He was a clumsy sod at times.'

Fiona paused before answering. Not because she wanted time to think, although she was happy to give Steve that impression. The way he was trying to disprove her allegation of murder spoke volumes. He could, of course, be in denial someone in the shelter had murdered his uncle, or it could be he was the person to have attacked Kevin and was trying to discredit her thinking.

'The bloodstained rock I found was at least five feet away from where Kevin rolled down the slope. I'm no expert on the trajectory of falling objects, but I think it's safe to assume Kevin didn't fall and hit his head off a fist-sized rock in a way that caused the rock to jump up and fly six foot across and twenty foot down the slope. I'd also think it was safe to assume that once his killer had struck they launched the rock – or if you like, murder weapon – away to be lost in the snow. It was only pure chance I found it.'

Lewis's forehead scrunched. 'Yeah, you're probably right. Kevin was murdered. It stands to reason it was Kevin's killer who battered Alice and left her to die. There was six of you out there. Sara can be a right cow at times, but other than a slap to someone's cheek she's never raised a hand to anyone. Not even me when I've pissed her off and probably deserved it.'

'Thanks a bunch, husband.'

'That leaves you, the long streak of piss there, Thomas, Steve and Ivor as suspects.' Fiona grabbed a handful of Jack's sleeve before he could react to Lewis's insult. 'You're a copper so you should be above suspicion. For the moment let's leave you out of it. Like you and the gobby cow, the long streak of piss is a stranger so far as we're concerned, so it doesn't make sense he'd kill any of us. Your mate seems to doubt your capabilities as a copper, but that's bullshit I'm putting down to her being scared shitless. You've twice made the news for solving murders in tough circumstances. That tells me you're a better copper than she thinks.'

'Thank you.' Fiona meant it too. After Donna's broadside it felt good to hear someone backing her, even if the backing came from a murder suspect. She flashed a quick glance and a nod his way. 'If you're discounting me, Jack and Sara, that leaves Thomas, Ivor and Steve as your suspects. Do you want to continue with your theorising?'

'I've not a lot more to add. I've known them three for years and I can't see any of them being a killer.'

'Why not?'

'Thomas is little more than a bairn and hasn't a bad bone in his body. Steve's the same and he's a nurse. Nurses help people not hurt them. Isn't there some line about doing no harm that covers them? Plus, Kevin is his uncle.'

'It's part of the Hippocratic oath doctors take. Nurses don't need to take any such oath, so it's a moot point.' Fiona only knew this because her friend Heather's little sister had told her all about it one drunken night. What Fiona didn't say was how pledges and oaths meant nothing to people such as Harold Shipman. If Steve was cut from the same cloth, he would think nothing of taking a life.

'And Ivor, what about him?'

'You're joking, right? Ivor doesn't give a shite about anything except his job at the hotel. Plus he was in the shelter with me and Sara when you arrived carrying Kevin, so he wasn't out there to attack him.'

'That's right – you all work together. What's the hotel called?'

'Inveraray House, Kevin's the owner. Ivor looks after the gardens and does any maintenance needing done. He can grow or fix anything.' Lewis slid a look in Ivor's direction. 'Mind, he'll not tell you how.'

Fiona knew Inveraray House. It was a former country house converted, as so many had been, into a top-end hotel. A guy she'd dated for a couple of weeks three or four years ago had taken her there for a meal that comprised fourteen separate courses. It would have been a wonderful experience were it not for the way her date had treated the waiting staff. He had been rude and overbearing; she'd supposed he was trying to be masterful in plush surroundings, when the truth of it was she'd have thought more of him if he'd been polite to the staff at a chip shop. She'd dumped him five seconds after he parked outside her house. Fiona dealt with too many arseholes in her professional life to tolerate one in her personal one too.

That was enough for Fiona. Their jobs at Inveraray House provided a connecting thread for them all which she could pull on. Instead of a public discussion like this, she would speak to every person individually until she knew a whole lot more about them all.

THIRTY-ONE

Fiona knew from personal and professional experience workplaces were a hotbed of secrets, jealousies and allegiances. Police Scotland was little different and she had colleagues whose company she adored and others she loathed.

When first stationed to Lochgilphead, she'd been partnered with an officer everyone called Ozzy. It was only when preparing for a court appearance her sergeant had taken her aside and explained Ozzy was a nickname. Ozzy was a derivative of Ozzy's constant mantra, "Oh Shit, Yeah". A genial and likeable person, Ozzy wasn't close to being classed as a competent officer. He forgot daft things all the time, and when these omissions were pointed out to him by either a nervous Fiona or a raging sergeant, he'd always give the same three-word response.

Fiona had encountered many hospitality workers during her career. Like the emergency services, hospitality was a vocation not a job. Both came with anti-social hours and dealing with the general public who, by turn, could be wonderful or obnoxious, depending on their circumstances.

After the pandemic and Brexit anyone she'd spoken to who

worked in the hospitality sector shared the same complaints. Customers were more demanding, and staffing numbers were lower due to there being fewer people willing to work with an ungrateful public.

If the same problems found elsewhere were prevalent at Inveraray House, there was every chance the group had been through adversity together. That they'd fallen out with each other, made friendships that would last years. Maybe there had been a workplace romance or two. That fit with the theory she had about why Lewis and Sara didn't show any affection for each other.

Fiona looked around the shelter trying to decide who to speak to first. Steve was busy attending to Alice, Frances and Thomas were the least confrontational of the others, but they were also the most nervous. Instinct told her if she picked either of them as the first person she spoke to they'd clam up, or stutter and stammer their way through her questions delivering nothing more than what they thought she wanted to hear.

Lewis and Sara were strong types who'd engage her in a battle of wits. The best thing Fiona could envisage happening now was that Alice would recover and identify her attacker, but Fiona couldn't delay her investigation in the hope she would.

'Ivor, can you join me for a quiet chat, please?' Fiona gestured to the doorway of the shelter's other room.

THIRTY-TWO

To question suspects in the hearing of other suspects was a million kinds of wrong. Fiona knew that and she made sure to keep her questions neutral and devoid of accusation. What she planned to do was gather information so she could identify the killer. She'd collected one of the Tilley lamps which she set on the floor and seated herself on a bench, gesturing for Ivor to sit opposite her. It was nowhere near as private as an interview suite but provided they talked in low voices, they wouldn't be overheard. Without the stove to heat it, this room was cold enough to fog their breath.

Other than this second room, the only other place she could have talked to each person was outside. That was a complete non-starter as it would at some point have put her into a one-on-one situation with the killer.

'You're a gardener and maintenance man at Kevin's hotel, right?'

'Aye.'

'What exactly do you do there?'

'The gardens and maintenance.'

'I was looking for a more specific answer.' Fiona allowed her tone to harden. 'Or are you trying to be deliberately obstructive?'

'No. I plant veg and flowers. Pick or prune them when they need it and fix owt that needs fixing. Do you want me to tell you about cutting the grass and painting ceilings, or do you want to cut to the chase and ask me if I killed Kevin?'

The laconic tone Ivor was using didn't escape Fiona's notice. On some levels he seemed amused by her questions, but he also seemed nervous about any accusation she might make. Were those nerves founded in guilt or fear of a miscarriage of justice?

'Not yet. I'll be honest, I've no idea who the killer is, and that's why I'm trying to find out about you all before I make any accusations. How long have you worked at the hotel?'

'Since Kevin got the place in ninety-five.'

'That's a long time. You must be good at what you do. How many of the others work there?'

'Lewis is in the kitchen with Kevin. Alice does the books, Frances is on reception.'

'And the others?'

'Thomas runs the bar and ponces about with fancy wines.' Fiona couldn't picture the nervous Thomas as a sommelier, but she'd been wrong about people before so she filed the fact away for later consideration. 'Sara does the rooms, and Neil used to run the restaurant until he was poached by the castle and given the manager's job there.'

'Steve's a nurse. How does he fit in?'

'Kevin brought him up. Steve's parents died in a car smash when he was ten. It was a miracle he survived. When help came he was trying to do CPR on his mother. Kevin took him in and looked after him ever since.'

'Does Kevin have any other family?'

'Nane. Everything he has will go to Steve, but if you're thinking Steve killed him so he'd inherit, you're wrong. They were like faither and son.'

The claim they were like father and son rang a familiar bell with Fiona, as she was as close to Aunt Mary as she ever had been to her mother.

'I wasn't thinking that, but it's interesting you raised the thought. That suggests you've already considered it. With the pandemic and everything, hospitality businesses have been having a hard time of it these last few years. Do you think the business is viable as a going concern?'

'I plant the veg and fix broken things. I don't know owt about the finances beyond the fact my wages are aye paid and Kevin was aye grumbling about the cost of stuff. Mind you, Kevin aye got a new Merc every other year, so it must've been doing alright.'

Fiona recalled it was Alice who did the books, therefore that line of enquiry was closed to her. The others would provide answers on the topic of how busy the hotel was, though they'd not know the financial situation of the business. If this was a normal investigation she'd be able to look up the accounts at Companies House, but stranded where she was and not being able to do so was the latest of a long line of things denied to her.

'All bosses grumble about the cost of things. You should hear my sergeant going on about the overtime budget.' The sharing was supposed to endear her to Ivor a little, but all it did was cause him to lift a bushy eyebrow a half inch north. 'You work there, you're friends with the staff. Did they tell you it was busy? Quiet?'

'I stopped listening as they talk shite. Sara reckons any more than five rooms is busy. Frances says anything less than ten is quiet. Car park was usually full, but that don't mean owt if customers aren't spending. My wages get paid every week and that's all I care about.'

'When you were paired with Sara to look for Alice, did the two of you split up at all?'

'Aye.' A concerned look passed over Ivor's face. 'You telt us to stay together and she said we'd search a bigger area if we didn't. I shoulda listened to you not her.'

Fiona could hear remorse in Ivor's tone, but that didn't mean she trusted him. 'When you split up, where did each of you go?'

'I went down the track. Sara said she was going to check the edge of the track in case Alice had went straight down.'

If what Ivor was saying was true, he wasn't well placed to have committed the attack. To do so he'd have had to sneak past Sara and the rest of the searchers. This logic carried for whomever had attacked Alice, but someone close to the shelter would have had fewer people to dodge.

'Did you see any sign of anyone having joined the track from up where Alice was found?'

Ivor's head shook. 'No. Wasn't looking for that.'

What he said made sense to Fiona. So far as they knew, Alice hadn't gone down the track so the snow wouldn't show any footprints other than the ones left by the attempts they'd made to get help, and those would have been getting covered by the falling snow.

'How far down the track did you go? Why did you turn back?'

'Mebbe fifty yards tops. No sign of anyone having been there so I came back.'

'Okay. One last question. Did you see any of the others when you were down there?'

'No.'

'Thanks. That's all the questions I have for you just now.'

As Ivor retook his usual seat, Fiona considered what she'd learned while also selecting the next person she wanted to speak to. As he was set to inherit Kevin's hotel, Steve was presented as a prime suspect, but other than Alice potentially having seen him strike his uncle, Fiona couldn't see why she'd been attacked.

THIRTY-THREE

Unlike Ivor who'd sat in a relaxed fashion, Sara was parade-ground stiff with her arms folded across her chest.

'This is absolutely ridiculous. You've placed under suspicion everyone except your mate and you have no idea who killed Kevin. I've seen *Line of Duty*, you're one of those bent coppers; stitching people up is probably how you get your results. Go on then, deny it.'

'There's no point in my denying anything as you won't believe me. However, as I'm an officer for Police Scotland, you probably want me to believe what you say.'

'I'm not answering any of your questions without a lawyer present.' Sara made a show of looking at her watch. 'I know my rights. If you haven't charged me within twenty-four hours you have to let me go. To charge me there will have to be a formal recorded interview.'

Fiona had dealt with more than her fair share of clued-up members of the public. Sara was right in what she said, but she was nowhere near as well informed as she thought. 'You're right. Or you would be if I had arrested you. I would have to let you go. But, just so you know the facts, there would be nothing to stop me or any other police officer from re-arresting you when more evidence comes to light. I'm going to ask you some questions. Whether you choose to answer them or not is up to you, but by answering them you may very well eliminate yourself and your husband from my suspect list.'

'What questions?'

'Someone clearly had a reason to kill Kevin. I don't know much about you and those with you, except you all work, or have worked, at Inveraray House. I want to know more about the hotel and how you all got on with each other.'

Sara's mouth curled into a close-lipped sneer. 'So you think his killer is one of us and not your mate's husband. That's blinkered thinking. He's the one who thumped poor Thomas. He's the one who's showing violent tendencies. That great thug is the one you should be arresting, not the rest of us.'

'I hear what you're saying, but Jack, Donna and myself are strangers to you, the same way you're strangers to us. Jack and Kevin only met on the way down the Munro. Do you think it's credible in that short period of time for Kevin, who everyone says is a decent guy, to have pissed off Jack to the point where Jack lashed out with enough force to kill Kevin?'

'Who knows? Jack was quick enough to clobber poor Thomas. And who's to say they didn't already know each other.'

'I was there when our group joined up with theirs. Neither Jack nor Kevin gave any sign of them having met previously. The reason Jack lashed out is because he thought Thomas had attacked me. Wouldn't you expect your husband to do the same if I was your friend?'

Sara's confidence drained from her face and body language as she considered what Fiona had just said. To press home her point and wrong foot Sara, Fiona chose an innocuous question next. 'I only exchanged a couple of words with Kevin. What was he like as a person? As a boss?'

'He was all right. He wasn't a tyrant, but he wasn't a

pushover either. You knew where you stood with him, and if you did your job right, he'd look after you. Most of us have worked there a long time which is rare in our line of work.'

'Did he shout and swear at staff? Ivor said he worked in the kitchen, and that's a pretty intense place to work. I've seen those programmes with Gordon Ramsay and he's always swearing and shouting at people.'

'Kevin hated Gordon Ramsay.' A wan smile touched Sara's lips for such a brief moment Fiona wondered if she had imagined it. 'Said he'd made it cool for chefs to behave like arseholes. Lewis worked in the kitchen with him, and he said the only time Kevin swore was when something like a cooker or dishwasher broke down.'

'Was that because of the inconvenience, or the cost?'

'Both usually. Everything in the kitchen is both vital and expensive, so if Ivor can't fix it, the nearest repair service is based in either Glasgow or Oban, which means there's usually a couple of hours travel on top of the callout fee.'

This rang true with Fiona's experiences of living in Lochgilphead. One of the disadvantages of living in such a scenic area was the lack of amenities and services which were readily available in cities or more populated areas. If Fiona wanted a new TV she either had to buy online, or travel to Glasgow or Oban and then fold down the back seats of her car so she could get the TV home.

'Was Kevin someone who was all about the money, or was he reasonable?'

'He was a good businessman. He knew the price of everything he bought, but he didn't buy rubbish. He's got new curtains coming for the rooms. I helped him choose them as he reckoned I've better taste than him when it comes to such things. They're over four hundred quid a pair.'

From Sara's telling, Fiona was starting to build a picture of what Kevin was like. A good businessman whose finger was on the pulse, he invested in his business, not just by spending money, but also by involving staff in decision-making processes. Whether Sara's taste was better than Kevin's when it came to soft furnishings was a moot point, as he'd got Sara on board.

'How did Kevin get on with his staff in general?'

'Well enough. He'd make time for you if you needed to speak to him about something, and he paid seventy-five pence an hour more than anyone else in the area. He got his pound of flesh from us, mind. He didn't suffer fools or shirkers. I liked that about him. Some of the places I've worked take anybody and then you find yourself working twice as hard to cover for folk who don't show up, or are lazy bastards who don't bother their arse to do a good job. You get a two-month trial when you start and if you're no good, you don't get to finish the trial.'

'It sounds like he was a decent boss. You must have all got on well with him to come up here together?'

'We did. This was a paid trip, as he wanted us all to contribute our ideas on which views would be best for him to photograph.'

'So who's running the hotel today?'

'It's closed for a week. It's quieter this time of year so he closes the first week in December and the first full fortnight of January. We get our holidays then, and two and a bit more weeks to take when we want.'

Sara's comment about the hotel being quiet gave Fiona the perfect chance to dig into the hotel itself.

'Is the hotel usually busy? How many rooms does it have? Is it a seasonal business?'

'It's busy most of the time. We get a lot of tourists throughout the year, and the summer is mental, although we usually host a wedding on Saturdays throughout the year.'

'Sounds like it's a good business.' As she spoke, Fiona thought back to Ivor's comment about Kevin getting a new Merc every other year. That was either a sign of a successful business, or someone treating themselves to a nice car rather than paying money to the taxman.

'It is. I wish it was mine.'

Fiona let the comment slide, but she did file the sentiment away. 'You never said how many rooms it has.'

'Twenty-four. Including a bridal chamber which is really a suite, four family rooms and the rest are doubles and twins.'

'What do you think will happen to the hotel now?'

A shrug. 'I don't know. Kevin was involved in everything, but he let us run our own departments without interfering, so we'll be okay for a few months, although we'll have to get a chef in to replace Kevin as Lewis won't be able to manage by himself. I guess it'll be up to Steve. He might sell it, or decide to take it on himself.'

'Are you worried about your job long term?'

'Not really. I'm good at what I do and having eight years at Inveraray House on my CV won't hurt when it comes to getting a new job.'

'What do you think about Steve?'

'He's a nice enough guy. What he plans to do with the hotel is up to him. I'll be okay either way.'

'Last few questions. Do you know of anyone here who had a grudge against Kevin?'

Sara's eyes slid left. It could be she was looking towards the person who had the grudge, or she was using the right side of her brain. The creative side. If that was the case, what she was about to say could be a lie.

'Lewis. Kevin was a fantastic chef and a good boss, but he never let Lewis contribute a single dish whenever he changed the menu.'

Fiona was left wondering whether she'd just witnessed a husband being thrown to the wolves, or had learned a potential motive for murder. Top level chefs tended to be highly strung and emotive perfectionists. Gordon Ramsay was televised proof of that. If Lewis's ambitions had been kept down by Kevin, resentment could have festered.

'Ivor told me you and he split up from the pairs I suggested. Where did each of you go?'

'He went to search down the track, and I checked the edge near the shelter in case she'd taken a path straight down the hill.'

'Did you see anyone else before Ivor came back up the track?'

'No.'

As Sara padded back towards her husband, Fiona cross-referenced the new information against the old. Sara's account of their movements tallied with Ivor's. But to Fiona's suspicious mind that didn't mean they couldn't be working together. Sara wasn't worried about her boss's murder in terms of her job, which suggested many things. None of which were good. And that was before Fiona factored in the way Sara had placed a potential motive in her husband's hands.

THIRTY-FOUR

The looks Fiona received when she asked Frances to join her next were a mixture of suspicion and incredulity.

'W... what do you want to ask me about? I was in here the whole time. I didn't attack Alice. I would never do that. And I didn't kill Kevin. He was a lovely man. He was very kind to me when my sister was ill. He gave me lots of time off to look after her and her kids.'

Frances's expression was one of fear. By far the meekest of the Inveraray House employees, she was someone Fiona expected to gabble away rather than give the concise answers she'd received from Sara and Ivor. That was fine by Fiona: sometimes gabbles could hold little nuggets of information that were clues.

Of all the potential suspects for Kevin's murder, Frances was the second bottom on Fiona's list, after Jack. While Fiona was too experienced an officer to discount anyone without proof, timid and mousy characters such as Frances weren't in-your-face killers. They either snapped at the hands of their abusers and lashed out with an iron or a carving knife, basically whatever was to hand. Or they used a more subtle method such as poison to achieve their goal.

It could be Frances's personality was nothing more than an act designed to throw Fiona off the scent, but she doubted that. All the others seemed used to Frances behaving the way she did. There were no surprised looks flowing her way whenever she acted in a certain way, which suggested the version of herself she was projecting was what they were all used to. To put on an act for a few hours was one thing, but to do so for weeks and months in the workplace was something else. All the same, until Fiona had evidence proving otherwise, Frances wasn't going to be crossed off her suspect list.

'I know you were in here the whole time, and therefore you weren't the person who attacked Alice. I just need to ask you a few questions. That okay?'

Frances twisted a ring around her finger and looked everywhere but at Fiona. 'If you must, but I don't know anything. I'm sorry, but I can't help you.'

'Ivor told me you take care of reception at the hotel where you all work. What is it exactly you do?'

'I answer phone calls and process the online bookings. You know, ones that come in through our website or through *Booking.com* and so on.'

'That sounds interesting.' It didn't, but Fiona wanted Frances to relax before she asked her a tougher question. 'Is it you who sets the rates? And what else do you do?'

'It is.' Frances sat a little straighter. 'Kevin allows me to use my discretion within reason. It's better to get ninety pounds for a room last minute than to have it unoccupied.'

'I see. And how often do you have empty rooms?'

'At this time of year quite often, but in the summer it's rare.'

'So you'd say your annual occupancy is quite high, would you?'

A self-indulgent smile caressed Frances's lips. 'Oh yes, last year we got eighty-seven per cent occupancy and we're on course to hit ninety this year.'

'That sounds very good. Do you know the industry normal?'

'I don't, but Kevin always reckoned we needed above fifty-five per cent to turn a profit.'

'Then you must be good at your job to get so far above what's needed.' Fiona saw no harm in complimenting Frances to keep her onside.

As they were talking, Fiona was crunching numbers in her head. The last-minute rate was ninety pounds so she added at least half as much again and got to one thirty-five. Say one fifty for easy counting and to account for the family rooms and bridal chamber. Times the twenty-four rooms got her to £3,600 a day, or just over twenty-five grand a week. Multiply that by the forty-nine weeks they were open and knock off ten per cent to match the annual occupancy and it was just over a million pounds a year on rooms alone. For a place like Inveraray House, a hundred and fifty quid a room was conservative to say the least. In peak season it could be twice as much. This line of thinking was backed up by Kevin spending four hundred pounds a pair for curtains. Fiona's first car had cost less than that.

There was also the fine dining to account for. Curiosity had made Fiona look the cost up when she'd been taken there. It had been a hundred pounds per person before a drink was bought, and there were at least forty other diners. Say they achieved those numbers five days a week every week they were open: that was another million on food and drink sales. Plus the weddings they had most weekends. Fiona knew very little about how much wedding venues charged, but she was sure a place such as Inveraray House would charge tens of thousands of pounds.

If what she'd learned about the hotel, and the figures she'd calculated, were correct, it was clear to Fiona the business was making very good money indeed. Enough it would be worth killing for.

'Do you have any other questions for me?'

'Just a couple.' Fiona's cheeks burned as she realised she'd spaced out when questioning Frances. 'Would you say Inveraray House was profitable as a business?'

'I would, yes. Kevin would occasionally grouse about the cost of things, but he never once said he'd had enough, or that he was planning to sell up.'

With her answer, Frances had eliminated the need for Fiona to ask her next question, so she moved to the trickier, more personal ones. 'As I understand it, Kevin had no family other than Steve. Was he seeing someone? Living with a partner?'

'No. I've never known him to have time for a relationship. He worked seven days a week from breakfast right through. It's such a shame he never got to find love. I'm sure he'd have made someone very happy.'

'It sounds like he would.' The banal comment tasted sour to Fiona, but she was doing what she had to do to keep Frances talking. 'Do you think he was ever lonely?'

'Goodness no. He loved what he did.' Frances leaned forward and lowered her voice. 'Maggie Gilmoure, who has the Lochside Hotel and Spa, was sniffing round him once upon a time, but as pretty as she used to be, she has a reputation no woman of decent upbringing could be proud of.'

Fiona tried not to pull a face at Frances's outdated thinking. She was no more than ten years younger than Frances and she'd never had a relationship lasting longer than six weeks. If Frances knew her dating history, she'd be lumped into the same 'fallen woman' category as Maggie Gilmoure. Although Lochgilphead was a rural town, Fiona thought attitudes like the one Frances had just expressed were consigned to the past. What made such thinking worse was the knowledge any man who behaved like Maggie Gilmoure would be classed as a stud or lad-about-town, yet any woman doing so would always be castigated.

'Do you know of anyone with a grudge against Kevin?'

'You mean someone who's here?'

'Yes, but if you know of anyone else, it won't hurt to mention them.' It was the people in the shelter Fiona really wanted to know about, but if Frances recited a long list of people Kevin had angered, it would present a different picture of the victim.

'He crossed swords with a few reps over the years, but I wouldn't say he actually fell out with them. He just stopped using their companies, or went above their heads to complain about service levels and so on.' Frances pulled a face. 'The only person I can really think of who'd have an actual grudge is Jake MacDonald, who has Inveraray Castle.'

'Do you know what the grudge is about?'

The corners of Frances's mouth twitched upwards for a heartbeat. 'Inveraray Castle is the main competition for us, and since Kevin took over Inveraray House, we've been much busier than them. Jake MacDonald reckons we've taken half of his trade.'

As much as Fiona believed such a grudge might exist, it was a professional one, and unless MacDonald was hiding out somewhere on the slopes of Beinn Bhuidhe, he wasn't a suspect.

'What about Neil? Ivor said he used to work for Kevin until he was poached to run the castle? I presume the castle in question is Inveraray Castle, but correct me if I'm wrong.' Fiona knew this was true, but the more facts she could check, the more she could learn who to trust. 'Why was he along on what was pretty much a team-building exercise?'

'Yes, it is Inveraray Castle he's at now. Neil and Kevin are friends, and have been as long as I've known them. Kevin was sad to see Neil move on, but he threw him a farewell party and picked up the entire bill. There were no hard feelings, and I bet they would have still bounced ideas off each other like they always did.'

Fiona didn't reply. Now she'd got Frances comfortable with answering her questions, she wanted to try silence for a minute or two, to see if Frances chattered some more details. Neil might have been a good fit for the murder of Kevin, but as he hadn't left the shelter, he wasn't the person who'd attacked Alice.

'Shit.' It was Steve's voice Fiona heard. 'She's stopped breathing.'

Fiona knew Steve could only be talking about Alice, which meant the killer had claimed their second victim.

THIRTY-FIVE

'She's stroking.' Steve's face was as grim as any Fiona had ever seen.

A silence fell over the shelter as every eye turned to Steve. There was not a sound beyond the quiet words of support Steve was speaking into Alice's ear.

Numbness at the situation engulfed Fiona, so she made a fist with her left hand and dug her nails into the palm. More than any other person in this shelter, Fiona had to keep her wits sharp. As the police officer in the group, it wasn't up to her just to catch the killer, she had to do so before they had the chance to strike again.

As much as Fiona wanted to act, to try and help somehow, she stayed back. Steve was a nurse, he'd be far better placed to look after Alice. Or he would be, if he wasn't riding high on her suspect list.

Steve was in line to inherit Kevin's estate. This included a successful business in Inveraray House, and if the business was as profitable as Fiona suspected, there would be investments or savings as well.

Money was one of the most common motivations for murder. By Fiona's calculations, Inveraray House turned over more than two million a year. If after taxation and costs, there was a ten per cent profit margin, Inveraray House would give Kevin two hundred thousand a year. Kevin had owned the hotel for the best part of thirty years. If he'd cleared that much every year, he could be sitting on three million, plus whatever the business was worth when sold. Some or all of that money could have been given to charity, or spent on a frivolous lifestyle, but everything she'd so far learned about Kevin showed him as a savvy businessman with a strong work ethic.

People were killed every day for a lot less than three million. Sums like that were the realms of fantasy for most people. For a nurse working in A&E, it would be a veritable fortune.

Like so many of the country's public sector workers, Steve would be expected to work long thankless shifts for a wage that was little more than liveable. Had he looked at his uncle's wealth and decided to take matters into his own hands? Without knowing if Kevin helped Steve financially, it was a possibility that had to be considered, although Fiona knew she had to keep an open mind.

Steve had said earlier he worked at Glasgow Royal Infirmary. Before she'd been posted to Lochgilphead, Fiona had been stationed in Glasgow. She'd attended the Royal Infirmary on three occasions to break up fights in A&E. On weekends and bank holidays, it was a regular call out. The A&E dealt with drunks who'd hurt themselves, people who'd received beatings and all manner of other injuries. The atmosphere had always been that of a tinderbox, and while the NHS staff had gone about their work with a smile on their faces, it was obvious the smiles were false.

It took a special kind of person to tolerate such an environment on a daily basis, and Fiona had seen the worn faces behind the false smiles. How tempting would it be for someone who could exchange that life for one of wealth and luxury?

All of this was a stretch. It implied a lack of morality in someone who'd chosen a career where helping people was the main goal. Sara had said Steve's parents were killed in a car crash when he was just ten. She'd also said the first people on the scene found Steve trying to give his mother CPR. It required no psychological deftness to work out Steve's career was a calling, because every patient he saved would in some way atone for not being able to save his mother.

Steve's story mirrored Fiona's own. That, more than any other reason, was why she doubted it was Steve who'd murdered Kevin. Aunt Mary had been the one to protect and care for Fiona in her darkest days. Kevin would have been the same for Steve. Under no circumstances could Fiona imagine herself doing even the slightest harm to Aunt Mary. Not a slapped face, not even a plucked hair. She could no more kill Aunt Mary than she could flap her arms and fly.

When it came to Aunt Mary, Fiona picked her words with care so as not to cause so much as the slightest offence.

Fiona knew she owed Aunt Mary a debt that could never be repaid, and she was sure Steve would feel the same way towards Kevin. That above anything else was why she doubted Steve was the killer.

There was no amount of worldly goods that would make Fiona even consider killing Aunt Mary. If offered the chance to learn the identity of her parents' killer, and reasons for their murder at the expense of Aunt Mary's life, Fiona wouldn't even stop to think. She'd keep her aunt alive and forego the closure whose lack dominated her life.

Once again, Fiona dug fingernails into the palm of her hand. She needed to stop thinking emotionally, and start thinking with the rational, logical part of her brain. Facts, not emotions, solved cases.

Steve had been calm when he'd found Kevin. There had been no histrionics, no outpouring of emotion to show his feelings towards his uncle. Instead he'd treated Kevin as a medical patient rather than a family member. It could be his professional training had kicked in, or it could be something more sinister. After Kevin had died, Steve's emotions had remained buttoned down. There were no tears for the lost relative, no anger or denial about Kevin's death. Everyone grieved in their own way. Fiona knew that only too well, but they still grieved and Steve didn't appear to be any more upset at the loss of his uncle than any of the others who knew Kevin.

Fiona was well aware she'd got lucky with Aunt Mary. Everything she'd heard about Kevin from the people she'd spoken to had painted him as a good boss and decent guy; he was also a successful businessman. To succeed in business, especially a high-end hotel like Inveraray House, would take no small amount of hard work, and at times ruthlessness. Chefs were known to work long, punishing hours and if there was a hotel to oversee as well as his work as a chef, there wouldn't be many hours left in the day for Kevin to care for his nephew.

Steve appeared to be in his early thirties, which would mean he'd gone into Kevin's care around the turn of the millennium. Say four or five years after Kevin had taken over Inveraray House. By then most of the hard work turning a business around ought to have been completed, but Kevin would still be a busy man. Fiona needed to get a picture of what life was like for Steve and Kevin at that time. Had the grief-stricken child been plonked in front of a TV or games console and left to amuse himself while his uncle carried on with his business, or had Kevin relied on his staff to keep the business steady while he devoted his time to caring for Steve? Had the boy been shipped off to a boarding school? Had Kevin been close to Steve's parents the way Aunt Mary was with Fiona's, or was he someone the boy hardly knew? Was he a kind and benevolent uncle, or one who'd made Steve earn his own way in life?

There were so many questions whirling around Fiona's head she barely heard Steve asking Ivor to help him move Alice onto the floor so he could start CPR.

THIRTY-SIX

Nobody moved, or spoke, or looked anyone in the eye as Steve went to work on Alice. Fiona knew that they were all expecting Alice to die on the floor of the shelter.

'Somebody check their watch. Let me know when ten minutes has passed.'

Fiona got why Steve wanted someone to monitor the time. Ten minutes was how long he'd chosen to give Alice the CPR that was keeping the blood and oxygen flowing around her body.

Ten minutes was a short amount of time to perform CPR. Fiona's training had been to continue until paramedics or a doctor was present. In her years as a police officer she'd never had to perform CPR, but it wasn't an omission she was unhappy about not having on her record. The last refresher course she'd been given had highlighted a few key numbers to her. The number she'd taken away was twenty minutes. People had responded to CPR long after this milestone, but there was a far greater risk of brain damage to the casualty after this point. The tutor had pressed home the number saying even in a surgical setting, CPR was usually halted after twenty minutes if there had been no response.

Steve had chosen to give Alice just half of the key number. Was the decision based on callousness, the fact that even if Alice did respond before then her chances of survival were negligible without proper medical attention, or a desire to strike another person down?

Ever since the attack on Alice, Fiona's thinking was the attack had been committed by the same person who'd murdered Kevin. Only four of the strangers – Steve, Ivor, Thomas and Sara – had been out looking for Alice along with herself and Jack, creating the opportunity to attack her and leave her for dead. Earlier on, Ivor and Sara had been at the shelter already when she'd arrived with Donna and Jack and the rest of their group, which meant it wouldn't have been easy for them to attack Kevin and then make their way to the shelter undetected. That left Steve and Thomas as prime suspects.

Steve halving the time he performed CPR on Alice was perhaps another way to ensure she didn't make it through the night.

Why Steve would want Alice dead was unknown to her, but Fiona guessed Alice might have seen something. Perhaps it had been his attack on Kevin, or something to do with the hotel. She did the books for Inveraray House. If Steve had been up to something, had she spotted it and threatened to tell Kevin? That tallied on a lot of different levels, and none of them bode well for Alice.

Sara's voice broke the silence. 'Five minutes.'

Fiona was wrestling with two dilemmas, was she watching a murder take place in front of her, and what ought she do when they reached the ten minutes Steve had allotted?

A glance round the room showed white faces set in fearful expressions. Even the inexpressive Ivor was stony-faced as he watched Steve perform rhythmic thrusts down onto Alice's sternum. Steve's face was beaded with sweat and his breathing was ragged from the exertion. Frances was drawing the back of her thumbs under her eyes as Thomas smoothed his hand down her back. Donna was cuddled into Jack, not that Fiona gave much concern to the woman who'd once been her closest friend.

'Eight minutes.' Sara's tone was more stretched than it had been three minutes ago. 'Come on, Alice. We're here. You can get through this.'

The comment from Sara earned her a vicious look from her husband.

'Say more, she might be able to hear you.'

At Steve's instruction, everyone joined in, urging Alice to cling on, to open her eyes.

The only movements from Alice were involuntary reactions to Steve's thrusts.

'Nine minutes.'

The entreaties to Alice deepened in their fervour as Fiona prepared herself to take over from Steve if he tried to call a time of death at ten minutes.

'Nine and a half.'

Fiona wanted to gag Sara, to prevent her from continuing her macabre countdown. To switch off the clock whose ticking signalled the end of Alice's life. The urgings were growing louder and more desperate as they all willed Alice to survive.

'Ten minutes.'

Steve didn't stop pumping Alice's chest. He kept on going, past twelve minutes, fifteen. Alice still didn't respond.

When Sara said *eighteen minutes*, Steve turned his head to look at Fiona without pausing his downward thrusts.

Fiona gulped at the enormity of his unasked question. As a police officer, she was the authority in the room, and he was deferring responsibility to her.

With a clenched jaw and a leaden heart, Fiona lifted her right hand and gave Steve the peace sign. In two more minutes

Alice would have had CPR for twenty minutes. To continue beyond that point wasn't likely to bring Alice back, and even if by some miracle she responded, they were still stuck up a Munro many hours from the kind of medical help Alice would need if she was to make it through the night.

All the same, Fiona wondered if she'd just given a murderer permission to kill again.

'Nineteen minutes.'

By now the entreaties were less fervent as everyone seemed to be coming to terms with the idea Alice wasn't going to respond to Steve's efforts.

Fiona wasn't speaking. Instead she was working out what to do and say when another minute had passed.

'Twenty minutes.'

Again Steve looked Fiona's way. And this time everyone else looked at her too, as they'd picked up on the unspoken conversation between nurse and copper.

'You're the nurse, Steve, I have to bow to your greater experience. I hate to say this, but if you think life is extinct and there's no chance of Alice coming back, you should call time of death.'

Even to Fiona's ears the statement lacked emotion and sounded like the kind of thing people said when they wanted to cover their arse. It was far from Fiona's proudest moment, but she had to protect herself. To insulate herself from any comeback when this was over and everything was picked apart by a team of detectives.

The only way Fiona would ever find out who killed her parents was by investigating the cold crime herself. And to do that, she needed to retain her status as an officer for Police Scotland.

THIRTY-SEVEN

Jack, Ivor and Thomas helped Steve place Alice's body on the same bench in the second room where Kevin's body lay. Hard looks were spearing Fiona's way but she ignored them. There was still an investigation to conduct and no matter what the others thought, she had a duty of care for them, and the only way she could guarantee their safety was to identify the killer.

Next on Fiona's list of people to speak to were Thomas and Steve. Neither were conversations she was looking forward to. Both were suspects, both had had the opportunity to attack Alice as well as Kevin. For Fiona, Steve had an obvious motive: money. Thomas on the other hand possessed no standout motive.

Due to the way Steve had slumped onto a bench Fiona stepped across to Thomas and tapped the arm he had draped across Frances's shoulders. 'Your turn.'

A hand grasped Fiona's shoulder from behind. Not hard, but firm enough to make Fiona tense as she whirled to see who it was.

'Can we talk? I'm so sorry about what I said before. I didn't mean it. You know that, don't you?'

'Not now, Donna.'

'Please, Fiona. You have to let me apologise.'

'I don't *have* to let you do anything. And I said, *not now.*'

Donna's lip wobbled as she retreated. Fiona felt no guilt at the way she'd spoken to Donna. At some point in the future she would let Donna say her piece, but she wasn't ready to hear it yet. If she ever would be. What Donna had said was the worst kind of betrayal, and as close as she'd always been to Donna, Fiona wasn't sure she could forgive her.

Thomas was on his feet, but his expression was one of fearful confusion. The hard tone Fiona had used with Donna wasn't a side of her she wanted Thomas to witness. He was nervous enough by nature and she needed him to be calm instead of a skittish fawn.

'Poor Alice.' Thomas's eyes were locked on the section of the bench where Alice and Kevin lay. 'Poor Kevin.'

'It's terrible what's happened. You do understand I need to work out who murdered them? That I have to identify and arrest the killer?'

'Of course. They need to be locked up.' Thomas gave a half-furtive look at the doorway to the shelter's main room. 'I can't believe anyone in here killed them, though. We all got on. We worked together for years. The killer must be someone else, or your mate. He was quick enough to lamp me when he thought I'd attacked you.'

Every word Thomas was saying got analysed by Fiona as he said it. He'd started off lamenting the murders, and that could be a distraction, or if he was smarter than he presented himself, a way of urging Fiona to solve the case. After that he'd denied the killer was one of his group. That was natural. Nobody wanted to think the worst of people they liked and respected. But it hadn't gone unnoticed by Fiona Thomas had pointed the finger of blame squarely at Jack. After being punched by Jack it was no surprise Thomas had his suspicions about him, but

Fiona knew Jack hadn't had the chance to commit the attack on Alice; therefore, if her theory was correct and there was only one killer, then Jack was innocent. Even if there were two, Jack wasn't close to the top of her list of suspects for Kevin's murder. It was typical, though, of a guilty person to try shifting the focus of an investigation onto someone else. And who better than a stranger who'd already shown a violent side to his personality?

'I can understand why you want to blame Jack, but he and I were together all the time we were looking for Alice.' Fiona allowed a silence to grow, as she wanted Thomas to eliminate Jack of his own accord. Even more than that, she was testing Thomas.

'And if you were together, you know he didn't attack Alice. The odds of there being two people up here who are killers are bound to be ridiculously low, therefore Jack is innocent.'

Fiona said nothing, but she did rotate her head to acknowledge Thomas's words. He'd arrived at her theory in no time at all. Therefore, he was nobody's fool, and a lot smarter than she'd previously thought.

It had been a mistake of Fiona's to assume Thomas wasn't as clever as his colleagues. Maybe it was his youth compared to the others, or the fact he seemed less confident, but when she'd learned he ran the bar and acted as a sommelier at Inveraray House, she ought to have recognised to do so would require what Dave Lennox referred to as 'live cells', and revised her opinion of Thomas.

How big an error that might prove to be was unknown, but the realisation just added to the dread Fiona could feel building in her stomach.

'When you and Steve were out looking for Alice, did you stay together or split up?'

'We split up. Both of us thought you were being overly cautious by telling us to stay in pairs. Besides, we both needed a piss so we went our separate ways. I went a little bit along the track and looked down the hill. Steve went further uphill.'

'When did you meet back up?'

'After I shouted to let everyone know I'd found the place where Alice had flattened the snow with her feet. Everyone came together at once.'

'Did you see anyone before that?'

'No.'

'Are you finished with me?' Thomas gestured to Frances. 'She's upset and none of the others are helping her.'

'You like Frances, don't you?'

'I do. She's always been good to me. She doesn't rip the piss like Sara or Lewis.'

Fiona had meant Thomas liked Frances in a more romantic way, but what he'd said about Sara and Lewis gave her a better line of enquiry. 'How do they rip the piss?'

'They don't like how much I know about wine and whisky. Before he left, Neil taught me a lot about them. Not just where they're from and so on, but how they're made, what to look for in certain grape varieties, what distinguishes a good whisky from a great one.' A sneer crept into Thomas's voice. 'Sara buys her wine in three litre boxes at the shop, and Lewis drinks whichever whisky is cheapest. I've given them a taste of the really good stuff, but they didn't appreciate it. They think I'm jumped up because even though I came from a shitty council estate, I learned to appreciate the finer things in life. The only reason I made it is because Kevin took a chance on me.' Thomas gave a huge sniff and let it act as a full stop on his sentence.

'Were they nasty to you? Or was it good-natured teasing?'

'They are never full-on nasty about it, but they never let it go either. Sara is the worst; she can be a right snidey cow when she wants. I've stopped reacting to it and they've eased off.'

'What flaws of theirs are you aware of?'

'She's got ideas above her station. To hear her speak it's her who should be in charge not Kevin. I've heard her try and tell Kevin what to do on a couple of occasions.'

'And how did Kevin react to that?'

'He thanked her for sharing her opinion, but said that if he wanted her advice in future, he'd request it.' The corners of Thomas's mouth leapt for such a brief second it might have been a nervous tic. 'She wasn't happy, but what could she do?'

'What indeed?' Fiona picked over what he'd said and added it to her picture of the various personalities. 'And what about Lewis, did he challenge Kevin at all? Someone said earlier Kevin never let Lewis add a dish to the menu. That doesn't sound like someone who's supposed to be a good boss getting the best out of his staff.'

Thomas's mouth opened and closed before he opened it a second time. 'It's the difference between a good and great chef. Lewis would be fantastic in a country pub with lots of home-made fare, but Kevin was on a different level. You should have seen the dishes he could create. Comparing the two of them is like comparing a bog-standard saloon to a Ferrari. For the fine dining, I match wines to each dish. Lewis's idea of matching food and drink is a pie and a pint.'

'It doesn't sound like he was that good a fit for a fine dining establishment. Why wasn't he let go?'

'Because he works hard, follows instruction well and is reliable. Say what you like about him, and Alice often did, he worked hard and never let anyone down. That's a lot more than you can say about lots of people who work in the hospitality industry.'

'I see. You said Alice often voiced her opinion on him. What did she have to say?'

'She always thought Lewis could make more of himself. That if he showed a bit more interest in the finer things in life, he'd get more pleasure out of what he did.'

'What about Alice and Sara, how did they get on? They were at each other's throats earlier, is that normal for them?'

'It isn't. They're normally like besties. Many's the time I've seen then having a cuppa and a craic.'

Fiona added the information to her profile and considered how it affected her opinions of everyone. Alice and Sara being friends was a surprise as both seemed vocal, and in her experience, two vocal people rarely got along well. As for the comments made to Thomas about his interest in whisky and wine, they could be passed off as petty jealousy from people who didn't appreciate the sight of someone bettering themselves.

'And what about Steve, how does he get on with everyone?'

'Fine as far as I'm aware. Whenever he visited he'd pitch in if needed. He'd moved out long before I started there so I don't know what it was like when he was there full time, but from what I've heard, if it wasn't for Kevin, Steve would have ended up in the care system. I've been there when my old dear's drinking got out of hand. Steve was bloody lucky to have Kevin looking after him.'

The revelation Thomas had been in the care system rammed home to Fiona how little she knew about all of the people on her suspect list.

It was Steve whom she planned to question next, and after him, Neil. As the oldest in the group and a friend of Kevin's, Neil would know more about Steve's early days living with his uncle.

THIRTY-EIGHT

Steve's eyes were hard when he sat down to talk with Fiona. To her they looked like dirty granite orbs. His expression was one of someone who was beaten down by life, and that figured considering he'd just lost his closest relative and had then failed to save a patient in his care. Or at least, it would figure if he was innocent.

'I've been waiting for you to speak to me. I saw how you talked to some of the others first. I expect they'll have told you Kevin was my uncle, and about how he took me in. I'm sure they've also told you that as I'm Kevin's only living relative, I'm like as not in line to inherit Inveraray House, unless there's any surprises in Kevin's will. You cops all look for means, motive and opportunity, don't you? I bet they're like a holy trinity to cops. You said before Kevin had been clobbered with a rock; that would be the means, the lack of visibility in the snowstorm gives the opportunity, and now you've learned I'm in line to inherit a very good business, you have your motive. So what happens now, do you drop your suspicions of everyone else and focus on me?'

Fiona was happy to listen to Steve. He was making sense and if his words were to be believed, he was expecting to be the focus of her investigation.

'They did tell me all that, and you're right, means, motive and opportunity are all factors detectives look at when working a case. However, I'm not a detective. I'm your bog-standard, run-of-the-mill police officer. I get sent to break up arguments between neighbours, wrestle drunks at kicking out time, and if any crimes of note happen in the area, I either get guard duty, or a task so boring and mundane it makes my teeth itch.'

'Nice try. I watch the news, read the papers. You've solved two murder cases in the last year. You're a poster girl for Police Scotland. A PR dream. You're not so pretty it looks like they drafted in a model, yet nor are you some hatchet-faced old cow. You're smart, a lot smarter than you're making yourself out to be. You might fool some of the others, but you're not fooling me.'

'I'll take your comments on my intelligence as a compliment. What you said about my looks could be taken either way, so I'm ignoring both your comments and whatever your intention was in giving them.'

Steve's expression never changed, but the forefinger of his left hand started tapping against his knee. 'I get I'm a good fit when it comes to Kevin's murder. I deny killing him; of course I do, but I don't expect you to believe me. What I will say, though, is while I had your holy trinity when it came to Kevin, I didn't have it so far as Alice was concerned. So why would I kill her? And let's be sensible about this, whoever killed Kevin has to be the same person who killed Alice.'

A sense of calm fell over Fiona. Steve had a sharp mind and was a quick thinker. It was clear he'd given the topic a lot of thought, which was logical whether or not he was the killer. These verbal jousts weren't something she got very often. Most of the interviews she conducted were with mouth-breathing Neanderthals whose idea of clever wordplay was an episode of *Catchphrase*. Steve on the other hand presented a challenge, and while she felt she could best him at leisure with a well-timed sentence or two, Fiona was happy to let him rattle on as she was more likely to hear things she could use when she needed to.

'You're not saying much, are you? Is it because you know I'm right about Alice?'

Time to drop the first bomb, to test whether Steve's confidence remained when his defence was put under some pressure.

'If Alice told you she'd witnessed you attacking Kevin and put the screws on you for a share of Inveraray House, or maybe a one-off payment to ensure her silence, I'd count that as a motive. Thomas said you'd split up when searching for her, which is opportunity. As for means, I established earlier all of us who looked for her grabbed an armful of logs.' Fiona made a point of locking eyes with Steve. 'And that's just off the top of my head. Like you pointed out, I'm not a detective, but lots of detectives will end up working this case. That's as certain as night following day. They'll ask about your relationship with Alice. Whether you liked her. Loved her even. They'll want to know if you and she ever had a physical relationship. If she ever touched you in an inappropriate fashion while you were growing up. Those detectives will have years of experience. They'll have seen and heard of things you and I couldn't begin to imagine. Make no mistake, when we get down off Beinn Bhuidhe, you're going to be asked an awful lot of questions by some very suspicious officers.'

Fiona stopped speaking and waited until Steve broke eye contact. It took less than a second as he contemplated his near future. It had been good to see the doubt in his eyes, to see him realise how easy it might be to find a reason for him to kill Alice as well as his uncle. What Fiona hoped more than anything was that she hadn't made a mistake in saying so much. If she'd given him forewarning of the questions coming his way, he'd have time to prepare answers. Worst of all, if he was guilty, he might try concocting some ridiculous story about how both Kevin and Alice had abused him and use it as mitigating circumstance to plead down his sentence.

'So what you're saying is, I'm screwed, aren't I?'

'I'm not saying that. You sat down here expecting me to accuse you. You even challenged my logic should I make an accusation. All I've done is show you how I or any halfway competent detective can guess what your motive for killing Alice might be.'

'What happens now?' Steve gestured at the shelter. 'You won't be able to do a proper police interview here, will you? I'm guessing this conversation is only happening because you think I'm guilty and you're trying to either trick me into saying the wrong thing, or you're putting pressure on me so I'll confess when one of your detective buddies starts with the real interviews.'

'I'm not going to lie, I'm trying both of those things. But there's something else I'll admit to you. I don't think you're guilty.'

Steve's mouth hung open as he stared at Fiona. 'You what? If you don't think I killed them, why are you giving me the third degree?'

'I actually wasn't. I haven't yet asked you a single question about Kevin's or Alice's murder.'

'You said yet, that means you plan to. But you haven't explained why you think I'm innocent.'

'I'll come to that in a minute.' Fiona wanted to lean back, but doing so would encourage Steve to either lean over her, or speak louder. Neither were things she wanted to happen. But before she got too far into the questions with Steve, she wanted to try and put his mind at ease a little, so he'd be more likely to say something that she could pounce on. 'First, I want to start with the whole third-degree thing you mentioned. Out of interest, did you know the origin of giving someone the third-degree stems from freemasonry? To achieve the third degree and become a Master Mason, candidates were subjected to intensive questioning.'

'Trust a copper to know that.'

'Touché. Now, getting back to my questions, you were taken in by your uncle after your parents' death. I believe you were ten at the time. How did your uncle juggle looking after you and running Inveraray House?'

'He didn't. For the first few weeks he was with me all the time. When he'd got me enrolled in a school, he'd look after the hotel while I was at school and be there for me the rest of the time.' Steve gave a shrug that also saw him tilt his head to one side. 'By the time term had finished, he was easing more and more back towards the hotel.' He'd spend a couple of hours with me and then leave me to watch TV, or do my homework, or play on the PlayStation he got me. Around half eight he'd come up to the flat we lived in, chase me off to bed and that would be it. He kept every Sunday afternoon free to be with me and if we didn't go out somewhere, we'd watch or play football together.'

Everything Steve was saying evoked bitter memories for Fiona. Aunt Mary had done for her pretty much what Kevin had done for Steve. Without Aunt Mary, Fiona had no clue as to how she'd have got through those first weeks. She guessed Steve would have similar thoughts about his uncle.

'It sounds very much like he put his life on hold to make sure you were okay and then eased back when the time was right. Was he good to you? I don't mean financially by buying you bits and pieces; I mean did he make sure you were okay, mentally as well as physically? Looking after a kid who's lost their parents is about a lot more than buying toys. It's about repairing their soul.'

Steve's eyes narrowed. 'Why do you ask that?'

'Because I think it's relevant. Because I don't think any amount of PlayStation games or any other trinkets are what you really needed then. Did he look after you in the ways that really mattered?'

Tears filled Steve's eyes but he made no effort to wipe them away. 'He did. I didn't know it at the time, I was just this daft bairn who was football mad and then when... when... After the crash, Kevin stepped up. He put his dream on hold and became mam and dad to me. When I look back and think of some of the shite he put up with from me those first weeks, he was a saint. If he hadn't taken me in, God knows where I'd have ended up. He didn't just save me, he made me. He put me through uni to get my nursing degree, and paid for all my accommodation and anything else major that I needed. The only thing he didn't pay for was my food and drink. He told me to get a job and pay for them myself. I guess it was his way of teaching me a work ethic and the value of money.'

Steve locked eyes with Fiona. 'I didn't kill him, I could never hurt him. Okay, we fell out from time to time, but usually over something stupid I'd done like getting a speeding ticket in his car. I could always go to him with anything. He'd grumble a bit and then give me solid advice. He was the first person I came out to.'

'How did he react?' Fiona hadn't thought about Steve's sexual preferences, as they didn't matter to her.

'He told me he'd guessed years ago, and then asked me to pass the remote.' Another tilt of the head accompanied by a rueful smile. 'That was Kevin all over, he never made a song and dance about anything but Inveraray House, and even then he was quiet and forceful. He was so clued up, he saw everything, had such a wise take on so many situations. Yes, I might inherit the hotel and whatever money Kevin has. I'd give it all up to have him back. To sit and watch a match with him. To once again have a last drink after the bar's closed and all the customers have gone to bed. Fuck the money. I don't want that. I want the man who saved my life to not be dead. With Kevin gone, I've lost everything, not gained a fortune. I'd commit suicide before I did anything to hurt Kevin. You've no idea what it was like for me when Mam and Dad died. Without Kevin, I'd have wound up in prison, if I didn't kill myself with drink or drugs first.'

'I do know what it's like.' Fiona rose to her feet and went to the narrow doorway. When she caught Jack's eye she waved him over.

Jack loomed over Steve, and Fiona could tell he was tense and ready to act at her command. 'What is it? Is he giving you a problem?'

'There's no problem. I just want you to tell him what happened to me when I was fifteen. Just the headlines, he doesn't need the gory details.'

Steve turned his head to look up at Jack.

'Her parents were murdered when she was at school. She ended up living with her auntie in some remote valley near Hawick. The cops have never found out who killed her parents and whether she admits it or not, that haunts her.'

'Thank you, Jack.' Fiona had to cut Jack off before he said anything more. He wasn't wrong, but it didn't mean the time was right for her whole sorry story to be laid out in front of Steve when the headlines would suffice. 'I'll take it from here.'

As Jack shuffled off there were unshed tears in Steve's eyes, but he was looking at Fiona with a new understanding. 'You *do* know what it's like. We crashed because my mam and dad were arguing and he was driving too fast. That sucks, but at least I've always known why they died, but you don't even have that, do you?'

'I don't. But you were there with your parents. You'd have seen how hurt they were. You were younger than me. We might have much the same story, but our versions are different. It's because I've lived a lot of the same things you have that I don't think you killed Kevin or Alice. But you have to admit, you being Kevin's sole inheritor makes you a highly placed suspect, and a perfect scapegoat.'

THIRTY-NINE

Steve's reaction to Fiona's last sentence made her question her opinion of his intelligence once more. The suggestion whomever had murdered Kevin might be setting him up wasn't one he'd considered and, now he was considering it, his emotions weren't hidden.

As soon as his lips began to thin and his head twisted towards the doorway, Fiona reached out a hand and grabbed his wrist to stop him from moving. 'Stay calm. You're doing yourself no favours by ranting and raving or throwing accusations around.'

When Steve looked back at Fiona she saw the defeat in his eyes, the anger in his jaw and the bloodless skin of someone whose emotional tank was empty.

The anger Steve felt would be a natural thing. If he was innocent, he'd feel not only a soul-crushing loss, but a fury against the person who'd robbed him of a loved one. A guilty person might affect the same emotions as a way to deflect any investigation, but Fiona's gut was telling her every one of Steve's reactions was genuine. She had just spelled out what would happen when they got back from the shelter, and unless Steve was planning to go on the run, the only way he wouldn't face a lot of awkward questions from the detectives who landed this case was if Fiona proved someone else was the killer. Innocent or guilty, Steve's best option was to retain control of his emotions and answer Fiona's questions.

Fiona had realised this a good while ago, but she gave Steve a couple of minutes to work it out for himself.

'Whether I killed him or not, I'm screwed. What you said before about me being the prime suspect will be right. I'll have to face hour upon hour of questions when I should be planning Kevin's funeral. Instead of being allowed to grieve, I'll be fighting to prove my innocence, won't I?'

'I'm afraid you will, unless...'

Fiona let the hook dangle to see if her bait was taken. The best way to enlist an ally was to trick them into making the alliance. Steve was still on her list of suspects, but after seeing him talk about Kevin he'd dropped down to equal last place with Jack. Robert De Niro or Meryl Streep may be able to act that grief-stricken at will, but no ordinary person could.

As well as the emotional part of her brain discounting Steve as the killer, the logical section was telling her that from Steve's perspective it didn't make sense for him to do it on Beinn Bhuidhe. From everything she'd heard, Kevin loved Steve, and Steve was in line to inherit Kevin's entire estate. He would be welcome in Kevin's home and probably had his own key. If he was plotting to murder his uncle, he'd probably have planned to sneak into the house during the night and slit his throat or bash his skull in. Steve would have worked to give himself an alibi, he may even have hired a hitman, but for someone who was savvy enough to know they'd be the first person the police would look at, it seemed reckless in the extreme for him to seize an opportunity that was granted only by a whim of the weather.

It could be the chance had been taken because Kevin planned to change his will cutting Steve out, but from what

Fiona could recollect, there had been no sour faces or lingering atmosphere when they'd first met Kevin, Steve and the others, and nobody who'd just lost out on millions would have been in good spirits.

'You have to help me, Fiona. Help me prove my innocence.'

'I'm a cop.' Fiona used the slang term on purpose. 'I'm not a detective. All I can do is try my best to investigate the murders until trained detectives take over. However, if I can work out who the killer is, then you'll be recognised as the innocent you claim to be. Now, everything you've told me so far about yours and Kevin's relationship will be very easy for detectives to prove or disprove. All they'll have to do is trace the payments he made to the uni and the place you stayed when at uni. If he paid the money to you and then you paid it on, that's just as easy to track. By speaking to former and current staff members, they'll verify what you said about him looking after you. My old sergeant who taught me the ropes is a canny beggar. He taught me a lot and he reiterated what we'd been taught at Tuliallan when it came to murders. It's usually about money or sex. There'll be the odd time when a domestic violence victim will lash out at their abuser and kill them, but those cases are fewer and further between than you might imagine. Sometimes there can be a gang killing, but most of them are either retaliation, or a warning to someone who's encroaching on a gang's turf. As they're to do with protecting the gang's territory, they're about money.'

'You're basically saying the detectives are gonna think I killed him so I'll inherit his money and Inveraray House. That's obvious, and as I didn't do it, the real killer must have had another reason. Sex isn't something Kevin ever seemed interested in to me. I've never known him to date, or even check out a good-looking woman. The odd time he'd joke about female sales reps who thought flirting was the best way to achieve sales, but that was about it.'

'So he didn't date anyone. That seems odd. We all need someone in our lives, even if it's for companionship rather than a physical release. Do you think he never checked women out because he was gay himself?'

'Kevin certainly wasn't gay. He told me once when we sat up to three in the morning drinking, he'd been married around the time I was born. He admitted she'd broken his heart and because he never wanted to risk being so hurt again he decided to put all his energies into his business. And that's what he did. Well, until I moved in at least.'

'I get that.' The words were out before Fiona could stop them.

Steve's look curled into shrewdness. 'Let me guess, you don't form lasting relationships because you're afraid of the pain when they go sour. Sure, you might go on dates and have some fun, but the minute someone starts getting serious, their arse is kicked into touch before you can experience a painful loss again. Am I right?'

'Let's just say you're not wrong and leave it at that, shall we?' Fiona caught the catch in her own voice as she recognised a kindred spirit in Steve. 'We've both been damaged by life, but I don't consider myself broken, and nor should you.'

'Fair enough. Now if the motive for killing Kevin isn't money or sex, what is it?'

FORTY

Fiona tried not to pull a face at the way Steve was so quick to rule out sex as a motive. For all he might have been close to his uncle she knew only too well how a loved one could keep secrets. Her own aunt, Mary, had withheld details of a relationship she'd started, and while Fiona wasn't ashamed of herself, there wasn't anything in the world that could force her to tell Aunt Mary how she'd pick up a guy when she felt the need for sexual release.

'If you're not the killer, we can rule out inheriting Kevin's money as a motive. That leaves sex.'

'Thanks, but you're not my type.'

The wan smile that accompanied Steve's joke almost broke Fiona's heart. The man in front of her was living her worst fear. He was hanging by his emotional fingertips and by sharing her thought processes with him she was asking for more than he could give. She got why he'd made the weak jest. He needed to keep things light, to keep himself on an even keel.

'Shame, I've always had a thing for nurses. I guess it's the scrubs, the way they really show off the figure.'

'Yeah, they're great. I pull whenever I slip them on.' A

flicker of amusement crossed Steve's face for the briefest of moments before it fell again. 'I can't see Kevin being killed over sex, though. Certainly not by anyone here. He always kept a professional distance between himself and his staff. Don't get me wrong, he'd work alongside them and have a laugh and everything, but he always knew where to draw the line. No way would he have slept with any of them. Nor would he have even tried. He was never one to hug them, even when they clearly needed a friendly hug because they were going through a tough time.'

To Fiona, Steve's words sounded like the lionising of the deceased that so often happens. After death all living sins were erased and arseholes became saints, abusers became wonderful providers and a thousand other such reinventions happened.

Fiona was aware she was being cynical. It could be Kevin had been as Steve described him. While Kevin wasn't being offered up for sainthood just yet, nor was he being painted as anything other than a decent guy who behaved in a responsible way. Inveraray House seemed to be his love affair and while it was possible he had a sex life Steve knew nothing about, none of the others in the group were flinging wild accusations around. In a close-knit work environment, there would be few secrets that could be kept for any length of time. Had one of them, say Ivor as an example, heard Kevin had slept with Sara, he was sure to have accused Lewis of killing him. That hadn't happened, therefore it was unlikely Kevin had slept with or made advances on any of his female staff, but not impossible. Despite their age difference, Thomas appeared to be sweet on Frances, but from what Fiona had seen, his was a case of unrequited love more than anything else.

Another reason to discount Kevin having had any romantic connection to Sara was Lewis had a twisted or broken ankle. Therefore, Lewis hadn't left the shelter to search for Alice which meant he hadn't been able to kill her, and that in turn ruled him out of having killed Kevin.

'Okay, let's take those present out of the equation. Do you think it's possible your uncle was seeing anyone at all?' Fiona tried a gentle smile to keep the mood light in consideration of Steve's fragile state. 'And if he might have been, who do you think that person was?'

'He might have been seeing someone, but I don't know when he'd see them, as he was always at the hotel. He certainly never brought anyone to the hotel to my knowledge. I asked him about it once. Why he didn't date anyone or invite a woman to join him there for dinner.'

'What did he say?'

'He laughed. Said he wasn't interested in dating anyone and if he did, there was no way he'd bring her anywhere near Inveraray House until he knew what she was really like. He said bringing anyone back to Inveraray House on a date was showing off. That he wouldn't do it, and I never should. He was always on about watching out for gold-diggers. Kept telling me to never reveal I was going to inherit a hotel one day. That I should always make sure of someone's real motives for being with me before I mentioned Inveraray House.' Steve gave a deprecating shrug. 'Like I was ever gonna risk getting hurt again.'

'That seems wise.' Fiona didn't just mean the risk of losing someone Steve loved. 'Is there anybody, anybody at all who you think he may have dated, or even wanted to date?'

'There's nobody. He never got over his wife's affair. He loved her. I think part of him always loved her no matter how much she hurt him. I never knew her. They split when I was around three, so I have no memories of her and how he was when I did see him.'

'We'll leave individuals for a moment. And I know you said there was no one. But if there was, what type of woman do you think he would go for? What would she have to be like? Tell me anything you can think of, we're talking age, personality, shape, whatever.'

Steve's brow creased, and Fiona used the time he spent thinking to take a run at a new theory she'd created. It was a stretch, a real stretch, but not beyond the bounds of probability, not when the payoff would be in the region of seven figures.

Kevin had built a successful business of Inveraray House. It was worth a couple of million at least, plus whatever he had stashed away. He seemed a canny operator and decent person. Aunt Mary worked at a solicitor's office and while she never blabbed about clients, she'd often regaled Fiona with tales about the legalities of various situations. As Fiona's chosen career was a police officer, she'd lapped up these stories and done whatever she could to learn as much as her aunt could or would tell her.

If money was the key reason Kevin had been killed, then the killer had to be someone who stood to gain financially from his death. That thinking made Steve the chief suspect. He was number one in line. Except Fiona knew from Aunt Mary few solicitors advised their clients to name only one benefactor when drawing up a will. There would be a secondary name or collection of names should Steve be deceased at the time of Kevin's death. The identity of the secondary name was unknown to her, but the more Fiona thought about possibilities, the less she liked where she was going with her thinking.

Steve had said Kevin's ex-wife cheated on him before he got Inveraray House. Was she bitter because she felt she'd made a mistake with her life choices? Had she watched from the side-lines and built years of resentment towards her ex? Had she felt she was owed a share of Kevin's money and business? Steve had also said he thought Kevin still loved his ex. Would he name her after Steve? Maybe even give her something alongside Steve? If not a share of the hotel, perhaps she was in line for a cash sum. If she knew or suspected this, she'd then be in the frame for Kevin's murder.

Fiona's mind flashed to the possibility one of the women in the group was Kevin's ex and then ground to a halt. Sara and Frances were both too young to have been married to Kevin almost thirty years ago, and Alice had been murdered. Plus, surely one of the group would have told her about Kevin's ex-wife being present.

What seemed far more probable to Fiona was the ex-wife had enlisted the help of someone who was here. If she was romantically involved with one of the men here, it would make sense for them to kill Kevin, set Steve up as the killer and then enjoy her inheritance together. Under Scottish law people couldn't inherit if they were found guilty of murdering their benefactor. It was this fact more than any other which kept Steve from the top of her suspect list. He was too good a patsy, and too smart to kill Kevin when he'd be a suspect.

'If he had dated anyone, she'd have had to be someone who appreciated the finer things in life. Someone smart, both in the way she dressed and education wise. He had no time for numpties who couldn't hold an intelligent conversation. She'd have to be clean; he kept his kitchen as clean as an operating theatre and his house was never anything less than spotless.'

Steve's words snapped Fiona away from her theorising. As she scrambled to digest what he was saying her mind took on another thought. *If Steve wasn't lined up to take the fall, did that mean he was a target and would be next to be killed?*

FORTY-ONE

It made a lot of sense to Fiona that Steve may also be a target, but for the moment she had to park such thoughts and focus on what he was saying. 'So can you think of anyone who fits that description?'

'There's a consultant at the hospital who does, but there's nobody around Inveraray I can think of.'

'Nobody at all?'

'Hang on a minute.' Steve's face creased, but he shook his head long before the prescribed time period had passed. 'No, no way. He'd never do that.'

'Do what?'

'The only person who's likely to come into his orbit who fits that description is a woman from Dalmally. She works as a rep for a family firm. They supply game meats to hotels and restaurants across Argyll and the southern highlands. She's exactly the kind of woman he'd go for if he went for anyone at all.'

'So why are you discounting her as a possible love interest?'

'She's married to the son who runs the business, and after the betrayal Kevin felt after his wife cheated on him, there's no way he'd ever get involved with someone who was attached.'

Had Fiona not kept such a tight rein on her own emotional attachments, she might have argued the heart wanted what the heart wanted or some other such cliché, but she couldn't bring herself to do it. What she could do was appreciate Kevin's principles. She'd twice felt herself developing feelings for someone that could be love. Both times she'd ended the relationship as soon as she recognised the depth of her feeling. Kevin's moralistic principles might sound trite to some, but to her they were beholden to an inner decency, and everyone she'd spoken to had portrayed Kevin as a decent man.

'Okay, let's discount her. Is there anyone else who might feature in his life?'

'There's nobody else I can think of and he'd have sooner had his eyes gouged out than try online dating. He always said he was happier on his own and if he ever did meet someone, it'd happen because the world intended it to.'

The last sentence struck a chord with Fiona. 'Did he believe in divine intervention, karma, that kind of thing?'

'Not at all. He just believed that if something was meant to be, it would happen and if it wasn't, it wouldn't. He was quite fatalistic that way.'

'Okay, let's leave that subject alone for now, but we can easily revisit it if you think of anyone else. I want you to tell me everything you know about his ex-wife. Are they still in contact? Does he send her money on a regular basis? Did she remarry? Does she live anywhere near here?'

Steve's face went blank for a second and then drooped with disappointment. 'I'm sorry, but I don't know anything about her. They lived near Stirling when they were married, but I don't know where she went after that. I believe Kevin paid the mortgage on the house, but once it was paid up, he didn't give her any money that I know of. I don't know where she is now, whether she married again, or anything about her. For all I know she could be in Australia or dead. Why do you ask? Why aren't you asking me this stuff about Alice?'

'I'm just trying to build as big a picture as I can. So far as Alice's murder is concerned, I think whomever attacked Kevin suspected Alice saw something that would reveal their identity and killed her to stay anonymous. Therefore, the key to identifying the killer is to find out who might want to kill your uncle.'

'Oh.'

As Steve fell silent, the cogs again began to whirr in Fiona's mind. Not for the first time that night she rued the fact she couldn't get anything she was told checked out by other officers. Every word she was told had to be taken at face value or discredited by a contrary story. Worse than that was the feeling of isolation. She was the one person who could prevent the killer from either striking again or escaping justice. Sure, some of the men in the shelter would step up if things got physical, but the killer was picking his moments to strike and so far there had been not even a hint of who might be responsible.

Fiona bent her mind back to the ex-wife theory. If she was in cahoots with the killer, it would be one of the men present. That meant Neil, Ivor, Lewis and Thomas were all in that particular frame.

Of the four, Neil and Ivor were of a similar age to Kevin and as such more likely to fall for a woman of their own age. However, there was little love showing between Lewis and Sara, which could be down to the fact Sara knew, or had strong suspicions, her husband was cheating.

The problem with putting Lewis in the frame was he'd already been more or less eliminated from her thinking due to his injured ankle. The same logic applied to Neil, who although looking to have got over the worst of his allergic reaction, hadn't been part of the search party when Alice went AWOL. That left Ivor and Thomas. Of the two, Ivor looked to be the better candidate. Not only was he around the same age as the ex-wife would be, his work as gardener and maintenance man would tone his muscles. Sure, Thomas would lift a few cases of wine or whatever on a regular basis, but there was no escaping the fact there was more meat on a butcher's pencil than his gangly frame. Another reason to doubt Thomas was partnering with the ex-wife was his mooning over Frances. In some respects it suggested he had a thing for older women, but if he was in cahoots to murder Kevin and frame Steve, he'd surely be infatuated with the ex-wife not the receptionist.

Whichever way she looked at it, Ivor was the chief suspect if her theory about the ex-wife was correct. And that's all it was, a theory. Fiona knew well enough to not pin too much credence on it, but so far as she could work out, it was the best theory she had to date.

Another thought was developing in Fiona's head and she didn't like where it was taking her, as it would cast suspicion on many, instead of a couple of candidates, such as her ex-wife theory.

The problem with this new idea was it made logical sense, and logic was something she always trusted.

If, instead of naming his ex-wife as a beneficiary should Steve have pre-deceased him, Kevin might have split the inheritance among his staff. Should that be the case, everyone was a suspect. There could be a couple of them working together, or any one of them could be working independently.

This new theory meant every person in the shelter, except Jack and Donna, was now a suspect. And those suspects were all potential targets, as the fewer of them who were alive to inherit their share would mean the size of the inheritance for those who survived would be larger.

FORTY-TWO

This new theory was sending Fiona's mind down roads she didn't want to travel. She could feel her heart thumping in her chest as Steve went to check Neil over once more. Fiona knew she ought to speak to one of the others to gain more information, but she needed to think first, to align her thoughts into a cohesive form instead of the chaotic jumble they were.

First on Fiona's list was to assess how the hotel and wealth might have been shared out. It could be it was done equal dibs all round, or divided on a meritocracy derived from such factors as length of service and contributions to the business. As a couple, Lewis and Sara both had credit in the bank, which could potentially mean a significant portion of Kevin's estate would end up in their hands, although Sara's gripe about Kevin not letting Lewis contribute to the menu could mean Kevin had his own views on Lewis's worth.

Alice and Frances were the members of staff who worked in the office, which suggested they were best suited to learning the contents of Kevin's will, either by overhearing a conversation or via a spot of snooping. If Alice had learned of the will and told another member of staff, it could mean she was killed to keep this point silent.

By the same thinking, Frances could have been the one who'd spread the news to someone. That brought Thomas back into focus as a suspect, as Fiona believed his infatuation with Frances was strong enough she'd be able to wrap him around her little finger at any point she desired.

The issue with that line of thinking was Frances had never presented herself as anything more than a dowdy mouse. If it was an act, it was one she must have maintained her whole time at Inveraray House, as not one of the others had commented on the way she was behaving, which suggested it was her norm.

If could of course be Frances had been playing the long game. That she'd spent years portraying herself as timid in order to achieve an end goal. To Fiona that wasn't credible. If Frances was going to embark on a plan to get her hands on a man's money, the easy way was to get the man to marry her, and then divorce the unlucky fellow, not kill him. Frances might not put herself forward as a leader of people, but she was pretty enough and Fiona suspected to a lonely man getting the right signals, those hypnotic green eyes Frances had would take a lot of resisting.

Along with all these theories about Kevin's money being the motive for his murder, Fiona was still wondering if sex had a part to play. How it was involved was something she couldn't yet figure out, but she knew she couldn't eliminate it from her thinking until she had more information. Maybe the one person here who Kevin classed as a friend would be able to shed a different light on things.

'Neil, do you think you're well enough to join me? I have some questions for you?'

'Of course, I'll be with you in just a minute.'

'How long is this all going to take?' Sara's head bounced from shoulder to shoulder as she spoke. 'It's bad enough being trapped up here without you going around like you're God's gift to policing. What's your plan, question all the suspects and then assemble everyone in the drawing room like you're Miss Marple?'

Fiona stepped across until she was in front of Sara. 'I plan to identify the person who's killed twice and arrest them before they kill a third time. If you have a problem with that, you're free to try and hike your way down. But if you're staying in the shelter, you'd better believe I'm conducting my investigation, and the process will take as long as it takes.'

As Neil heaved himself upright, Donna blocked Fiona from returning to the second room. 'Please, Fiona, I need to talk to you.'

Fiona skewered Donna with a look. 'Later.' Whatever Donna had to say could wait until they were off Beinn Bhuidhe, maybe forever. She hadn't had time to give Donna's incendiary accusation any thought, and whenever it tried to creep into her mind she found her jaw clenching and fists balling. Of all the hurtful things Donna could have ever said, she'd chosen the worst, and there was no way Fiona was ready to hear whatever apologies Donna tried to make.

FORTY-THREE

Neil shambled into the second room and took a seat opposite Fiona. His face was ruddy and looked to be swollen, although as Fiona had only seen him swaddled in a scarf against the cold, she didn't know if it was from the allergic reaction or his normal look.

'How are you feeling now?'

'Poorly, but it is good of you to ask.'

Fiona couldn't help but return Neil's grin. Away from rescue attempts he was a charmer and had a twinkle in his eye that would make him easy to like. As someone who worked front of house in a hotel or restaurant he'd be perfect.

Had Alice been alive, Fiona would have suspected Neil a lot more than she currently did. It could be he was in cahoots with either Alice or Frances, and they'd seized a chance to thin the herd by feeding him an allergen, but if that was the case it didn't explain who'd murdered Alice. Incapacitated as Neil was by his reaction to the soup, he hadn't left the shelter for hours which put him out of the frame for killing Alice.

'The allergic reaction you had, do you think Alice or Frances fed you the soup hoping you'd have that reaction?'

'Heavens, no. I've had the peanut allergy for years, but the celery one is quite recent. I only got it after being put on a new set of pills for my gout. The pills work wonders, but I have to be careful about what I eat. I don't think either of those ladies wanted to do me any harm. It's my own fault, really. I should have brought my epi-pen, but as I didn't expect to eat anything except from what I brought myself, I left it in the car.'

What Neil said made sense, but as it was Kevin she really wanted to talk about, Fiona was glad this line of enquiry could be shut down. It could always be reopened later if any amount of suspicion fell Frances's way.

Fiona's instinct was to think Kevin's closest friend might be someone he'd confided in. Therefore, there was a chance Kevin had told Neil outright about his will. A better chance was he'd told his friend about his love life. Both past and present. That more than any other reason was why Fiona wanted to talk to Neil.

'I understand you and Kevin were close. I need to ask you about Kevin's life. I know he may have spoken to you about certain things and asked you to keep them to yourself, but I need the truth if I'm to find his killer. You understand that, don't you?'

'Of course I do, my dear. Ask your questions and I'll answer as if in court, but I very much doubt I'll be able to provide you with the insight you're seeking. I want whoever killed him to face justice every bit as much as you do. Not just for myself, but for poor Steve as well.'

From anyone else's lips, a patronising and dated phrase like 'my dear' would have set Fiona's hackles off, but the gentle way Neil spoke and the open expression on his face made the outdated term as comforting as a warm bath.

'How long did you know Kevin?'

'Since he took over Inveraray House. I was a head waiter then, but we got on well enough and he promoted me two years later. We then worked together until I left. Do you know, I didn't really want to go to Inveraray Castle, but they offered me a package that was too good to resist. Bless Kevin, he shook my hand and wished me well when I told him I was leaving. Do you know, the night of my last shift there, he got a bottle of Macallan eighteen-year-old from the shelf and the two of us set about it somewhat. I don't think I've ever tasted a finer whisky or enjoyed better company than I did that night.'

'Sounds like he was a good guy.'

'The best. The very best.'

'You remained friends even though you left his employ to go to a rival. Doesn't that seem a little odd to you?'

'Not at all. Kevin never saw any other establishment as a rival. The way he saw it, those who don't know better would get Inveraray House and Inveraray Castle mixed up, and if his hotel was getting mistaken for another, or attributed something that belonged elsewhere, he wanted that place to be every bit as good as Inveraray House. In fact, if either venue was fully booked, we were both confident in recommending the other. Kevin was about bringing a bigger pie to Inveraray rather than fighting for a larger slice of the existing pie.'

Like so many of the other details Fiona had learned about Kevin, this last piece of information only made his murder seem all the more sad. Kevin was someone who was a force for good and had an altruistic nature. Perhaps Neil would know of a different side to him, but if such a side existed, it was more likely Sara and her antagonistic nature would have revealed it.

'How much do you know about Kevin's personal life? I'm talking specifically about any romantic relationships he might have had and whether or not he remained in contact with his ex-wife.'

'Kevin wasn't interested in dating. If he had dated it would have been about the experience itself, not the usual conclusion. Do you know, he'd have been more interested in savouring a delicious meal, sampling fine wines and enjoying intelligent company than any romantic or carnal activity.'

'You make it sound like he was happy being alone. Didn't he ever get lonely?'

'If he did, he never mentioned it. He liked his own company and he worked brutal hours. I've seen people half his age wilt trying to match him. He was around people all day long and was only alone when he went home. He cared about people. He knew all there was to know about his staff and he remembered it. Birthdays, wedding anniversaries, where they'd been on holiday and what their sister's dog was called.'

'Okay so he wasn't interested in dating per se, but that doesn't mean he didn't date from time to time, even if it was for the experience of having a nice evening rather than any lustful motive. You never actually answered my question, did Kevin to the best of your knowledge go on any dates with anyone?'

'Not for the last eight or so years. The last time he took a woman out, he brought her to Inveraray Castle for a meal.'

'What was she like?'

'Do you know, she was a very handsome woman. Very well turned out and from our brief conversation I recall her having a sharp mind.'

'Did they date another time?'

'I'm afraid not. As I understand it, Kevin found her to be an excellent dinner companion, but when he told her he worked late on a regular basis, she found that unacceptable. You never knew Kevin, but Inveraray House was everything to him. He could no more envision taking time off work to date than he could severing his own throat.'

Fiona recognised a bad line of enquiry when she saw it so she moved on to the other part of her query. 'What about his ex-wife? What can you tell me about her?'

'Ahh, Claudia. Simultaneously the one who got away and the one he never wanted to see again. He was head chef at an

up-and-coming restaurant and she managed the front of house.
They married young and in a hurry. What is it they say? Marry
in haste and repent at leisure?' The twinkle in Neil's eye extin-
guished itself. 'He loved her. Properly loved her. I only met him
some years after they split up, but I could see the wounds of her
betrayal had never healed. I don't think they ever could. Kevin
was the nicest, kindest man you could ever meet, but he wasn't
able to forgive Claudia for what she did to him. With a kitchen
porter, no less.'

'And what does a kitchen porter do?'

'Pot washing and veg preparation. They also clean and mop
the floors. To make matters worse, they were caught in a store
cupboard at a Christmas party and everyone knew.'

The picture became clear to Fiona in a flash. Claudia hadn't
just cheated on Kevin; she'd cheated on him with someone
whose station in life was lower than Kevin's. As nice a guy as
Kevin may be, he was an excellent chef, and chefs have egos.
That showed by his not allowing Lewis to create a dish to put
on his menu. For his wife to cheat would have been bad enough,
for her to cheat with a pot washer would have been worse. And
for Claudia's infidelity to have become public knowledge at his
workplace would have added a healthy dose of humiliation to
the pain.

'Do you know if they split right away, or if they tried to
make a go of it?'

'Right away. Kevin told me he quit on the spot. Went home
and packed his bags. Do you know, he once told me walking
out on her was both the hardest and best thing he'd ever done.
She'd followed him back to their house and begged and
pleaded and apologised. He'd walked out and told her she
could keep the house and everything in it, he'd pay the mortgage and he'd file for divorce the next day. I won't ever forget
the day the final mortgage payment was paid. After cleaning
up the kitchen at the end of service he took off his wedding

ring, walked down to the bottom of the garden and tossed it into Loch Fyne without a word, then he came back and poured himself a glass of water and chatted to the guests as he always did.'

Once again, it was Kevin's decency Fiona took from the tale. Not only had he paid a mortgage he had no need to pay, but also he'd worn his wedding ring until the day he'd judged he was free of all connection to Claudia. A psychologist may have made a lot of his actions that day, but Fiona liked the understated way Kevin had dealt with his emotions. There had been no roar of 'freedom' or anything trite, no glass of champagne or a fine malt whisky, just a glass of water and a resumption of his role as *mine host*.

'The poor man. He did look after Claudia, though, even after what she put him through. That says a lot about him, as most men would have booted her out for what she did. Do you know if there was ever any contact between them?'

'Not one word so far as I know. Do you know, in the early days I was always waiting for her to turn up and beg for another chance. She never did, and I don't believe Kevin would have given her one if she had. It's such a tragic story, isn't it? And it's made all the more tragic by the fact it happened to such a fine man.'

'It is.' Fiona was keen to finish up with Neil as soon as she could. The man never used one word when twenty could be spoken. 'Do you know if she's still alive? Where she might be?'

'She died four years ago in the Cumberland Infirmary. Kevin went to her funeral. According to what he told me, he slipped in at the back of the church and then out again before any of her family saw him. He never said it, and I never raised the subject, but I always did wonder if he wanted to see if she had children and what ages they might be.'

'And had she children?'

'No.' Neil's face adopted shame. 'I looked up her death

notice in the *Cumberland News*. Like Kevin, she was never blessed with children.'

'Kevin brought up Steve, though. He seems to have done an excellent job.'

'He did. Considering what the poor boy went through losing his parents like that, Kevin worked wonders to make him the man he is today. Wonders I tell you.'

'Was there any friction between them about Steve being gay?'

'None whatsoever. Kevin didn't care about such things. He loved Steve because of who he is, not in spite of who Steve was attracted to.'

'What about Kevin's will? What can you tell me about that?'

'Do you know, that's one area where I may actually be able to really help you. He asked if I could be named as executor. Of course, I agreed. Poor man had nobody else except Steve, and as much as he loved the boy, he recognised his failings.'

Fiona's heart beat faster at this little tit-bit. 'What failings do you mean?'

'Steve is a warm, caring young man, who has found his vocation in life. It saddens me to tell you, Kevin soon worked out Steve has no head for business. When it comes to dealing with any kind of bureaucracy he's lost. Kevin had to sort all kinds of things out for him like utility suppliers, his Sky subscription and his mortgage payments. Steve paid the bills, but when it comes to sorting out legalities, Steve couldn't arrange the proverbial party in a brewery.'

'I see. Do you know the contents of the will? Who would inherit if Steve wasn't able to?'

'I do. In the event of Steve predeceasing Kevin, Kevin's estate was to be split equally between two charities. Cancer Research and Headway UK were his chosen beneficiaries. Kevin's mother died of cancer, and his sister, Louise, who was

Steve's mother, succumbed to massive head injuries in the crash that killed her. It was Kevin who had to make the decision to switch off her life support system.' Fiona couldn't help but pull a face at Neil's words. His expression hardened as he glared at her. 'I hardly think it is necessary for you to grimace the way you have. Both charities are worthy recipients; however, the point is moot. Steve is alive and well and it will be he who inherits Inveraray House. There is a codicil to the will that states he is to have the business valued and then sell it for ninety per cent of its market value before he can inherit a penny from it. Kevin loved Steve, but he didn't trust him to take care of his life's work.'

'Forgive me, Neil. I grimaced because I've been working on the theory someone knew they were in line to inherit if Steve couldn't. I believed they'd tried to frame Steve for Kevin's murder, which if he was convicted, would mean he couldn't inherit. Because the money is going to charity, my theory has been blown apart. As you say, both charities are worthy causes and were obviously chosen for personal reasons.'

'I see. And what of your theories now? Do you have another?'

'I do and I don't. Everything you've told me has been very helpful, but I need more from you.'

'Ask and you will receive.'

Neil's words were a familiar quote to Fiona, but she didn't know their origin. Whatever that might be could be googled when she got off this infernal Munro; for now she had other things to think about.

'Would you say that after Steve, you were closer to Kevin than anyone else?'

'I would. Although after me telling you Kevin had named me as executor of his will, the question does appear to be rather redundant, does it not?'

'Perhaps and perhaps not.' Neil's good manners didn't hide

the man's sharp mind or steely nature, so Fiona chose her words with care. 'We've already established he wasn't dating to your knowledge. What can you tell me about his relationships with his team at the hotel?'

'He got on fine with them. Occasionally someone would need a sterner word than usual, but for the most part they rubbed along just fine. He retained staff much longer than most establishments, which shows you just how much they thought of him as a boss. This area has plenty of places where staff can get another job, but the key people at Inveraray House all have years of service. I should think that tells you all you need to know.'

'I don't doubt he was a good person to work for. Everything I've heard about him suggests as much. What I don't know is his opinion of them. In my experience, successful businesspeople tend to be very good at weighing people up. They can tell a slacker from a grafter in no time at all, spot a troublemaker a mile off and so on. So, I'm asking you what his private thoughts were about the people in this shelter.'

'Do you know, he would have a grumble about any of them from time to time, but that's all it was, a grumble. Sometimes it would be about Lewis's presentation of a dish, or Alice missing a payment to a supplier, or Frances making an error with the rates, but he saw the good in people. Not once did he speak about them with any serious negativity.'

'Okay. What about them? Do you know of any grudges they might hold against him? According to Sara, Lewis isn't allowed to contribute to the menu. Surely that's going to rankle him.'

'Would Da Vinci let a house painter display their work alongside the *Mona Lisa*? Kevin tried all he could to encourage Lewis to create some magnificent dishes, but Lewis was content to follow. Some people are like that, and that's fine, not everyone can be a leader. If you ask me, and you more or less have, Sara's the one who wanted Lewis to be Kevin's equal.'

The direction the conversation had taken was perfect for Fiona and she didn't miss her opportunity. 'Do you think she resented Kevin because he was a better chef than Lewis? Because he'd done well enough for himself to buy his own place while Lewis was stuck working for him?'

'Sara is a... difficult woman to like at times, but I never heard her say a bad word about Kevin. Lewis on the other hand...'

Neil didn't need to finish his sentence for Fiona to know what he was about to say. All the same, the unspoken words gave her a line of enquiry to follow, albeit one that wasn't central to her investigation.

FORTY-FOUR

Fiona took a moment to look through the doorway to where Sara and Lewis were sitting either side of Ivor. They appeared to be fighting sleep and that was little wonder. Now the stove was warming the shelter, there was a cloying heat that sapped energy. In an ideal world there'd be a window that could be cracked open to let in some fresh air, but whomever had transformed the old bothy into the shelter they were now in hadn't gone to the expense of fitting windows that opened. A constant draft blew in from the door, but it was the only indication of the intensity of the weather outside.

'Can you elaborate, Neil? Is Lewis and Sara's marriage in trouble, do you think?' As a by-product of Neil's speech patterns, Fiona couldn't help but tailor her own choice of words.

'Do you know, it's not something I'm sure about. For as long as I've known them they've always seemed to be dissatisfied with one another, but neither one has chosen to leave the other. Sara always seemed to be accusing Lewis of infidelity. Whether she was right to do so or not, I couldn't tell you. But he had an eye for the ladies that's for sure. He was always more chatty with females than males. When he cooked for staff the girls always got a larger portion than the boys, and there was this woman who used to deliver for Johnstone's, the fruit and veg lot.'

'I've seen their vans.' Fiona nodded for Neil to continue and gave herself a mental kick for interrupting.

'Well, this woman was very pretty, and Lewis would flirt with her something rotten. Sara caught him flirting on more than one occasion and boy did she give him what for. I've incurred the wrath of my wife a couple of times over the years, but I've never seen anyone speak to their spouse the way Sara spoke to Lewis.'

'I see.' And Fiona did. Despite all the accusations of infidelity, Lewis and Sara were still together. Those accusations spoke of a deep love and a shallow insecurity. Several times over the years Fiona had been called to what were once referred to as domestics, where things had kicked off because of a jealous rage. In every instance the accusing party had driven their loved one further away rather than drawing them closer. For Lewis and Sara's marriage to have survived this long suggested that somehow they both managed to endure a love-hate relationship without ever going so far as to isolate the other. 'And how long have they been like this?'

'As long as I've known them. Say ten years or so.'

'And what did Kevin make of it?'

'Do you know, he had the good sense to stay out of it. He'd listen if Lewis talked about it, but I understand that only happened a couple of times. What he did do was joke about how he liked the way they both reacted to their anger.'

'What do you mean?'

'When they were angry, both Lewis and Sara would scrub their rage away. Lewis has a touch of OCD when it comes to keeping the kitchen clean at the best of times, and when he was pissed off he'd grab a cloth and clean things until they shone. Sara was the same with the rooms.'

'So you think the accusations were groundless?'

'Absolutely. Lewis might flirt something terrible, but I don't think he'd have ever cheated on Sara. For a start, he'd never have dared sleep again.'

'Okay, that's been a help. What about Thomas and Frances? He seems to be sweet on her. Is there anything in that?'

An indulgent smile filtered onto Neil's face. 'You've spotted that, have you? Take it from me, there's nothing there. Frances's only loves are her cats and her job. She was dumped at the altar twenty or so years ago and since then she's settled for a spinster's life. Personally, I think he sees her more as a mother figure than anything else. His own mother was a drinker, a big drinker, and if it hadn't been for the lad's own initiative in getting a job as a KP at Inveraray House, I dare say he'd have followed her path. I believe that to him Frances is a better version of the mother who never looked after him. Bless the lad, any feelings he has for Frances are misplaced, as what he's really seeking is a mother figure to love him.'

Fiona guessed KP was hospitality industry slang for kitchen porter. 'Do you know if he's ever asked her out, or chanced his arm at a Christmas party, or some other staff function?'

'Goodness, no. When he's working he's great with customers, and really knows what he's talking about, but take him out from behind his bar or remove a wine list from his hands and he's terribly shy when it comes to speaking to females. Kevin once told of a time when he had to pitch in behind the bar at a big wedding. There was this bridesmaid whose eye was caught with Thomas. The girl mooned over him all night, and all Thomas could do about it was blush. Kevin told me he suggested Thomas give the girl his number and Thomas flat out refused. According to Kevin, the girl was good-looking and a nice person, but even so, Thomas wanted nothing to do with her. Do you know, I think the lad may still be factory fresh, so to speak.'

'Thanks. Is there anything you think I ought to know about any of the people here? Any reason you can think of why any of them would want to murder Kevin, and Alice?'

'None at all would want to kill Kevin. They all thought of him as a good guy. As for Alice, she could be spiky at times, but everyone was used to her ways. She might have had a sharp tongue, but she was good craic, and was always the first person to offer help whether you needed it or not.'

'What about your allergic reaction? You maybe couldn't hear the conversations at the time, but it would appear everyone knew of your celery allergy. You said you're sure it wasn't a deliberate attempt to harm you. Is there a reason why Alice or Frances might want to kill you?'

'Heavens no. It was a mistake, nothing more. I cannot envision either Frances, or Alice rest her soul, trying to do anyone harm, much less myself.'

'Thanks. I've no more questions for you.'

Fiona stayed put as Neil lumbered back to his previous seat. Of the group, the only person she had yet to question was Lewis, but before she spoke with him, she needed a moment to think.

With Kevin's wife Claudia dead and buried, and Kevin's estate charity bound if Steve wasn't around to inherit, there was no financial motive for any of the others to murder Kevin. Although, he could have been killed on the assumption that if Steve didn't inherit his estate, and there was no other family member to inherit, then everything might be shared out among his employees.

That theory was a leap, and not one Fiona had confidence in. For the vast majority of the human race, to run the risk of being imprisoned for murder, there would have to be a guaranteed payoff, either financial or emotional if revenge was the motive. To maybe inherit a share of a business wasn't close to being the payoff a killer would look for if murdering for money.

With money off the table, the only thing left was sex. Steve was gay and had no obvious motive. Frances had chosen the life of a spinster due to a broken heart. Lewis and Sara were married, although Sara had serious issues regarding Lewis's fidelity. Thomas was smitten by a mother figure, and Neil said he was married. Had Neil not been incapacitated and unable to search for, and kill, Alice, he would have been a suspect for the murders, with his motive a possible revenge killing for Kevin sleeping with his wife, but everything Fiona had learned about Kevin refuted the idea he'd any interest in a sexual relationship and certainly not one with someone who was married, much less married to his closest friend. Ivor's marital status was unknown, but wouldn't be hard to find out. Gruff and taciturn he exuded common sense and while he might be in a relationship with someone, other than his businessman's haircut, he didn't come across as any kind of lothario. Ivor's clothes were a long way from new, and while his boots looked sturdy, the hat on the seat beside him bore grubby marks. That was fine while gardening, but if he had any sexual connection to one of the women present, he'd have dressed better. The haircut was a sign of his vanity, and nobody who was vain about their appearance ever did things by half when they wanted to impress someone.

That left Fiona with a whole bunch of unknowns. There were four people who'd had the chance to kill Alice, and Fiona was firm in her belief Alice had been killed because she'd seen the killer strike Kevin, or knew something that would incriminate them when she was interviewed by the police about Kevin's death. Of the four, none stood out as a strong suspect. Fiona didn't believe Steve would have killed his uncle, not for any inheritance in the world. Thomas appeared to worship Kevin for the chance he'd been given to better his life, and there was no obvious motive for him as a suspect. Ivor also had no obvious motive. Which left Sara. If what Neil had said about Lewis's flirting was true, and Fiona had no reason to assume otherwise, there was a potential motive in Sara's fears about Lewis being unfaithful: perhaps they were based on the fact she herself had cheated.

If Sara had cheated on Lewis, was it with Kevin? Sara had ambition, not just for herself but also Lewis. According to Neil, Lewis was content to follow rather than take the lead. Kevin was a leader, he had to have been to turn Inveraray House into the place it was.

By this thinking, Kevin would have made an ideal target for a climber like Sara. Had she inveigled her way into his bed? Spun him tales of how Lewis made her feel unloved? From there it stood to reason things had come to a head whether their relationship was a one-time thing, or a full-blown affair. If either Kevin had threatened to tell Lewis if Sara refused to leave him, or he'd ended the relationship, Sara could have killed him to protect her marriage or seek revenge for a broken heart. As theories went, it was a stretch, but it was the best Fiona could come up with given the list of suspects she had. Alice could have caught them and was killed to ensure her silence, or perhaps she witnessed Sara attacking Kevin. Whichever it was, her fate was sealed when Sara caught up with her outside the shelter.

Another possibility was Lewis had taken revenge on Kevin for sleeping with Sara and killed him. Sara had worked this out and when Lewis confirmed it and mentioned Alice may have seen him, Sara had then attacked Alice to keep her husband out of jail.

The main thing going against this latest theory was what everyone had said about Kevin: he wasn't interested in dating, and he seemed too professional to engage in any kind of personal relationship with a member of his staff.

Nevertheless, Fiona had plenty of questions for Lewis.

FORTY-FIVE

There was an openness to Lewis's face when he sat opposite Fiona. For her it struck the wrong chord. Until taking the seat he'd never looked anything but grumpy. At first she'd put his nature down to a combination of their being trapped by the snow and him falling out with Sara. After he'd hurt his ankle she'd figured pain was also playing its part.

'How can I help you?'

'I've been speaking to everyone to get a picture of all your personalities. Someone among your group murdered both Kevin and Alice. I'm trying to identify that someone.'

'So you should. It's awful what happened to them. If you ask me, which I'm sure you're about to, I'd say it was Steve. He's the one who'll inherit Inveraray House and all of Kevin's money.'

'You think that's what's behind the murders, financial gain?'

'I do. What other reason could there be? Kevin was a decent enough fella. He didn't suffer fools but he wasn't one for shouting and roaring and carrying himself on. If someone pissed him off he'd just disengage with them or the company they represented. I tell you, it's got to be Steve who killed them. No one else stands to gain. So far as I'm concerned, I might get a temporary promotion, but in the long run, whoever ends up owning Inveraray House will need to bring in a top chef. I'm good at what I do, but I can't create the dishes Kevin could.'

'I hear what you're saying, but I'm sure you understand I have to keep an open mind.'

'Of course you do.' A weak smile touched Lewis's mouth but left his eyes unchanged. 'Sorry, I guess I've been in the room too often when Sara's watching her true crime shows.'

Fiona was grateful he'd mentioned his wife. It gave her the perfect chance to bring Sara into the conversation. 'Would I be right in saying things are tense between you and Sara just now?'

'They're no worse than usual. We're always bickering about something or other.' He gave an unconcerned shrug. 'It's how we are, how we've always been and likely how we'll always be. It's shit at times, but the making up is usually good fun.'

With comments like the last one Lewis had made, Fiona was accustomed to a knowing look or a leering expression. Lewis was expressionless and his tone was flat. It was as if he was trotting out an old and tired line he no longer believed. That more than anything made Fiona suspect their marriage was in far deeper trouble than either of them realised.

It could of course be both of them had settled for their shared existence and the accusations of infidelity were more about maintaining their pride than anything else. Whatever it was that kept them together, Fiona was certain she never wanted to have that kind of relationship with anyone. Not that she ever planned to have a lengthy relationship.

'I've asked the others a lot of questions about Kevin, but not many about Alice. What can you tell me about her?'

'She was good at what she did, she kept the books right and my wages were always spot on, but I never found her easy to like. She had a few ideas above her station, mind, and although she acted all prim and proper like butter wouldn't melt, the truth of it is, she was a horny old goat. It's maybe not common knowledge, but I know of a few occasions where she's been playing hide the sausage with someone she shouldn't have.'

Fiona hadn't ever heard sex being described like that before, but it was a phrase that needed no explaining, even if it was on the crude side.

'Are you saying Alice slept around? Was there ever anything between her and Kevin?' Fiona's mind raced as she pictured Alice and Kevin together. If that happened and Steve knew, would he have killed Kevin and Alice to protect his inheritance? 'She was a right one when it came to it. From what I've heard, she's broken up more than one marriage.' Lewis leaned forward in a conspiratorial fashion. 'My cousin told me she joined his mate and the wife for a threesome. Apparently she was up for anything, dirty cow. For me, the one saving grace about her was she kept her work and her sex life separate.'

Fiona kept her face immobile to hide the disgusted wince she wanted to give. As a cop she'd heard a lot worse, but that didn't mean she enjoyed hearing such outdated thinking and terminology. 'I see. How did she get on with the others?'

'All right, I guess. I know I've made her seem like some kind of slag, but she was all right. When I was ill last year and couldn't get out of bed, Alice brought round a few meals for me and Sara. The wife won't thank me for saying so, but she couldn't cook a salad without burning it. Apart from the times when she gave someone what for, nobody complained about Alice. One way she kept in our good books was her baking. She'd bring in scones or cakes she'd made. They were delicious. Even Kevin said they were better than the ones we made ourselves when we did afternoon teas.'

'Thanks. When I asked if you thought there was anything between Alice and Kevin you never answered. Could you answer that now?'

Lewis didn't answer for a moment and Fiona attributed the delay to him trawling through his memory.

'If there was, they kept it from us all. I've never heard of, or noticed, anything between them. He treated her the same as the rest of us. Once the work stuff was dealt with he'd have a craic or a joke, and then we'd get on with the next job.'

'You worked alongside him in the kitchen. I'm guessing the two of you spent a lot of time together. Would you class it as a friendship?'

'Aye and no. We got on well enough, but Kevin always maintained a distance, we'd laugh and joke and so on, fall out with each other from time to time, but he always held something back. He was the boss and kept things professional.' A shrug. 'I'm sure you've got sergeants or inspectors who you get on with, but never see away from work. That's what it was like with me and Kevin. With Kevin and all the staff. Except Neil. The pair of them were thick as thieves.'

'Did it bother you he treated Neil as a friend when he didn't treat you the same way?'

'No. I've got other mates, so long as we could work together, and we could, that's all I give a shit about. I've worked with some chefs who were a nightmare. Shouting abuse all the time and throwing pans. Fuck that for a game of soldiers.'

'Indeed.' Fiona didn't miss the way more swear words were creeping into Lewis's vocabulary the longer they talked. 'What about other staff members, did it bother them?'

'Not as far as I know.'

'What can you tell me about Ivor?'

'I don't see him that much unless he's fixing something in the kitchen or delivering veg from the gardens, but like everyone Kevin employed, he's good at what he does. The veggies he grew were always far better than any we bought in, and if he couldn't fix something, it was generally buggered.'

'What about Ivor's personal life? Is he married, living with someone?'

'He lives with his wife of forty years. Dotes on her like they are still teenagers. Their daughter and grandson moved back in with them a few months ago when her marriage went tits up.'

'Thanks.' Time to try ruffling some feathers. 'I heard Sara has accused you of having affairs. Is there any truth in the accusations?'

'Nah, they're all bullshit. Sara's a passionate woman with trust issues. I'd never cheat, but I'm a flirt at times and it winds her up. Be honest with you, sometimes I do it for the sole purpose of winding her up.'

Fiona didn't trust herself to comment. Lewis's way of playing with Sara's emotions left her feeling nothing but pity for Sara.

'What do you make of Thomas and Frances?'

'As a couple or work mates?'

'Both, and as people?'

'There's more chance of Miss World turning up and making eyes at me than that pair getting together. They're both all right. Considering how his old dear dragged him up between drinks, he's done well for himself. Kevin gave him a chance I wouldn't have. All that posh wine is a joke to me. I'd sooner have a pint of lager, but he's good at selling it. Kevin was always pleased with how much of it Thomas flogged. Frances is a bit wet, no real craic about her, but she's a decent sort. Both of them would help you out if you were stuck, but you'd ask someone else first.'

'And Neil, what about him?'

'He's decent enough. Got the top job at the castle and made a success of the place. Bit of a fanny if you ask me. I mean, the way he speaks, do you know?' Lewis's mimicry of Neil was spot on. 'I believe he's going to retire in a couple of years and start touring in his motorhome. He's got one of them big articles you can never get past for miles.'

'Ivor's around the same age. Is he planning to retire?'

'I dunno, you'd have to ask him, but if I had to guess, I'd say he'll leave Inveraray House feet first in a pine box. He loves those gardens near on as much as he loves his wife.'

'What about your role in the kitchens at Inveraray House? I've heard Kevin never allowed you to put a dish on the menu, and also that you were happy to follow his lead rather than try and outdo him. What's the truth of it?'

Lewis's eyes hardened. 'I'm guessing it was Sara who said Kevin never let me contribute to the menu. That's typical of her. She's never satisfied with what she's got. Kevin wanted me to create dishes for the menu, but he was so good at coming up with fantastic dishes that I just couldn't compete. I think he wanted me to push him to even greater heights, but that's not me. Don't get me wrong, I enjoyed the challenge, but I knew I'd never be as good as him, and after a while he realised it too. He never said as much, he was too nice for that, but he eased off and we fell into a routine where he'd create a dish, show me how to put it together and then we'd serve it. I'll miss working with him, not just for what he taught me, but because he was good to work with.'

Fiona got what Lewis was saying. She thought of Dave Lennox the same way Lewis thought of Kevin. No matter how good she got at her job, Lennox would always be steps ahead of her while making everything look effortless. It was a shame for Lewis's sake Sara felt Kevin held him back. She, of all the staff, had been the only one to voice even the slightest negative about Kevin. But was that a cover to hide their affair, or the truth if she was innocent?

With Lewis hobbling back to his usual seat, Fiona leaned against the wall of the shelter and fought to keep her eyes open. She was exhausted from the exertions of the day; the cloying warmth of the shelter carried a soporific effect lulling her towards sleep. Now it was after midnight, most of the others were visibly drowsy and there was a series of head jerks as they all fought to stay awake.

Fiona had a lot to think about. As well as catching the killer and getting everyone safely off the Munro, she was determined to do so soon enough she could still attend the dreaded appointments in Glasgow. She dug the nails of her right hand into the back of her neck and forced herself to stay awake. Whatever may be to come before dawn, she had to remain alert and ready to deal with it.

FORTY-SIX

Now all seven strangers had been questioned, Fiona had a lot of information, but very little of it was useful. Other than money, nobody had an obvious reason to kill Kevin, and Steve was the only one who'd benefit financially from the murder. Alice had to have been collateral damage for something she knew or saw.

None of the group had any clear sexual motive for either murder; and if revenge had been at the heart of the motive, it didn't seem credible none of the others knew about it. From her time working in a small police team out of Lochgilphead, Fiona had learned few work-based secrets about her colleagues were kept more than a few hours. It would be the same for the staff of Inveraray House.

Where things may differ would be if there was another way of looking at things. Fiona didn't have a detective's training or experience, but as that was her ultimate goal in the police, she'd done all she could to train herself to think like a detective, to follow the evidence like a detective and to keep her mind open at all times.

Fiona's fingers drummed on her knees as she examined all the little details she'd learned, the facts about each person and their life. In a lot of ways there was nothing too remarkable about any of their stories. They were a bunch of people thrust together in a work environment and they all had their own histories. A lot of their stories verged on the tragic, but perhaps it was the glue that held them together as a group. A shared and unspoken empathy that ran throughout all their tolerances.

No matter how Fiona probed and tested motives for each of the seven, she couldn't find anything close to a credible motive for any of them murdering Kevin. The exception to this was Steve, as he'd inherit, but after seeing the pain in his eyes and hearing it in his voice when he talked about how Kevin brought him up, she couldn't get her head around him being the killer.

A conversation with Heather came back to Fiona. Heather was a DC who worked out of Lochgilphead, and one of her closest friends. Many times Fiona had mined Heather's experience and discussed various techniques detectives used. One such snippet Heather passed on was if no obvious solution presented itself, take a couple of metaphorical steps back from the issue to look at the whole picture rather than focusing on one specific detail. Another pearl of wisdom she'd passed on was to try flipping a theory on its head to see if it made more sense looking at it from a different perspective.

Instead of thinking of Kevin as the primary victim, Fiona gave that role to Alice and tried to think of what Kevin might have known that got him killed. As the person who did the accounts at Inveraray House, Alice would have been the person most likely to uncover any fraudulent behaviour by another staff member. Whether it was a bottle of wine that had been pocketed instead of being sold, or a longer con such as Frances getting a kickback from a booking agent wasn't the heart of the matter. What mattered was it had happened, and to such an extent the guilty person had taken preventative measures to ensure their guilt was never uncovered. Any discrepancy Alice found would also be uncovered by her successor or Kevin and that's why he was killed first. He'd also make an appealing target, as with Steve set to inherit, there was a ready-made scapegoat to take the fall for his murder. Plus, in a close-knit environment as existed at Inveraray House, the others would soon learn of Steve's inability to think as a businessman.

The amounts of money stolen had to be significant enough the guilty party would fear a prosecution. As principled as Kevin might be, he wouldn't have got to where he was in life without understanding the way the world worked. Theft was theft, but Fiona knew from bitter experience many petty thefts from the workplace went unreported, as the hassle involved wasn't worth the payoff as the courts tended to only give offenders a slap on the wrist. If this theory was correct, the sums of money involved would have to run into the tens if not hundreds of thousands. No matter how Fiona tried to imagine such sums of money being swindled from a hotel, she couldn't see how it would happen.

Most workplace thefts started small and built over time. A box of staples here, a bottle of wine there. Over time the thefts would build to the point where they'd become more and more profitable. It would be a case of wine and perhaps a delivery to the person's home address was invoiced to the company.

The problem with this line of thinking was in a well-run business such as Inveraray House, it wasn't even close to probable the thefts would have gone on long enough to be worth killing over. Not unless the guilty party had a record that would go against them should their crime be discovered. Even so, it was a stretch to imagine them getting any more than a few months of jail time. With the penalty for murder being far greater, it didn't compute.

Nor did it add up Kevin had been killed. If he'd known about the thefts, then he'd have dealt with the thief, not invited them on a team-building hike up Beinn Bhuidhe. To carry on this line of thought, Alice must have confronted the thief and either given them a chance to confess to Kevin, or, and Fiona didn't like to think ill of the dead, cut her in on their deal.

Fiona preferred to think Alice had given whoever the thief was a chance to speak to Kevin. That she'd tried to persuade them confessing their crime was the best chance they had. It was this altruism that cost Alice her life.

Except.

Very little about this theory stood up against scrutiny. Alice wouldn't be put in charge of the accounts if she wasn't trusted. To learn of the thefts after a trip such as the hike up Beinn Bhuidhe would make the pill of betrayal far more bitter to swallow. It would be fair for Alice to expect some backlash from Kevin. If the thefts had been worth enough to kill for, Alice's first duty would be to Kevin and Kevin alone. It made no sense Alice had done this, unless, and Fiona hated to think this way, the thief was someone Kevin trusted above all others: Steve.

With Steve in the frame as the thief, other possibilities raged into Fiona's mind. Of all those present in the shelter, Steve would have the greatest access, have the most trust in the bank. Neil had said Kevin recognised Steve was rubbish when it came to business and dealing with any kind of legalities. How far did that rubbishness extend into Steve's personal finances? Had he run up gambling debts? Had he chased a big win with promises of a long-term boon coming his way? Were his debtors calling in his debt and trying to claim a piece, or even all, of Inveraray House? While Steve perhaps wouldn't have killed Kevin for money alone, it wasn't impossible he'd done so because his own wellbeing had been threatened by those he owed money to.

This all made a lot more sense than any other theory Fiona had come up with so far. A gambling debt could have seen a pair of heavies lay some threats on Steve. Desperate to keep whatever part of his body was threatened in working order, he'd brought up the fact he was due to inherit a fortune. The screws would have been turned and he'd somehow stolen enough from Kevin to keep himself unharmed. If Steve was the thief Alice had uncovered, it stood to reason she would give him a chance to explain himself to Kevin. Nobody would want to be the bearer of such news.

As the person who'd inherit Inveraray House and the rest of Kevin's estate, Steve would then be in a position to destroy evidence of his theft and he'd be confident Alice hadn't confided in anyone, as even worse than breaking the news to Kevin herself, would be for him to hear it elsewhere and know she hadn't told him first.

Fiona needed to speak to Steve again, but as she crossed to where he sat, she made sure to give Jack's boot a subtle dunt as she passed by him. With what she was about to accuse Steve of, she wanted backup not just on hand, but fully alert.

FORTY-SEVEN

Fiona waited in the doorway to the second room while Steve plonked himself down. Before moving to her usual seat she cast a quick glance in Jack's direction. He'd disentangled himself from Donna's embrace and was sitting erect. Good, if the accusation she was about to throw in Steve's face struck home, there was no telling how he'd react.

There was no easy way of segueing into a topic such as this, so Fiona decided to use blunt force and the element of surprise. Whatever Steve was expecting Fiona to say, she was confident he wouldn't be expecting what she planned to ask.

'How much did you steal from your uncle to pay off your gambling debts?'

'What?' Steve's face was the dictionary definition of bewilderment. 'What the hell are you on about? I haven't got any gambling debts. I've never been in a bookies and I don't use any of those online apps. The last time I played cards for money was on the school bus, and even then it was ten pence stakes for pontoon.' The confusion fell away from Steve and his brow furrowed as his voice rose. 'Do you really think I stole from Kevin and then killed him and Alice to cover it up? Fuck you. I thought you understood what Kevin meant to me. You've gone through much the same, but you're sick. Twisted. I haven't got any debts bar the mortgage on my flat and the HP on my car. I don't gamble. It's a fool's game. If you don't believe me, ask Ivor. His wife had it bad for the online bingo a couple of years ago. She ran up thousands of pounds on his card before he found out and stopped her.'

Fiona was tensing as Steve rose to his feet, his left hand pointing at her face. Over Steve's shoulder she could see Jack was poised at the doorway to grab him if necessary. Ivor was also in the doorway, his face a mask of fury.

'Sit down, Steve.' Fiona kept her voice even and gestured at the bench Steve had occupied seconds ago. His outburst was so sudden and had so many of the hallmarks belonging to a genuine reaction she now doubted her theory. 'If I'm wrong, I'm wrong, but you agreed earlier I have to consider every angle.'

'You *are* wrong. You couldn't be more wrong if you... you...'

'Then sit down. Help me work out where I've gone wrong. Prove your innocence to me if you can.'

'You're a bitch. A cold-hearted little bitch, you know that? I loved Kevin. He was everything to me and you think I stole from him. That I killed him. Your friend was right to say it's no wonder you've never caught your parents' killer.'

Neil pushed Jack and Ivor through the doorway and aimed a finger at Steve. 'Do yourself a favour and sit down and listen to what she's got to say. I think she's wrong on this, but you, out of all of us, must want her to catch Kevin's killer the most. Behaving like you are helps nobody and certainly not you. Do you know, if Kevin could see how you're reacting now, he'd be ashamed of you. The lass has a job to do, and she's all by herself and no real way of verifying anything any of us is telling her. She'd have to be superhuman not to bark up the wrong tree from time to time.'

The glare Steve sent Neil was returned without animosity.

It took all of Fiona's self-control to look at Steve. After what he'd said about her parents she wanted nothing more than to punch and gouge and beat him until exhaustion stopped her. It was bad enough Donna's histrionics had put the words on her lips, but she'd been filled with immediate remorse. Steve wasn't. Steve held her stare, daring her to call him out on the insult.

'I'm an officer for Police Scotland in the middle of a murder investigation.' That sentence was as much to force calm into Fiona's twitching limbs as to put Steve back in his box. 'You're the prime suspect as you stand to gain the most from their deaths. I'm looking at every angle I can, and if you don't like those angles, tough, because, as I told you when we spoke earlier, a lot better detectives than me will be asking a lot more annoying questions than the one I just asked. Now before I continue, I need you to listen to me for a minute or two without speaking. You'll see why I'm asking this by the time I'm finished talking. For the record, asking that question was a test. A test any of my colleagues would believe you failed. You were very quick to work out I thought you'd killed your uncle and Alice to cover up the theft I'd accused you of. To a detective it would suggest the preplanning of a defence in any possible situation. It's the kind of thing a guilty person would know to say, whereas an innocent one would be too surprised at the accusation to think straight.'

'I knew it. I knew you'd end up stitching me up.'

'I'm not trying to do that.' Fiona wiped a hand across her brow then adopted a softer expression. 'I've lived a life that's been very similar to yours. I know exactly what Kevin meant to you because I have my own version of him. My colleagues wouldn't understand that. My Aunt Mary isn't my mother, and she's never tried to be, but I love her as much as I loved my mother. Everything I've heard about Kevin suggests he was a good person. Nobody here has a bad word to say about him and that's unusual because he was in a position of power over them, although his power wasn't something I understand he wielded unless necessary. You're not a fool and I think that like me and everyone else in here, you'll have been running your own ideas on who killed Kevin and Alice. That's why I think you used the term cover up so quickly. I think you too had the idea Alice found something amiss and gave the person responsible the chance to confess. A chance they didn't take. As I said, whether you like it or not, you're the number one suspect for your uncle's murder as you have the most to gain.'

'I've also lost the most. I don't give a shite about the money and the hotel, they're his not mine. I've lost my uncle. The man who made me what I am today. You know the score, you've been there, without Kevin I'd have ended up in the care system. After the crash, it was tough enough having to live with someone I hardly knew. If it had been strangers, it would have been ten times worse. And that's providing I was lucky enough to end up living with a good family instead of a bunch of scrotes, or worse, a children's home. At the Royal A&E, we get kids in from children's homes all the time. They're either smacked up on whatever hit they can get, or they're so badly battered by the older kids they take weeks to get better. Without Kevin that could have been me. Or you if you didn't have your aunt.' Steve jerked a thumb over his shoulder. 'You should ask Neil what Kevin was like with me when it came to money. I had to insist on buying my own flat and car. Kevin wanted to buy them for me. He was so generous financially I actually had to have a row with him so I could stand on my own two feet. Neil was there that night. If I had been stupid enough to run up gambling debts, Kevin would have bailed me out. I dare say he'd have given me a hard time about my stupidity, which would have been fair enough, but he'd have asked how much and then paid up. I remember him telling me about Ivor's wife and her gambling. Kevin described it as the addiction it is. He didn't judge, he just gave me the heads-up Ivor was going through a tough time and that's all he said; although I do know he loaned Ivor ten grand so he didn't lose his house. That's the kind of man Kevin was. A gentleman.'

'I'm sorry, but when you've had more time to think everything over, you'll see I had to ask that question, and I thought throwing it at you was the best way to catch you unawares. I did say a minute ago you'd probably been thinking along the same lines as me. Do you have anyone in mind as someone who may have had their hand in the till so to speak?'

Steve's head sawed left and right. 'No. Kevin had a stocktaker come once a month and he'd detail everything, but there was never anything out of place. And there's not much cash used these days. It was one of Kevin's hobby horses, the way everyone uses cards all the time. He told me it cost him a fortune in credit card fees whereas the bank charges for depositing cash were a lot less. Is there anything else? I get you're just doing your job, but right now I can hardly look at you.'

'No, we're done, but there may be other questions I have to ask you later on.'

Fiona was settling down to think about a new idea when she saw Jack was still on his feet and coming over to talk to her. She hoped it would be a brief conversation, as she wanted to crack on and think about how hotel staff might be able to enact credit card fraud from the numbers they gleaned from customers.

'What is it, Jack? I'm busy.'

'You need to let Donna say what she's got to say. I'm not asking for her, I'm telling you, you need to hear it.'

'She's got one minute. I've enough to think about without dealing with her trying to apologise for what she said.'

'It's about the case. She knows you're angry with her and

she hopes by helping you, she'll be able to fix things between you.'

'Just tell me what it is, Jack.'

'No. You need to hear it from her, and she needs to be the one to tell you.'

'Fine. Send her through.'

FORTY-EIGHT

There were tears in Donna's eyes when she sat opposite Fiona, but that didn't remove any of the tension in Fiona's jaw. On top of not having a clue about who the killer was, her left arm and shoulder were a fiery ball of agony from all the times she'd aggravated the injury she'd picked up on Luing.

To add to her list of woes, Fiona couldn't decide if the knot in her stomach was from hunger or a grave foreboding things would get worse before they got off this infernal Munro. The hike with Donna and Jack had been planned as a way to destress before the dreaded appointments and the agonies they would elicit. Instead she was cold, hungry and once again in the middle of a murder case without any backup. Donna's words had cut deep, and while Fiona had pushed them from the forefront of her mind, seeing Donna in such close proximity again brought them back to Fiona in all their sneering contempt.

The one, lonely positive Fiona had was that she could rely on Jack to pitch in and help her should things with the other group take a physical turn. Or at least, it would be a positive if she could keep herself from venting at Donna, and thereby alienating her husband. If this confrontation were to have taken place anywhere else, she would have spoken her mind and to hell with the consequences, but Fiona might need Jack to help her out and, no matter how gangrenous Donna's words had been, Fiona daren't risk losing his backing. That didn't mean she planned to make things easy for Donna.

'Spit it out, Donna. I don't have time to listen to your apologies, I have a killer to catch.'

'I'm sorry, Fiona, but I won't tell you what I know until you let me apologise.'

Fiona knew Donna well enough to take her at her word. When she wanted to be, Donna could be more stubborn than any mule.

'You do realise, don't you, that right now, I don't have the brain space to deal with any apology you make? My every thought has to be on identifying and arresting whoever killed Kevin and Alice. I need time to work out how I feel about what you said. Whether I can ever bear to look at you again, whether I can trust you not to throw other things about my life into my face when it suits you. You've been my closest friend for as long as I can remember and now, now I feel like I don't know you. Can't trust you. Don't want to be anywhere near you.'

Fiona could feel her eyes prickling and decided to wrap up what she was saying before she unleashed a torrent at Donna. 'Even now, when you reckon you have something to help me solve a murder case, you're holding it back unless I agree to your terms. Just get on with it, Donna. Say what you have to say, and when you're finished with that, tell me the only thing I can bear to hear you say.'

'I'm sorry, Fiona. I never meant to say such a horrible thing. I was scared and stressed and hungry and stupid. So stupid I said a ridiculous thing and hurt my dearest friend. I knew I shouldn't have said it as soon as the words came out of my mouth, but I was so scared. Scared for you, for Jack and for myself. I love my life, and my husband, and *you*. I was scared of losing any of that. You're so brave. You always have been. I've never told you this, but I watched you as you shook hands and exchanged hugs outside the church when it was your mum and dad's funeral. Your Aunt Mary was at your side, but you stood there in the rain being so brave and tough when I knew your heart was breaking. I cried my eyes out for you right there and then, but you just stood there shaking hands and thanking people for coming. You were fifteen years old at the time and you got through it. There must have been two hundred people there, and you spoke to them all. Even at the tea afterwards, you went round the room to speak with people and thank them for coming. I know it's no excuse; that nothing can excuse those stupid words and how much they will have hurt you, but I was terrified. I still am, I'm not brave like you, Fiona. You're the bravest person I've ever been lucky enough to know. To call a friend. You deserve better from me, I know I hurt you, but you have to let me put things right between us. Whatever it takes, tell me what I can do to fix this, and I'll do it.'

There was nothing Donna could do to fix things except give Fiona time and space. Time to calm down, to assess how deep the sense of betrayal ran, and space to work out if Donna could ever be forgiven.

'You can tell me what I really want to know, and then go and sit with Jack. Twelve hours ago, I'd have placed you second only to Aunt Mary as the most special person in my life. You maybe saw me being brave at the funeral, but you also saw how broken I was. I'll always thank you for what you did back then, what you said earlier won't erase all the good times, but right now listening to you while I'm looking at the floor is all I can bring myself to do. Remember all the times I told you my biggest fear was not ever finding out who killed my parents? What you said before turned all those times you offered me reassurance into a pack of lies. You would never have said such a hateful thing if you didn't believe it.' Fiona lifted her head and bored a look into Donna's red-rimmed eyes. 'Now, what do you have to tell me about the case?'

Donna made no move to swipe the tears from her cheeks. 'Before Alice stormed out, Lewis had nipped out for a pee and he didn't come back in until after she'd left.'

The introduction of a new suspect ought to have fired the neurons in Fiona's brain, but she was too weary, both in a physical and emotional sense, to leap to any conclusions. Fiona had already considered Lewis as a suspect, either acting alone or as part of a team with his wife, and found little in the way of a motive. Just because he had the opportunity to kill them both, it didn't mean he had.

Donna's revelation held only bad news: to follow up and ask questions, Fiona would have to spend more time talking to Donna, and instead of her field of suspects narrowing, it had just widened.

FORTY-NINE

Fiona's mind raced as she went through what Donna had revealed. First on her list of priorities, was to establish a time-line. 'How long after Alice stormed out was it before Lewis came back?'

'A minute, two maybe. It wasn't long.'

Fiona had the questions lined up in her mind. She'd digest their answers once Donna was back beside Jack. 'Why did he go out?'

'He needed a pee.'

'Didn't Sara or any of the others offer to help him get outside?'

'No. Things were kicking off at the time. Alice and Frances were taking a lot of stick about the soup they'd given Neil. Do you think he's the one who killed Alice?'

'Was Lewis limping when he came back in?'

'Of course, you know how you asked me about his limp when he helped separate Sara and Alice? I remembered that and paid attention to how he was moving. He was definitely still limping.'

'Did anyone comment on how long he'd been gone?'

'No.'

'Did he ask where Alice was?'

'Yeah. Sara told him. By then they were all sitting with faces like thunder. I thought at one point it was going to end in a fight. It was horrible, Fiona, they should have been pulling together not tearing each other apart.'

Fiona made sure she held Donna's gaze. 'That's human nature for you. People under pressure and stress lash out without thinking about the consequences of what they say or do. It's usually those on the receiving end who get the worst of it.'

Donna broke the stare first, her head ducking away and down. In another time and place Fiona may have felt guilt for the way she'd twisted the knife in Donna, but not today. Today Fiona was the wronged party and whatever she said to Donna was deserved.

'I'm sorry. You know that, don't you?'

'I know, but right now, you being sorry isn't enough. Are you sure it was only a couple of minutes after Alice left that Lewis returned?'

'Yeah. Please, Fiona, we've got to find a way to put this behind us. We can do that, can't we?'

'I haven't yet begun to deal with the hurt you caused. How you made me feel. How we can possibly find a way forward after what you said. I need time. Time to think. Time to work out if I can ever trust you again. Time to decide if I want you in my life any more. You know that, don't you? I've never done it, because he's with you and I'd never do anything I thought would hurt you, but can you imagine how you'd feel if you found out I had tried to seduce Jack a few times over the years, including on your wedding day? What you'd feel towards me after learning everything you ever thought about me was tainted? That a whole bunch of your memories of me were soured by betrayal. That's where I am, that's where you put me when you opened your mouth to spout your cruel bullshit.'

Fiona pointed at Donna and then the doorway. Words could no longer be trusted lest they turn toxic. Gestures would have to suffice. As furious as Fiona might feel, there was no way she was going to allow her anger a position of dominance. The worst thing she could do now was to lose her temper and bring herself down to Donna's level with a string of invective.

As Donna sulked away to join her husband, Fiona pulled in a couple of deep steadying breaths. As she drew the breaths into her chest, Fiona's hands were flexing in and out of fists.

To sate the burning in her chest, Fiona bent all of her mental energy towards what Donna had said about Lewis.

Foremost in Fiona's thinking was the timeline. If Lewis killed Alice, and therefore Kevin, he would have needed more than a couple of minutes to follow her to the point behind the shelter where she'd been found, and then return to the shelter. In Fiona's mind there wasn't even close to enough time for that to have happened. Plus, Lewis had a gammy ankle, slowing him even further.

Lewis had left the shelter to pee, according to Donna, yet when she'd checked the toilet at the back of the shelter, there were marks in the snow showing the door had been opened, but only enough for someone to look inside, certainly not enough to allow someone of Lewis's size to enter. That was a small detail which might make a lie of Lewis's reason for exiting the shelter apart from two facts: Lewis was a man, and it's easy for men to pee anywhere they choose; Lewis was lame from the injury to his ankle, so it didn't make sense he'd trudge all the way round the shelter to access the toilet when he could just turn his back to the wind and let fly.

Fiona could picture him hobbling a few feet away from the door, and not even knowing Alice had passed behind his back.

The more Fiona tried to picture Lewis killing Alice, the

more she found herself foundering against the timings; and he also lacked a motive to kill Kevin. Lewis might have had the means, but he had nothing else.

Fiona's heart began to ache. Maybe Donna was right. Perhaps she wasn't cut out to be a detective, to finally solve her parents' murder case.

Rather than succumb to self-doubts, Fiona set her jaw firm and concentrated all her brain power on trying to work out who the killer was before they struck again.

FIFTY

No matter how much Fiona tried to dispel them, negative thoughts about her own ability were forming clouds in her mind far darker than any of the ones dumping snow on Beinn Bhuidhe.

To combat the insecurity Fiona went back to the start and tried to work out how any of the potential suspects might achieve a financial gain sufficient to warrant murder.

Steve was set to inherit Kevin's estate, which put him in the frame, but it was too obvious. Rather than rehash previous thoughts and end up with the same result, Fiona tried thinking about how the others might achieve financial gain.

With so many transactions now being paid with credit or debit cards rather than cash, it stood to reason the thief had perhaps targeted the cards, as the amount of cash used would be minimal. Another reason cards would be used a lot at Inveraray House was the sums of money involved. To stay and dine there would cost at least three or four hundred pounds. Few people carried that amount of cash on them. Fiona rarely had more than twenty quid on her at any time, and it was a handful of shrapnel and a fiver or two reserved for parking meters and tipping waiting staff.

There were sure to be security measures in place when it came to storing customers' card details. The thing was, all the key staff at Inveraray House had long service records. They'd be familiar with each other and would have built up years of comradeship and with it, trust.

Of those present who were involved in the use of cards, it would be Frances and Thomas who'd handle them most on a day-to-day basis. From its size and number of rooms, Inveraray House would almost certainly have some form of computerised diary. It was no stretch to imagine the system storing card details for future payments. There'd be protocols and user passwords to protect the cardholders, but with levels of trust built up over years, some of those protocols could become lax thereby opening a window of opportunity.

The problem Fiona ran into with this line of thought was she couldn't figure out how someone could use stolen card details without running the risk of being caught. Online goods could be bought with anonymity, but they'd be easy to trace once the cardholder learned of the purchase.

A potential way to delay this was to use a credit card rather than a debit card. Fiona's own bank card was linked to the app on her phone and a notification was sent for every purchase she made within seconds of the card being used.

To make online purchases a safe delivery address was required. A hotel receiving numerous parcels or deliveries for a guest would be memorable, but somewhere like an Airbnb could be booked last minute with stolen card details and the cardholder's name, and then the deliveries could all be received with low odds of them being traced. The chances of this being a perfect crime would increase if the Airbnb was in a country location where the neighbours were too distant for twitching curtains to be a factor.

The purchases could then be sold on via eBay or another online sales platform and the money banked.

Another way to profit from card details would be to sell them on to criminal gangs. Such gangs didn't really exist in places like Lochgilphead and Inveraray, but that didn't mean the numbers couldn't be sold to a gang from anywhere else. With Messenger, text, WhatsApp, Snapchat and email, Fiona's own mobile had five ways of communicating beyond making a call and reciting the card details.

Thomas was the one Fiona was thinking of as a suspect for such a crime. He was the one who'd had a rough upbringing, and while he might have crawled from a mire to escape his childhood disadvantages, he might never have really shaken the mud off his boots. As bar manager he'd have a credible reason to access the computer diary to check pre-orders for weddings and functions. His apparent sweetness on Frances may be a ploy to engender trust so he could harvest the card details. If Alice had received a call from an irate customer she would have gone to Kevin. Had the customer only used the card with Thomas he'd have been in the frame and, while he would have denied everything, he'd know he was in danger of being discovered and could have murdered both his accusers.

While this made a certain amount of sense, it still didn't stack up for Fiona. If it was Thomas who was the thief and killer, it didn't add up he'd target people who only spent with him. To do so was to put a noose around his own neck. Plus, for the endeavour to be worth killing over, it had to be hugely profitable. That meant it must have been going on a long time before it was discovered.

For someone to repeat a crime over a long period of time and go undetected takes a lot of cunning. It requires discipline and a limiting of risks to the point where they became negligible. Someone involved in card fraud on a long-term basis would be savvy enough to sit on stolen details for a cooling-off period before using them. If a month or two had passed and the card in question had been used another twenty or fifty times since its use at Inveraray House, there'd be a lot less chance of the card details being pinpointed as having been collected from Kevin's hotel.

Where this whole train of thought fell apart for Fiona was the realisation someone tasked with investigating credit card fraud for one of the major card providers would eventually have stumbled upon Inveraray House as a common denominator in their investigations.

Fiona had no idea how card fraud was investigated, but she was sure the card companies would take it seriously, and she imagined they'd have some kind of computer algorithm to cross check all places affected cards had been used. That left two scenarios: she was barking up the wrong tree with the idea about card fraud, or, she was on the right track and someone from the card company had contacted the hotel.

While the latter scenario made a certain amount of sense, Fiona didn't believe it would happen that way. If a specific business was a common denominator in several investigations, the card company wouldn't call the business, they'd call the police. As Inveraray was covered by her station at Lochgilphead, it would have fallen to one of her colleagues to investigate. Although she'd been off shift for a few days, Fiona was kept abreast of what was going on and when she'd spoken to Heather yesterday, she'd not heard any mention of such a fraud.

Even if the credit card companies weren't as good at investigating frauds as Fiona suspected they were, any would-be thief might expect they were. Organised crime gangs would know better and would be cautious about buying from someone who kept drawing from the same well.

As she couldn't find a way to make card theft a credible theory, Fiona tried another idea. It was a complicated one, and saw Steve as Alice's murderer, but not his uncle's.

FIFTY-ONE

If Alice had been embezzling money from Kevin at Inveraray House, it was possible he might have noticed something amiss. As the person overseeing the hotel's accounts, Alice would be in a position of great trust. To that end, she'd have the most opportunity to help herself to a share of Kevin's wealth.

Kevin was accepted as a good operator, and he knew enough about business to recognise Steve hadn't the skills to take over Inveraray House from him; hence the sale clause in his will. Therefore, Kevin could be assumed sharp enough to spot whatever Alice was up to. While he might suspect she was stealing from him, he'd no doubt want proof of some kind. That proof would come in the form of a trap to give Alice just enough rope to hang herself.

If Alice had seen the trap, she could have sidestepped it while recognising what its existence signified. To not give herself away, she'd have had to carry on as normal, pausing her theft until she could move on, or once again stick her hand in Kevin's till. However, it was plausible Alice had opted for a more drastic solution. By murdering Kevin she put herself in a win-win position. Not only did Steve lack the business acumen to uncover her crime, but as inheritor he would be the prime suspect for Kevin's murder. The plan made sense and if she'd had a hand in making sure Neil had the allergic reaction, she could have done so in the hope of creating a distraction from the murder she'd committed.

Where Alice's plan had fallen apart was the presence of Steve. Kevin could have confided his suspicions about Alice stealing from him to his nephew, meaning Steve had motive as well as opportunity and means to kill Alice. If that was the case, what must have been going through his mind as he did the chest compressions while trying to save her life? Had he been praying for her to pass? Or had he been worrying it might be recalled how quick he'd been to give up on the CPR? Had that, above all other reasons, been why he'd looked to Fiona for permission to halt his efforts?

Not for the first time that night, Fiona felt the oppressive weight of guilt pressing down on her shoulders. If this theory was correct, and of all the ones she'd concocted it was among the most credible, then she'd not just failed to identify Alice as the person who'd attacked and ultimately killed Kevin, but she'd also had an unwitting hand in Alice's murder.

Fiona knew she was being harsh on herself, but the knowledge didn't help salve any of the guilt she felt. Donna's words had been cruel, but right in this moment, it very much seemed to be a case of the truth hurting.

A soft snore came from across the room. When Fiona looked around she could see all the other occupants of the shelter were losing the battle against the soporific warmth emanating from the stove. Heads were drooping and while Steve's and Jack's eyes were still open, their eyelids were heading south like geese in autumn.

She took the fact people were sleeping as a compliment. Even though there was a killer in their midst, they trusted her to keep them safe.

As much as Fiona wanted to employ Jack as a bodyguard, she realised letting the others all sleep was a good way to ensure the killer didn't strike again. She would stay awake, and keep a watch. When morning came, she could reassess their situation. A sleepless night would be a small price to pay if she could prevent another life being taken.

To Fiona it was telling Steve was fighting sleep. If he was a killer he would be terrified of discovery, and if he wasn't, he'd be grieving his uncle and wondering which of his so-called friends had murdered Kevin. Either way, sleep wouldn't come easy to him, and that's why Fiona pressed her fingernails deep into the palms of her hands. Whatever may or may not transpire during the night, she had to stay awake to face it.

One benefit to everyone sleeping was it gave Fiona peace to think. To probe at her various theories from as many directions as she could.

After a check of everyone's status, even Steve had succumbed to sleep by now, Fiona took a look at her watch. It was ten past three. Sunrise would be around half past eight. If the storm had passed, she could strike out for support with someone. The question was who?

Thomas, Steve, Ivor and Sara were all major suspects. Lewis was lame and Neil recovering from his allergic reaction. That left Frances, Jack and Donna.

Fiona could only see Frances as a hindrance on a trek down-hill, and while Jack would be her preferred companion, if she left, she'd need Jack to stay behind and keep all the shelter's occupants together until help arrived. That left Donna. Whether her former friend would leave her husband was questionable, but Donna was the only logical choice as a companion.

Except Fiona couldn't bear the idea of Donna accompanying her. There would be hours of pleas for forgiveness, entreaties and, while Donna was fit enough to hike up a Munro in good weather conditions, she'd struggle with the effort of wading through snowdrifts for hours on end.

Fiona leaned back against the shelter wall until her head rested against the stone. If there was any decent amount of visibility when the sun rose, she'd head down alone and leave both Donna and Jack to guard the others. It was riskier, and somewhat foolhardy, but Fiona would rather take the risk than endure hours of Donna's company. They might have been friends for almost as long as Fiona could remember, but Fiona couldn't bear to spend hours alone with Donna. Not after what she'd said.

FIFTY-TWO

The pain of her injured shoulder being shaken with vigour snapped Fiona's eyes open. She hadn't planned to fall asleep, but it must have happened. Thomas was in front of her and there was movement in every part of the shelter.

Fiona rubbed a hand across her chin as she flexed her pained shoulder. Steve was bent over someone at the far side of the shelter. It was where Ivor, Sara and Lewis had been seated. Ivor stood off to one side, his face stern as he looked down at Steve whose hand was at Sara's throat checking for a pulse.

'What's happened?'

'Sara's dead and Lewis is missing.'

Fiona rose and pushed her way forward until she was standing behind Steve. 'Dead? How?'

The scream from Frances was high-pitched enough to shatter glass. It woke Neil, Donna and Jack and all of a sudden the shelter was filled with noise as everybody shouted or screamed. As she'd done earlier, Fiona banged two of the tin mugs together to bring order to the rabble.

Steve eased himself upright, his expression harder than any of the rocks comprising Beinn Bhuidhe. 'I'm no pathologist, but

I'd say she was strangled.' Steve's open palm gestured down at Sara. 'There's bruising on her throat and her eyes are bloodshot.'

Fiona didn't need to hear more. It was now time for action instead of speculation and deliberation. Sara's death was on her. It was she who'd fallen asleep and allowed the killer to strike again.

Lewis may have been the murderer, or he might have limped outside for another pee and been killed there, with Sara strangled as she'd stirred when the killer re-entered the shelter. Another idea was Lewis had left to get help before Sara had been murdered, but the injury to his ankle refuted that idea. Even if Lewis had woken and felt no pain, he'd be sure to know it would flare up again long before he got to the bottom of the mountain.

Whomever had killed Sara would have been conscious of her making a noise, so Fiona guessed they'd used one hand to clamp her mouth shut while the other constricted her throat.

Unlike the movies where someone who is being throttled takes an age to succumb, the reality is when the carotid artery in the throat is compressed blood can't travel to the brain and the victim passes out in a few seconds. If Sara had been asleep when the killer grabbed her throat, she'd have barely had time to wake up and react to what was happening before the effects of the strangulation took hold.

Whatever the sequence of events, and the identity of the killer, Fiona wasn't going to make any conclusions until she had more facts. And the only way to get those facts was to investigate.

The first thing Fiona did was lift each of Sara's hands and take a careful look at her nails. Not the top, the undersides. Under three nails of Sara's right hand, Fiona saw what looked to be scrapings of skin. Fiona powered up her phone and used a couple of precious percent of the battery to take photos of Sara's throat and eyes.

Fiona lay the hands back down on Sara's chest then turned to face the entire group.

'Sara is not to be moved under any circumstance until a forensic team get here. Her body is officially a crime scene, and if the skin under her nails matches Lewis's DNA, then we'll have a cast-iron case against him for at least one of the three murders. You're all to watch each other. Anyone who tries to move her is to be considered a killer trying to destroy evidence.'

With the stark warning given, Fiona aimed a hand at the door as she zipped her jacket up.

'Jack, come with me, please. We need to see if we can find Lewis.'

As Jack reached for his coat, Fiona stole a glance at her watch. Quarter to nine. After sunrise, but that meant little if the snow was still falling.

Although the shelter had cooled with everyone asleep and the stove burning out, the cold when Fiona opened the door was enough to take her breath away.

Fiona had to slit her eyes against the sunlight glittering off the snow. Gone were the heavy clouds depositing foot after foot of snow. They'd been replaced with a sky so blue it looked to have been photoshopped above the hills and Munros from a tropical land far away. The air was now so clear Fiona could see for miles in every direction she looked. There was only one direction she was looking: downhill, her eyes following the path of the track down to the glen floor. All Fiona could see was white. There was no flash of colour from Lewis's orange jacket.

Against the pristine snow, Lewis's jacket would be a beacon, but she could see no splashes of colour. To have found Lewis descending the Munro would have been the best option. Guilty or innocent, if he was moving away from the shelter, he was alive.

Fiona took a breath and ran through things for a moment as she looked around. If Lewis had absconded, then he'd have been sure to leave tracks. When Fiona cast her eyes along the snow-covered path she could see fresh tracks leading down the trail.

'Jack, can you follow those tracks for a couple of hundred yards? I want to know if they continue onwards or come to a halt. If they come to a halt, you'll probably find Lewis's body somewhere near where they end.'

With Jack given the task of gathering more intel, Fiona assessed what she knew and tried to work out if Lewis was the killer or not.

Whatever Fiona worked out, she knew she'd have a decision to make: to pursue Lewis herself, or to stay put and trust he'd send help.

On the grounds British justice worked on the principle suspects were innocent until proven guilty, Fiona fit what she knew against a sequence of events that happened while she was asleep.

At some point in the night the killer, who must have feigned sleep, strangled Sara. If Lewis had been awake he'd have tried to prevent it, and that would have woken the whole shelter, so if innocent, Lewis must have woken up and found Sara dead. From there he must have made the decision to go for help himself. Whether that was a desperation to have the police catch his wife's killer or a desire to remove himself from the shelter lest he end up either murdering the killer himself, or becoming a victim was unknown. Either way, he'd gone. While all of this was possible, to Fiona it didn't stack up. Lewis ought to have woken her, a police officer. While it was obvious the marriage wasn't in a good state, for him to react to his wife's murder without making a sound or alerting a cop on the scene was every kind of suspicious.

All of this made perfect sense until one fact was brought into play: Lewis's injured ankle. After the fall from the bridge, he'd limped with every step; his face a knot of stoic endurance. For him to wake up fit enough to hike down the Munro alone showed either superhuman powers of recovery, or that he'd feigned the injury all along.

Piece by rapid piece Fiona applied logic to every step of the events since they'd wound up in the shelter. By having the fall at the bridge, Lewis had prevented them from continuing on downhill. The later attempts had been thwarted by the snow and the failing torches, but it was the first where success had seemed most likely and Lewis had put paid to that by leaving them no choice but to turn back. After the stramash over the soup continued in the shelter while she and Jack were striking out for help again, Lewis had maintained his gammy ankle act and limped out for a pee. From there he'd lain in wait until taking his chance to murder Alice.

Donna had said Lewis was only outside the shelter a couple of minutes after Alice had left, but fully fit, it wouldn't have taken too long for Lewis to crack Alice on the head with a log and then carry her body to a place it could be dumped. It was the distance and his injury that had led Fiona to discount him from murdering Alice, but without the gammy ankle to slow him down, there would be a far larger window for murder.

Another thing supporting this thinking was a truism Dave Lennox had oft recited to Fiona. When it comes to people's recollection of time or the date an event took place, always add at least half.

Now she was having this thought, Fiona recalled a recent conversation with Heather about a trip to Oban cinema to watch *Bohemian Rhapsody* upon the film's release. Heather had it the film was released in early 2020 before any of the lockdowns were imposed. A quick Google search had shown the film had been released in October 2018.

Fiona had spotted there was no love lost between Lewis and Sara, but as she'd never believed Lewis was the killer, she'd seen no threat from him towards his wife; a mistake that added more guilt to an already intolerable burden.

Whatever reason Lewis may have had for killing his wife was something that could wait for an explanation. Now Fiona had worked everything through, the only way she'd believe Lewis was innocent, was if she found his body and it was obvious he'd been murdered.

'Fiona.'

Jack's yell carried up to Fiona with ease and as she set off towards him, her feet crunched their way through a crust of frozen snow, but it was her eyes that were absorbing information not her ears.

As she powered towards Jack she was looking at where he was pointing. A half mile away an orange blob was just visible above the brow of a slope, but when Fiona paused to watch the blob she saw it was moving, And not towards them. That was all the proof Fiona needed and there was no doubt in her mind what she must do.

Jack was coming back to her, but Fiona didn't halt.

'You go back to the shelter and look after the others. I'm going after him.'

FIFTY-THREE

Fiona had no real plan other than to catch up with Lewis and formally arrest him. A plan could be worked out as she descended Beinn Bhuidhe. Lewis had a half mile head start, and on a summer's day, she could reel him in with comfort. But it was December. Sprints had never been Fiona's thing, but at least once a week she ran a four-mile circuit to keep herself in shape. As things were, Lewis was having to create a path through thigh-deep snow. Fiona could follow his trail and as the going was easier, she'd make better time.

With no cuffs, or even a rope to bind Lewis, she'd have to improvise when it came to the arrest, but she had an ace up her sleeve. As she forged her way along the path Lewis had cut in the snow, she reached into her pocket and checked the ace was still in play.

Fiona's mobile battery was down to six per cent; more than enough to summon reinforcements as soon as she had a signal. The battery wouldn't hold out if there was a protracted conversation about location, but she planned to call Heather and raise the alarm that way. It wasn't the correct way to communicate, but it'd save her from being routed through Control. To preserve the battery, Fiona powered it down and continued after Lewis.

From the position where Jack had spied Lewis, Fiona had taken mere seconds to work out that after following the proper trail for a short while, Lewis had struck out in a direct line to the point where the A83 curled around the most northern point of Loch Fyne and continued down the loch's western shore towards Inveraray and Lochgilphead. The old bridge over the River Fyne was a popular place to park, and where Fiona had left her own car before heading down the road to pick up the track leading to the summit of Beinn Bhuidhe. The going would be harder than following the track, but it'd shave at least two miles off the journey, plus there was a power station and a quarry in that area, so there'd be a chance of a decent road to walk along when he got to the glen floor.

There was a frozen crust on the snow, and Fiona's breaths steamed from her mouth in the low temperature, but she was pushing herself more than hard enough to generate warmth. Fiona's nose and ears nipped in the cold, but they were minor discomforts.

Not once as Fiona trudged along in dogged pursuit did she question her actions. Yes, the man she was apprehending had killed three people; yes, he was bigger and stronger than she was; yes, he might be desperate to escape justice. All of these things faded into darkness so far as Fiona was concerned. She had to catch Lewis to stop him from disappearing into the wind. To bring the right kind of closure to Steve and everyone else who cared about Kevin, Alice and Sara. Most of all, she had to catch Lewis to prove to Donna – and in no small part herself – that she was a good copper who could solve cases.

Lewis might have the advantage in a one-on-one fight, but his kills had all been done with the element of surprise in his favour. He'd never met resistance of any form. No doubt when he'd throttled Sara he'd clamped a free hand over her mouth to ensure she didn't cry for help. Maybe he'd looked in her eyes as she'd died. Whatever the case with Sara may have been, Lewis had never killed when his victims had a chance of defending themselves. The skin under Sara's nails was as close as Lewis had come to facing resistance during his three kills.

Fiona's focus was on three key things: making safe passage along the trail Lewis had left through the snow, keeping an eye on Lewis – both to make sure she was closing the gap between them and to make sure he hadn't spotted her coming after him and set an ambush – and the motive for his kills.

To Fiona the three victims must have all been party to the same secret. Alice might have witnessed Lewis strike Kevin and been too scared to speak up, but if that was the case, no way would she have stormed out of the shelter when she knew Lewis was outside alone. Sara would be the person who knew Lewis best, and if she knew the reason why he'd killed Kevin and Alice, she'd be in danger by the same reasoning. Perhaps after everyone had fallen asleep she'd challenged him in whispers and told him to give himself up or she would turn him in.

While this thinking stacked up to a certain degree, Fiona wasn't convinced by it. To her there had to be a thread connecting all three victims. That thread would either be a huge rope of the kind used to moor large ships, or a fine filament binding them all in the same tangled knot.

Money was out as a motive; if Lewis had been on the take, he'd have been fired or Kevin would have turned him over to the police. As a chef he would have at best limited access to money, and even less to customers' credit card details.

There was a possibility Lewis had learned of something illegal Kevin had done with Alice's input and had tried blackmailing them only to be rebutted. Anger might have made him lash out or seek a brutal revenge, but there was no way Kevin would have retained his blackmailer as an employee, much less bring him on a works jaunt. The blackmailing may have been anonymous and Kevin may have worked out who his black-mailer was and confronted Lewis while on Beinn Bhuidhe, but that was stretching the theory well past its breaking point. Nobody had reported any confrontation or fall out between Kevin and Lewis, and there was sure to be some ill-feeling between the two if Kevin had accused Lewis.

That left sex as a motive, and no matter how she tried she couldn't imagine the three victims being involved in any situation where sex was happening between all three. Unless one of them knew of an affair concerning the other two and all three were killed to keep the affair secret.

When Fiona gave one of her periodic glances forward she saw the gap between her and Lewis was closing. He was perhaps a third of a mile ahead of her now. A quick calculation informed Fiona that if they both continued at their current pace, she'd catch up with Lewis more than a half mile from the bridge he appeared to be heading for. That was good news, but what wasn't good news was as Lewis neared the quarry and the power station, his going would be easier than hers. Worse still, as much as she'd do it if she had to, the solo takedown of a murderer with no handcuffs, pepper spray or collapsible baton – much less backup – was the stupidest of all stupid ideas.

FIFTY-FOUR

Fiona didn't falter, didn't slow her pace in the slightest at the thought of a physical confrontation with Lewis. A part of her wanted to push harder, to stretch every sinew, to work every muscle to capacity so she could take down the killer she chased.

The thrill of the chase was something Fiona had experienced before and she knew better than to listen to its siren song. Far wiser and safer to stick to her plan and trail Lewis until mobile signal returned and she could summon backup. Should it look as if Lewis was going to make it to his car before backup arrived, Fiona could then engage him, but as a tactic, it had to be a last resort.

Fifty yards ahead of Fiona, the ground dropped away into one of the many burns that tumbled down the side of Beinn Bhuidhe. Unlike a couple she'd already crossed, this one was both wide and deep enough to make it impossible for Fiona to step over the frothing waters descending to the River Fyne.

With no option but to put a foot into the water or risk a lengthy delay while she found a narrower section, Fiona gritted her teeth and plunged her right foot into the water. The cold drew one gasp and two curses from her, but she didn't halt and hardly slowed. A chilled foot wasn't the end of the world. In another hour or so, she'd be at the glen floor and would have either caught up with Lewis and captured him, or she'd be his fourth victim. Either way, frostbite and gangrene wouldn't have time to be a worry.

Fiona was now close enough to see Lewis turn and look back. It made sense he was watching for anyone who might pursue him. Anyone in his position would. All the same it was unnerving for Fiona to see a killer looking at her, even if there was at least quarter of a mile between them.

On a good day, it took the best part of an hour to drive from Lochgilphead to the head of Loch Fyne; with blues and twos on it could be shaved down to forty-five minutes, forty if traffic was light. With snow and ice likely to be affecting driving conditions, it could take twice the usual time for backup to arrive. The urge to check for a mobile signal was strong, but Fiona wanted to make sure she preserved every scrap of battery life possible until she was sure there would be a signal. Like everything else since Fiona deduced Kevin had been murdered, the decision as to when to test for a signal was a balancing act with no safety net.

Fiona's calves burned, her thighs ached and her right foot squelched with every step, but as hard as her limbs were working, it was her mind that was putting in the toughest shift. A memory of something Lewis had said to her, and the manner in which he'd said it, had sparked a new theory about how the three victims might be connected by sex.

As with so many of the theories Fiona had developed, it wasn't one which filled her with certainty, but the more she thought about it in the crisp clear morning air, the more she grew confident she'd either worked out the motive for the murders, or was close enough to it that when more investigating was done the pieces would all fall into place.

The realisation she might have cracked the case sent fresh

energy around Fiona's body, and the adrenaline boost was just what she needed to salve her exhausted muscles and keep them meeting the demands she was making of them. It didn't escape Fiona's notice the clouds of mist coming with each breath were getting bigger as she pushed her body to the limit.

Another burn appeared ahead of her. This one wider and faster than the last. That was to be expected, the lower down the slope she crossed each burn, the more it had built in size as it made its way down Beinn Bhuidhe.

As before, Fiona didn't hesitate as she led with her right foot and stepped into the tumbling burn. But when Fiona's left foot was about to break the surface, the rock she was standing on shifted and plunged her sideways into the frigid water.

FIFTY-FIVE

A hard jolt in the right hip brought a pained gasp from Fiona as she landed. The one saving grace about her fall into the burn was she'd only been submerged belly deep. Her first thought as she clambered from the water was for her phone. It had been in her left pocket beside the rock used to attack Kevin – the side of her that bore the brunt of her fall and had gone deepest into the raging burn.

Fiona didn't unzip her pocket until she was three paces past the burn. It would be bad enough if her numb fingers dropped the mobile into the snow, but for it to fall into the burn would be unthinkable.

The first thing Fiona noticed about the phone as she went to power it up was the screen now bore a spiderweb of cracks. That wasn't too concerning as she'd seen plenty work with damaged screens, and all she needed the mobile to achieve was a single call.

No matter how hard, or often, Fiona pressed down on the power button, no trace of colour flickered across the phone's screen. It remained as black as the snow around her was white.

The lack of functionality could be from the blow that broke its screen, the immersion in water, or a combination of the two.

Whichever it was, the point was moot. She was now left with no option but to catch up with Lewis herself and do whatever she could to stop him from getting away.

Fiona's teeth chattered as she kept pushing on. One positive she was finding was that as she descended the Munro, the depth of snow was shrinking. It was now knee high and while a hindrance to forward momentum, she knew she was making a better pace than when she'd first left the shelter. It was a blessing in disguise as she could see Lewis was much lower on the slope, and he'd be making the same pace she was, if not better.

As a way to close the gap, Fiona considered plotting a course straight down until she reached level ground. Then she'd be able to achieve a faster pace along the glen floor where the snow would be shallower still.

It was a nice idea in theory, but Lewis would reach the glen floor a good ten minutes or so before she did, and he was a quarter of a mile ahead of her. That quarter of a mile would take a lot of reeling in when she had to forge her own path through the snow. It didn't help Fiona's hip was stiffening from where she'd landed on it, and her injured shoulder was sending jolts of pain throughout her left arm and torso with every step taken. On a summer's day and without injury, Fiona would have backed herself to make up the quarter mile with ease. Today, exhausted and hurt as she was, Fiona doubted she'd have enough left in the tank to stop Lewis getting away.

Fiona's foot skittered beneath her and she had to arc her body to remain upright as the ground beneath her feet slid ten yards downhill. With measured steps, Fiona carried on, her every movement cautious not to disturb the scree slope she must be on.

As soon as the ground felt firmer, Fiona increased her pace

as much as she dared. She had to catch up with Lewis before he made it to his car, but she also had to keep something in reserve; it would be no good to catch Lewis if she was fit only to give him a laugh at her panted efforts to stop his escape.

Lewis was only a hundred feet above the glen floor now, but Fiona had at least thrice that before she'd reap the benefits of level ground. Fiona increased her pace yet again, her breaths long ragged flumes of mist hanging in the morning air.

As often as she dared take her eyes off the trail she was following, Fiona was casting glances at Lewis, every look an attempt to track his progress, to discern if he was opening up a greater lead or if she was closing on him.

By her best estimation, she was closing on him.

And then estimation became irrelevant.

Lewis had halted at the bottom of a wide crease in the landscape. Every step Fiona took brought her closer to Lewis: good.

Lewis was waiting for her in a hollow that would shield the pair of them from the view of anyone in the glen floor looking their way: not good.

FIFTY-SIX

Fiona eased her pace for two reasons. First, she wanted to be in the best physical shape she could achieve when she confronted Lewis. Second, even though her mobile was dead and none of the shelter's occupants had been able to raise the alarm, someone was bound to have missed one of the people who'd been trapped on Beinn Bhuidhe. That someone would surely have alerted Mountain Rescue, the police. If that had happened, people would be looking for them.

So far Fiona had seen no great amount of activity on the road leading up the glen, but she hadn't looked hard and her focus had always been on the course Lewis had chosen, rather than the trail up Beinn Bhuidhe which now lay miles behind her. If a search party had set off at first light, they'd have several hours of slogging uphill to reach the shelter.

Lewis no doubt suspected the same as she did. He must have calculated the risks involved in waiting for Fiona were less than the ones he'd face if she caught up to him in a place where search parties may be forming.

It crossed Fiona's mind to skirt around Lewis and deny him the choice of battleground. The idea was abandoned as soon as it came to her. For all she might manage to get past him, there would come a point where she'd have to face him down. Better to do it when she still had something left in the tank than when she was running on empty.

Fiona had none of the usual police tools to help her take down Lewis, but she had something she deemed better. Her mind.

Lewis didn't know her phone was dead. He sure as hell wouldn't know she'd worked out why he'd murdered Kevin, then Alice and finally Sara. When she confronted him with the knowledge of what he'd been trying to cover up – that it was known to everyone in the shelter – the fight would be sure to go out of him if he believed the lie. She'd present his situation as over. Tell him police were a mere ten minutes away. In short, she'd bluff him into submission.

As plans went it was risky; Lewis might call her bluff and try to kill her. Fiona had the first half of an idea as to how she might deal with that. Since embarking on the pursuit, she'd been assessing what she had on her person that might be useful in a fight and while she'd be the first to admit her plan had more holes than a sieve, everything that happened next was always going to have to be improvised as events unfolded.

When Fiona got to within fifty yards of Lewis she noted he was standing on a level patch of ground maybe fifteen feet in diameter. That was his chosen arena, his assumed domain.

Fiona gave no thought to how Lewis had set the terms. She had terms of her own.

Forty yards away. Now Fiona could see the tendrils of breath mist from Lewis were controlled and even.

Twenty yards. Lewis's hands were drawn from his pockets, and he drew himself up to his full height.

Fiona let the intimidation tactic pass by her as she drew her mobile from her pocket and held it up so Lewis could see what it was.

Ten yards from Lewis Fiona drew to a halt and unzipped her jacket. She planned to keep this distance between them. On a flat dry surface those ten yards could be covered in no more than two or three seconds. To travel the same ten yards when the going was uneven and there was shin-deep snow would take twice as long, unless Lewis threw all caution to the wind and gambled on not tripping before he got to Fiona. After the hike they'd endured, Fiona doubted he'd take the risk.

'It's over, Lewis. Before I came after you, I explained to everyone why you'd killed Kevin, Alice and Sara. It was Sara's murder that explained everything to me. I've already called it in. There's cops on their way here. The last I heard they're about ten minutes away from the top of Loch Fyne. Unless you fancy hiking over the hills, there's no escape for you now.'

'You don't know nothing. When I woke up, I was shocked to see my Sara had been throttled. That's on you, you were the copper there, you shouldn't have fallen asleep. You should have stayed awake to guard us all. I told you all along it was Steve who was the killer.'

Even though Fiona had expected some concocted story, it still stung to hear Lewis blame her for a murder he'd committed. Fiona guessed the sting came because she knew that on some levels he was right. 'Then why are you striking out like this?'

'So my Sara gets the justice she deserves. It wasn't safe for any of us in there and you were doing bugger all about it, so I took matters into my own hands.'

'Do you really expect me to believe that? You woke up, found your wife murdered and left everyone else with the killer. Not just that, but in leaving, you snuck out. Why didn't you wake me? You think Steve is the killer, you've said so more than once, so why didn't you try and punch his lights out for murdering your wife?'

'I'm not a fighter. Yeah, I may be quite big, but I've never been any good at fighting. I was always the one who got picked on at school, even though I was the tallest in my year.'

Fiona could see what Lewis's plan was. He would bullshit her until she fell for his lies, and then when he had a chance to attack her by surprise he would. And victim number four would be claimed.

'And what about the affair Sara was having?' Fiona let her expression harden. 'That's what all this was about, wasn't it?'

'What affair? You think my Sara was shagging Kevin and topped him when he binned her? You don't know what you're talking about, you stupid cow. And how does that explain why Alice and Sara are dead?'

'I've been cooped up with you all for a few hours. I questioned you all. I paid a lot of attention to everyone's body language. How they interacted with each other. Nobody once suggested Sara and Kevin were having an affair. In fact, everyone I spoke to about Kevin told me he wasn't interested in dating on any level. However, during the course of my investigation and the time spent observing you all, I came to some conclusions. You and Sara were nobody's picture of a happy marriage, which, quite frankly, is your business and nobody else's. However, last night wasn't a normal night. Couples fall out and make up, that's part of life, but at no point I saw was there any attempt by you to comfort your wife. When everyone was falling asleep, she was on one side of Ivor and you the other. That's hardly in sickness and in health, is it? Except, you weren't worried about her getting killed in the night, because that's what your plan was. Your last words to me a moment ago were "what affair", the answer to that question is: the affair between Alice and Sara. You yourself called Alice a dirty cow when telling me about a threesome she'd allegedly had with another couple. By discounting Steve as the killer and inheritance as the motive, I could find no other way anyone could profit financially from Kevin's death. After money, sex is a close second when it comes to the reasons people commit murder.

'When I had three victims to link together, that story of yours about Alice had me wondering if she was bisexual. Everyone had already told me Kevin had no sexual appetite, so any affair must have been between the two female victims. From there it was a case of seeing who would profit in any way from the murders. With no financial gain to be had, the profit would have to come in another way. Either a covering up of the affair, or as revenge for it. Who'd want to conceal the affair, or take revenge for being dumped so badly they'd kill?'

'Surely you don't believe that load of bollocks.'

'There was a widening of your eyes when I told you about Alice and Sara having an affair. You didn't shake your head as if in disbelief; instead you showed shock that I knew. I suspect Kevin somehow found out about the affair, and being the decent guy everyone said he was, told you about it, or at the very least threatened he would, to make Sara come clean to you.'

Lewis's top lip pulled upwards at both sides, his eyes becoming hate-filled lasers. 'So what if I heard my wife had an affair? That doesn't make me a killer, though, does it? Explain that if you're such a fucking smartarse.'

The vulgarity creeping into Lewis's language was enough to make Fiona tense. He was getting angry, and that meant she was on the right track. There was no telling if he'd try attacking her or would continue to scoff at her deductions.

'Your pride makes you a killer. Your wife's verbal assaults may have made you one. The way the others tell it, she spent years accusing you of having affairs. She told me Kevin kept you from contributing to the menu. You yourself passed that off as Kevin being so good you couldn't compete with him on professional terms. It galled Sara, though, and I bet it galled you a lot more than you let on. Sara had ambitions, not just for herself, but for you as well. How does it feel to know you've disappointed your wife so much she sought comfort in the arms of someone else? A woman you thought of as a dirty cow, no less? That would gall anyone. I'd say her affair with Alice was one slight too many. You could take the verbals from Sara. They could be ignored, but what you couldn't ignore, couldn't face, was everyone knowing your wife had cheated on you with another woman. You may work in a high-end hotel, Lewis, but you're not cultured as a person. In some ways you're way behind the times. I'm not criticising you for the way you are, it takes all kinds of people to make the world interesting, but I think you killed all three of them in an attempt to hide what you believed was a dirty little secret. Kevin because you didn't trust him to keep his knowledge of the affair quiet, and Alice because she was the one who was sleeping with Sara.' Fiona aimed a hand in the general direction of the shelter. 'I bet up there in the snow with Steve a ready-made scapegoat, you thought it was all a brilliant idea. But then you still had to deal with Sara, didn't you? She was loyal at first, she covered for you. But you didn't know how long that would go on for, did you? Once you'd killed Alice, there was no going back. Sara would have to die too if you were to have any chance of escaping jail.

'It's over. Turn around, get on your knees and put your hands on your head. Lots of cops are on their way here and it'll go easier for you if you don't do anything stupid.'

'No.'

Without another word, Lewis was on the move. Fiona had half expected him to run away. He didn't turn away; instead he was coming straight for her. At pace.

FIFTY-SEVEN

As Lewis charged, Fiona was swinging her plan into action. The longer the conversation had gone on, and the more Lewis was getting irate, the more she'd allowed her jacket to slip from her shoulders and down her back.

Fiona knew that as a police officer her plan was all kinds of wrong, but this was shaping up to be a fight for her life and she was prepared to do whatever it took to survive. There could never be too much wrong in making sure you weren't killed.

Lewis was within five paces of Fiona when she used her right hand to grasp the inside of her jacket's sleeve as her left arm slid clear of it. Now the jacket was where Fiona wanted it, she yanked her arm forward and whirled it anti-clockwise above her head.

By the time the jacket had completed its first rotation Lewis had closed the distance to two paces, leaving Fiona just enough time to direct the jacket's arc downwards so it took a sideswipe at knee level. As Fiona planned, the jacket connected with Lewis's knee.

The material of the jacket had no weight to inflict enough of a blow that would slow or incapacitate Lewis, but the contents of its left pocket were different. It was in this pocket Fiona had stored her phone, and the rock that had been used to assault Kevin.

To use a murder weapon in an act of self-defence wasn't something that would play well with Fiona's bosses, but sometimes the needs of a situation far outweighed the morality of doing the right thing.

Lewis went down with a pained yelp; that would have been a good thing had his momentum not carried him into Fiona, his shoulder slamming into her hips and flattening her into the snow.

The landing was soft, but with her legs pinned beneath Lewis, Fiona had no chance of escaping him as he dragged himself up to a position above her body. The jacket was trapped between them, and Lewis used his good knee to pin Fiona's left arm.

Already injured, Fiona's left shoulder was aflame as she tried to wriggle her arm free, but on the whole she was glad it was that arm Lewis was focusing on as he wound up a punch.

Fiona used her right arm to deflect the first punch, but Lewis's second punch snapped her head to the side when his fist collided with her cheek.

Despite the explosion of fresh pain, Fiona never let her mind dull. She knew two or three more blows like that from Lewis would leave her unconscious, and then he'd either beat her to death, or wrap a hand over her throat and squeeze the life from her.

The next blow was a left hander that landed near Fiona's temple. Even as Lewis was pulling his arm back upwards to relaunch it while sending his right at her, Fiona's hand was snaking upwards. With her shoulders against the snowy ground, there was little chance of Fiona putting a lot of power behind her strike, but it wasn't power she was aiming for – it was accuracy.

Thanks to her police career, Fiona kept her fingernails short, as there were far too many ways to break a nail or snap a false one off. Even so, there was enough length about her nails for the finger she jabbed into Lewis's eye to cause him to rear back with an unholy scream of agony.

To lengthen her moment of advantage now Lewis's face was out of reach, Fiona dropped the hand and used her fingertips to apply a pincer grip on the knee she'd targeted with the contents of her jacket pocket. Dave Lennox had shown her a pressure point at the knee, and she'd made sure to locate it before exerting every muscle her hand possessed.

As Fiona planned, Lewis screamed again and rolled off her to escape the latest round of pain she was inflicting.

Fiona rolled onto her side and was in the process of rising to her feet when a boot slammed into her hip, toppling her onto her back. The next strike from Lewis's boot landed on her knee, and even though he was using his good leg to bear his weight, Lewis still managed to put plenty of force into his kick.

To escape his reach Fiona rolled over three times in quick succession, both her knee and shoulder protesting at the violent movements as she sought to evade his reach.

Lewis was hobbling after her, but Fiona had made sure to drag her jacket with her and, as she sat up, she once again whirled the jacket towards his knee.

Unlike the first time she'd swung the jacket, Lewis halted his advance. 'You're a right bitch, you.'

Fiona didn't respond. Rather than waste time on words, she was fighting to find a solution to this impasse. Both of them had an injured knee, but Lewis could stand on his. She didn't know if she could do the same. The improvised medieval mace of her jacket would keep Lewis from attacking her for the time being, but he'd know he'd have to get off Beinn Bhuidhe soon, and it made sense for him to make sure she couldn't follow him for round two before he left her.

Even as she was working this out, Lewis's foot was swiping arcs through the snow. Fiona couldn't wait until his foot found a rock or stone he could throw at her head, so she eased herself into a position where she could attempt to stand.

Once on her feet she'd be in a far better position to dodge anything he threw at her, and perhaps launch a counter-strike of her own.

Halfway to her feet, Fiona's injured knee gave out on her and she flumped back into the snow, the jacket still arcing above her body as she sought to deter another attack from Lewis.

As she forced herself back to a sitting position, Fiona saw Lewis looking at her with a smug grin.

'Looks like your knee's way worse than mine.'

He bent down and picked up a stone from under his boot. The stone was fist sized, but Fiona's fist rather than Lewis's. All the same, if thrown with the force a man as tall as Lewis could generate, it was more than big enough to concuss Fiona and leave her at his mercy. Or lack of.

'Thing is, I don't trust you not to be faking how bad your injury is. I've already shown you the way on that one, after all.'

Lewis's arm bent back, and in a blur pitched forward.

Fiona had expected the stone to be aimed at her head, but Lewis had selected another target.

The stone bounced off Fiona's leg, its lower portion colliding with her injured knee.

It took all of Fiona's self-control not to drop the jacket and clasp the knee in both hands.

'You swine. You're not going to get away with this. You're already going to do hard time for the three people you've killed. If you kill me, you'll end up doing twice as long.'

'I won't be doing any time. And I'm not going to kill you; although if I thought I was going to jail, I'm sure the notoriety of being a cop killer would mean I'd get an easy ride with the other inmates. Your knee's fucked now, isn't it? I'm going to leave.

When I get to the bottom I'll disappear. I know people who can help me do just that. Maybe you'll freeze to death before they find you, and maybe you won't. Doesn't matter, I'll be long gone by the time you can tell anyone anything, provided you're alive to do so, that is. Your friend was right when she said you're a shit cop. She was right when she said you'll never solve your parents' murder. After you knew Kevin had been murdered and hadn't fallen, I still managed to kill two people right under your nose. You're a failure as a cop, and as a daughter. You should be glad your parents are dead and not alive to witness your uselessness.'

It was all Fiona could do not to launch her improvised mace at the back of Lewis's head as he turned away and limped downhill.

FIFTY-EIGHT

Fiona's lip trembled as she watched Lewis hobble away. It wasn't from the pain she felt, nor from the fact he'd callously left her to die, but from what he'd said about her parents. Right now, in this specific moment in time, Fiona hated Lewis more than the killer who'd slaughtered her parents.

When Donna had criticised Fiona's skill as a detective, she'd done so out of fear for herself and her husband. Steve had echoed them in anger at the accusations she'd made against him, but Lewis had said what he said for no other reason than to wound, to torment.

The cruel words ate at Fiona, but until Lewis was a good hundred yards away she made no attempt to stand. Until she got into an upright position and put weight on the knee she wouldn't be able to assess the damage.

Fiona knew she had to harness the anger within her chest, but before she did anything, she had to give Lewis a chance to be far enough away she'd have time to prepare a defence should he turn and come back to finish her off.

Lewis turned twice to look back and then he was out of sight, hidden by the contours of the land. Fiona wasted no time in rolling onto her front and, from a push up position, using her injured leg as little as possible, worked herself upright.

Shards of molten lava lanced through her left knee when she put weight on it, but they cooled as she gritted her teeth against the pain. Step by ungainly step, Fiona set off after Lewis with a stream of vindictive mumbles pouring from her lips.

As she'd risen Fiona had made sure to keep hold of the jacket, and she shucked it back on as she hobbled along.

The one thing Fiona had going for her was Lewis was injured too. He would be making progress every bit as slow as she was. What he'd do when he looked back and saw she was back on his trail was unknown, but Fiona had her makeshift mace as a defence weapon plus Lewis would be wary of tackling her again after the way he'd not been able to kill her with ease.

Lewis would also be conscious of time. Not the numbers on a clock, but the time he had to get away from the head of Loch Fyne.

There were only two ways for Lewis to go once he got to his car. He could either take the A83 west towards Inveraray and Lochgilphead, or east towards Loch Lomond. Whichever way he went there were small roads he could turn onto and lose himself in the wilds, but these small roads were more than likely to be blocked by snow. As a local Lewis would know this, and therefore it would be imperative to him he got away before the police could be notified of his crimes, as he'd be sure to expect roadblocks to prevent him escaping.

If Fiona was just a couple of hundred yards behind Lewis when he drove off, she'd be able to go to Fyne Ales, the brewery near the mouth of the glen, and alert other officers, but while that would lead to Lewis's arrest, it wouldn't give her the satisfaction she craved. After what he'd done, what he'd tried to do to her, what he'd said to her, she wanted to be the one to capture him, to stop him from evading the justice that was his due.

As much as Fiona wanted to close the gap on Lewis and stop him, she was also wary about getting into another fight with him too far from help. It wasn't so much she was afraid for herself, more that she was smart enough to want the odds on her side. The perfect scenario would be to catch up with Lewis at the same time he reached his car. After the snowfall, he'd probably have to dig his vehicle out unless he had a four-wheel drive SUV or pickup.

Fiona's teeth chattered as she limped after Lewis. The ducking in the burn had soaked her lower half and the icy wind was chilling her skin through the fabric of her clothes, but the cold wasn't a worry to her. The effort of pursuing Lewis was generating heat and, while the cold added an extra level of discomfort, it was the injury to her knee that concerned Fiona the most.

Due to the way she was limping, Fiona wasn't catching up with Lewis, and while the pain had subsided a little when she'd first set off, it had now returned with an unholy vengeance. Although the pain from her knee had a position of unassailable domination, Fiona knew her shoulder wasn't in a good way, and she could feel her right eye swelling itself shut.

First though, she had to close the gap between her and Lewis, but not so much he felt the need to turn back and confront her again.

By now they were both on the floor of the glen and while the going was easier on the more level fields, there were snow-drifts, walls and fences to contend with. The snow drifts could be dodged round or waded through, but the effort involved in clambering over the walls or climbing the fences sapped Fiona's fast disappearing reserves.

Ahead of her, Fiona saw Lewis reach an old footbridge over the River Fyne. He was maybe a hundred and fifty yards ahead.

Lewis raised a hand and gave what looked to be a cheery wave as he set off across the bridge.

FIFTY-NINE

The foot bridge was a game-changer for Fiona. Where she'd expected to have another half mile of pursuit to close the distance between her and Lewis, the bridge changed everything. She'd clocked the bridge on her way up the glen. Dilapidated and bearing a notice of condemnation from some authority or other, either side had been sealed with metal gates that were padlocked. The gates would prevent the average walker from using the bridge, but to a man desperate to flee from the police, they'd be a minor obstacle.

If Lewis could scale the gates, Fiona knew she could too. It was what they'd encounter at the other end of the bridge that raised concern. A hundred yards from the other side of the bridge was a small farm. After the murder of her parents, Fiona had spent her latter teen years with her Aunt Mary in a glen every bit as secluded as this one. Farmers were far from the most security conscious people. They left keys in the ignitions of their tractors, jeeps and quad bikes. For a desperate man like Lewis, there would be no reason not to steal a vehicle that would either get him to his car quicker, or act as a substitute for his getaway.

With time suddenly a far greater issue, Fiona dug in and forced herself to hobble forward as fast as she could. From hip to toes, her left leg was a turbulent sea of agonies as every movement brought crashing waves of torment. On and on she went, her eyes flicking between the terrain a few feet in front of her and the figure crossing the bridge.

As much as she willed the ancient bridge to delay Lewis, Fiona could see he was making steady, if slow, progress across the aged structure. Any delay he faced, she would too, and it was clear he was aware of this when he stopped in the centre of the bridge and turned her way.

Fiona's heart ran cold; the narrow bridge wasn't wide enough for her to use her jacket as a mace again. If Lewis was planning another showdown, he'd picked the perfect spot.

When Fiona saw Lewis stamping down and the timbers of the bridge decking fall towards the River Fyne she realised what he was doing.

On and on Lewis stamped as he moved his way to the far bank. By the time Fiona reached the bridge's gate, Lewis had knocked out several more pieces of bridge decking with his stamping, and had thrown another cheery wave in her direction.

The metal gate would have offered Fiona little challenge had she not been in such agony from her injured knee, but today it was a major obstacle. The one bonus she could take from the laborious climb up and over the gate was Lewis was in every bit as poor a condition as she was.

Lewis limped across the last timbers of decking ahead of her, but even if Fiona had been fully fit, the section of decking he'd knocked loose and the bridge's fragile condition would have made it impossible for her to sprint across and confront him.

Fiona set foot onto the timbers with care. They might have supported Lewis's greater weight, but that didn't mean she was going to trust them. Her right hand was gripping the railing and, as cold as it was, it felt good to Fiona to have something to cling to should the timbers give way.

As much as Fiona daren't take her eyes off where she was stepping, she couldn't resist taking occasional glances ahead of her. Lewis was six feet from the far side when the timber decking he was standing on gave way beneath him.

Lewis dropped, but the paunch he carried was too great for him to pass through the gap and for a couple of seconds he was wedged between the timbers of the decking, before his efforts to save himself and his weight combined to suck him down through the hole he'd created.

Fiona would have cheered in delight at Lewis's misfortune had she not just reached the section of the bridge where he'd stomped the decking away. The knowledge she might also suffer the same fate and drop into the icy waters of the River Fyne wasn't far from Fiona's mind as with both hands she gripped the wire rope that doubled as support for the bridge decking and a handrail, and slid her injured left leg onto the girder the bridge decking had rested on.

To achieve the necessary sideways motion Fiona slid one foot at a time and then repeated the process with her hands before starting over again. The old climber's maxim of always having three points of contact was at the forefront of her mind as she crossed the six-foot section of missing decking.

Such was Fiona's concentration on getting to the other side of the chasm Lewis had created, not once did she look to see where he was, or if he'd fallen beneath the surface of the water.

Her first thought when she got across to the other side was relief. Her second, Lewis's whereabouts. She looked ahead of her as she crossed to where he'd fallen through and saw Lewis clambering up the slope. He wasn't dripping water which told her he'd landed on the far bank rather than in the river itself, but from the way his limp was much more pronounced, it was obvious he'd hurt himself further.

'Good.'

Instead of dropping through the hole Lewis had, Fiona skirted it and steeled herself for the climb over the gate. At this, more accessible, side someone had taken the extra precaution of wrapping a couple of strings of barbed wire across the top of the gate, but with all her other agonies to contend with, the prospect of a few scratches didn't worry Fiona enough she planned to find another route.

Lewis had now crested the bank and was heading towards the farm at a slow but steady hobble. Unless he was again faking the injury, Fiona judged she had time to scale her way up the gate and down the other side before he could return and attack her.

Fiona got over the gate without incident beyond a few scrapes from the barbed wire and immediately looked ahead of her. Lewis was now just fifty yards from the farm, and forty from the aged farmer who stood with a shepherd's crook in one hand, and a shotgun slung over the crook of his elbow.

The shotgun was what Dave Lennox referred to as a farmer's special: a twelve bore with side-by-side barrels and triggers for each inside the trigger guard.

SIXTY

The shotgun held by the farmer was broken open, and while the man looked too frail to withstand the kickback of the weapon, Fiona didn't doubt he'd know how to use it.

What happened when Lewis got closer to him was another matter. Ahead of her she could hear Lewis's voice and she could see the farmer's mouth opening and closing as he replied, but she couldn't make out what either was saying with any degree of clarity.

When Lewis's arm pointed back at her and when the farmer turned her way, dropped the stick and used both hands to snap the shotgun together, Fiona knew Lewis had spun the old man a lie.

Fiona kept going, but when she got to within twenty yards of the farmer he lifted the shotgun to his shoulder and aimed it her way. 'You just bide where you are. I've heard you killed three people up there. It's the jail for you, lassie.'

Now two yards away from the farmer, Lewis turned and looked at Fiona with triumph in his eyes.

'Look out!' Even as she yelled the warning, Fiona let herself drop to the snowy ground lest the farmer pull the trigger.

Not hearing the blast of a shotgun, Fiona rotated her head so she could see Lewis and the farmer. Lewis had grabbed the barrel of the shotgun and held it where the farmer couldn't aim it his way. No matter how much wiry strength the farmer might possess, Lewis was taller, younger and heavier than him and as they grappled over the weapon, their bodies drew closer together.

Even as she was scrabbling to her feet, Fiona could see Lewis's back arching and knew what was coming. The farmer's knees buckled at the impact of the headbutt and he fell to the ground, leaving Lewis holding the shotgun.

Fiona was on her feet, but she was unable to move in any direction. As well as the fear coursing through her body, there was helplessness and a cold fury it had come to this. She was in no condition to run the five yards across to the wall on her left and dive behind it for cover. Nor was she close enough she might get to Lewis before he could train the weapon on her. This was it. The end of her time on earth. If she'd had faith, she might have believed she'd be reunited with her parents, but Fiona couldn't accept the existence of a deity who'd be so cruel as to snatch both parents away from their child.

More than anything, as she stood waiting for the inevitable, regret was the emotion coursing through Fiona. She'd never identified the person who killed her parents. Never told anyone except Aunt Mary that she loved them. Never heard anyone but her parents and Aunt Mary say it to her. She'd lived a life defined by murder, and now it would end that way. So many of the chapters she could have written on the pages of her life had never been started, much less brought to a finale. There were so many things she'd wanted to do and hadn't found the time. Instead of lying in an untidy heap on the couch with a remote control and bowl of crisps resting on her belly, she could have learned another language, taught herself to cook meals that didn't come in a tin or a microwavable dish, or a million other things.

'Not going to run? I'd ask if you wanted to beg for your life, but we both know what the answer would be so I'll save you the bother.' The mockery in Lewis's voice was clearer than his intent as he shouldered the shotgun. 'I'd ask if you had any last words, but I don't care.'

Fiona could see Lewis's index finger slide inside the trigger guard. This was it. In a second or two he'd pull the trigger. The gun would explode and she'd die. The urge to run was huge, but Fiona knew all hopes of escape were a falsehood, a mirage that flickered in the distance only to remain out of reach no matter how much you travelled towards it. There was only one thing Fiona could do, so she did it as Lewis's finger curled around the trigger.

Lewis's eyes were full of gleeful menace as he looked down the shotgun's sights at her, but terrified as she was, Fiona held his stare. She didn't cry, she'd didn't beg for her life and nor would she. The war had been lost, she'd die. Fiona was positive that's what would happen, so the only victory she had left was to not show any fear, to stand tall and not cower before him. After her death, wherever Lewis ended up, be that in his planned new life or a jail cell, she wanted him to be haunted by the victim he couldn't scare.

Fiona's mouth was parchment dry when she opened it to speak. 'Hey, dickhead, if you're going to shoot, shoot. If not, you're under arrest for three murders.'

Fiona saw a flash of fury in Lewis's eyes and then his index finger whitened as he depressed both of the shotgun's triggers.

SIXTY-ONE

Nothing happened. Lewis tried again, his eyes tar pits of impotent fury when the repeated action returned the same lack of results.

Whether it was a safety catch he hadn't released or the gun wasn't loaded wasn't something Fiona had time to consider. She had a second or two, three at the most, before Lewis figured out how to fire the gun or that he could use it as a club to beat her to death with.

Fiona's injured knee protested with lava spikes and threatened to collapse beneath her as she charged. Behind Lewis she could see the farmer levering himself to his feet with blood pouring from a shattered nose.

Lewis was trying the shotgun's various levers and it was clear to Fiona he was trying to locate a safety catch. Just as she reached him and launched herself into a headlong dive at his midriff, the gun hinged open, its barrels rotating out of line from the stock into the position the farmer had it when carrying the weapon.

Fiona digested this in a flash as she thumped into Lewis, driving him backwards and off his feet. Before Lewis could mount any kind of defence, Fiona was thrusting a palm strike at his nose.

The palm strike landed but had little effect. And then Lewis crashed the shotgun into the back of Fiona's head. With a hand clutching the shotgun either side of her head, Lewis kept butting the weapon into Fiona's skull.

There was only so much of this Fiona could take without succumbing to either a single blow or the cumulative effect of repeated assaults and she knew it, so with gritted teeth she lifted her hips by resting both knees on the ground and snaked a hand downwards.

When Fiona had a grip of Lewis's crotch she twisted and pulled at the sensitive organs until Lewis gave up trying to use the shotgun as a club and thrust his head up at her.

Fiona was ready for the move and ducked her head down until her chin rested on her chest as Lewis's head slammed forward. Instead of him shattering her nose with his forehead, hers collided with Lewis's nose.

With his tactic proving fruitless Lewis released his grip on the shotgun's barrel and tried to shove Fiona off him.

Fiona had been waiting for this moment and with a farewell twist of Lewis's crotch she rolled off him, making sure to trap the shotgun beneath her body so it couldn't be used by Lewis. Even before the roll was complete, Fiona's left elbow was arcing away from her body and into Lewis's face. As the elbow landed Fiona hoped it hurt him more than it did her.

Not wanting to wait and see how effective the elbow had been, Fiona wasted no time in following it up with a pair of right-handed palm strikes aimed at Lewis's chin.

The second palm strike was overkill as her first caught him with enough power to send a mistiness to his eyes.

With Lewis stunned even if for a moment, Fiona used the time she had to roll clear of him and wrench the shotgun from his grasp. As a precaution against there being an accident she checked the exposed tops of the barrels ready to pluck the cartridges out.

Both barrels were empty. Those hour-long seconds when she'd been waiting, terrified, for Lewis to end her life were among the worst Fiona had ever endured, and they'd been for nothing.

Now she knew the shotgun wasn't loaded, Fiona teased it closed and prepared to club Lewis if he showed any signs of resistance or escape. For a brief second she let her eyes leave Lewis's prone figure and locate the farmer. He was ten feet away, his stick back in his hand and a look of amazement on his bloodied face.

'I saw how you faced him doon. Did you ken it wisnae loaded?'

'No.' Fiona aimed an arm back towards the farm. 'I'm an officer for Police Scotland, have you a phone and some rope up there?'

'Aye. I'll phone the polis for you and bring the rope.'

'We'll need the Mountain Rescue as well. There are people trapped in the shelter and his three victims' bodies to bring down. Make sure you mention the bodies.'

Whomever took the farmer's call would know to send a forensic team as soon as they learned of the bodies. The skin under Sara's nails would implicate Lewis in at least one murder, and after that it shouldn't be too hard to build a case against him for each of the others.

The farmer looked Fiona up and down. 'You might be a lassie, but you've one hell of a pair of balls on you.'

As the farmer strode away Fiona let his comment wash over her. She took it for the compliment he intended, and started to shift her focus onto what would come next.

With the farmer's help she'd tie Lewis up and they'd get him to somewhere he could be held safely until cops arrived. The rescue of the others could be handed over to the Mountain Rescue team who were specialists at such things.

The cops would bring medical care with them, and hours upon hours' worth of questions. After that Fiona would be allowed to return home to rest. Except she wouldn't get much rest, not with tomorrow's dreaded appointments hanging over her. In the condition she was in, there was nobody she could think of who'd criticise her for rescheduling.

The way Fiona saw it, if she was able to survive the two encounters with Lewis, she'd be able to face the appointments, painful as they may be.

SIXTY-TWO

ONE WEEK LATER

A small town like Lochgilphead was lucky to have a restaurant at all. That the restaurant was Marco's, was the culinary equivalent of a winning lottery ticket. There were also hotels and pubs that served food, and considering the size of the population, there was a definite over-provision when it came to places to eat out, but that didn't ensure the quality of their offering.

Marco's was Italian at heart and Scottish by birth. Marco himself was a rotund man with an infectious smile and more bonhomie than any one person deserved. He spoke Italian with a Scottish accent and vice versa. Diners at Marco's weren't just made to feel welcome, they were treated like long-lost family members.

Fiona had planned this evening with care. After the events on Beinn Bhuidhe she'd attended her appointments, survived the ordeal, and found perspective on Donna's harsh words, although she knew their relationship may never regain its former closeness.

At Fiona's left as she hobbled into Marco's was her rock, the indomitable Aunt Mary. Nothing life threw at Aunt Mary could ever phase her, she just took things in her stride and steamrollered events through sheer force of personality.

On Fiona's other flank was Heather Andrews. Sharper than any surgeon's blade, it had been Heather's brain Fiona had picked night after night as she developed her detecting skills in the eternal quest to identify her parents' killer.

Fiona's smile was genuine when she saw the two men waiting for them at the bar. She was in the act of waving to them when a large man stepped in front of her.

'Miss Fiona, you've once again graced my humble abode with your heroic presence. I would say I'm honoured, but honoured is too small a word to use in the face of your achievements.' Marco's eyes caught sight of Heather and then flicked to Aunt Mary. 'While it is always a pleasure to see the lovely Miss Heather, you must, and I insist it is a *must*, tell me who this delightful lady is. Were I twenty years younger and some stones lighter, then I would pursue her to the ends of the earth for just one kiss on the cheek from her.'

'This is my Aunt Mary.' A streak of devilment crept onto Fiona's shoulder and whispered in her ear. 'I must warn you, she blushes like a beacon when she's embarrassed, and she embarrasses easily.'

'Tish and tosh, Miss Fiona. Signora Mary has a captivatingly classic beauty and timeless grace no woman should ever feel embarrassment for. Now if you'll follow me, I'll show you to your table and arrange for a wine so crisp you could snap it.'

Fiona nudged Aunt Mary's elbow. 'I think he's smitten.'

'Give over with you and your nonsense.' Aunt Mary's eyes sparkled. 'Signora means madam. He called you two miss. Do you know what that means?'

'That he's showing you more respect than us.'

'No. It means he sees me as old.' Aunt Mary could only hold a stern expression for a couple of seconds before creasing with laughter.

The two men from the bar walked over. Both tall and burly, Lennox with greying hair and Edwin with long white. They were the two men Fiona held dearest. She made the introductions and hammed it up about Edwin Hamilton having saved a life while on Luing earlier in the year. Poor of education, but strong of decency Edwin was a kind-hearted soul who'd never really outgrown childhood.

'And ladies, I'm sure I've bored you both many a time with tales of my grumpy-arsed sergeant, Dave Lennox; well it's time to finally meet him in the flesh. Sadly, I must warn you that while a fountain of worldly wisdom, Lennox – and that's the only way he likes to be addressed – knows far too many Chuck Norris jokes, and if left unsupervised, will turn the conversation to *Star Wars* in a heartbeat, so consider yourselves warned.'

Lennox held his hands wide. 'What can I say after an intro like that, except she's a liar? By the way, did you know Chuck Norris can dig a hole in water?'

The next three hours passed in a blur of laughter and stories interspersed by Marco's shameless flirting with Aunt Mary. Edwin's simplistic outlook on life was a perfect counter for Lennox's weary cynicism, but they were both content chatting about *Star Wars*, and when Fiona heard the words 'Chuck Norris' and 'roundhouse kick' in close succession from Lennox, she knew it was time to explain why she'd invited them all to dinner. To get their attention she clinked a spoon against her wine glass.

'Listen up a minute, everyone. As much as I have loved this evening, I invited you all together for a reason. I have a few pieces of news to share with you. First, I heard from Steve today. Inveraray House will reopen next week. He's got agency chefs in to run the kitchen and has lured Neil to manage the front of house for him. Kevin's funeral is next week and I'll be attending. When questioned, Lewis realised the evidence against him was overwhelming and confessed to all three murders, and the assaults on me.'

'I can't believe you worked out his wife was sleeping with the woman he killed. That's some connection to make.'

'Thanks, Heather. Anyway, everyone who was left up there got down safely in the end thanks to a Mountain Rescue helicopter.'

'You didn't invite us here to tell us that, Fifi. Get to the meat of the sandwich.'

Fiona smiled at Lennox; he was the only person she allowed to call her Fifi. 'You're right, I did have another reason, but before I tell you what it is, I've spoken with Marco about this, and none of your money is any good here tonight, because you're here to help me celebrate two things. Three if you count what happened on Beinn Bhuidhe. First off, I had a couple of appointments in Glasgow last week.' Fiona took a breath to steady herself. From nowhere, nerves had crept throughout her body and were putting a tremble into her limbs and voice. 'I got the results two days ago. The first appointment was a detective's exam. I passed it.'

All four of them started clapping and cheering her news, but for Fiona, the way Aunt Mary's eyes shone with a bright-ness far greater than any of Marco's comments had elicited meant everything.

'I'm so proud of you, Fiona. Your mum and dad would have been too.'

The words from Aunt Mary sprung tears to Fiona's eyes, but she refused to shed them, even if they were happy tears.

'Does this mean you'll be coming to work with me as a DC?'

Fiona steeled herself. 'That's actually the second piece of news I have to share, Heather. Once I'd taken the detective's exam, I took the sergeant's one as well. I passed it too. DI Baird has agreed to let me join your team.' Tears rolled down Aunt Mary's cheeks at this news, but Fiona could sense a falseness to

Heather's smile. It was one thing for her to join Heather as an equal, another to leapfrog her on the promotion ladder. 'Don't worry, Heather. I'll only be your sergeant in name.'

'Of course you won't. You're too smart for that. You'll be Chief Constable before we know it.'

Heather's brave face didn't fool Fiona, but she'd deal with rivalries another time. Right now she had Lennox standing beside her, his right hand extended and waiting. Behind him Edwin had also risen and was clapping his great hands together as he whooped. Aunt Mary was making no attempt to wipe the rivers of tears from her cheeks.

Marco appeared with another bottle of wine, and a J20 for Edwin, and the evening fell back into groaning at Chuck Norris jokes and laughing at the various tales Fiona had heard her guests tell before.

With Heather's good mood returning, Fiona counted the evening as a success, but she knew the promotion to detective was nothing more than a stepping stone for her. Once she had a few months' experience under her belt, she'd begin to properly work the one and only case that truly mattered to her. The murder of her parents. Theirs was a killer she could not allow to go unpunished.

A LETTER FROM G.N. SMITH

Thank you, dear reader, for getting this far. It means the world to me that you've stuck with the characters and story and seen it through to its conclusion. When I sat down to begin writing *The Shelter*, I had already created an outline of the story that had been approved by my editor.

That outline bears no resemblance to the final novel as once I'd got about ten per cent of the way into the story, things changed. Certain characters took more of a central role and the more and more I wrote, the further I was from my outline. By the time I hit a quarter of the way into the story, the outline was nothing more than a distant memory.

By abandoning my outline I was able to listen to the characters, Fiona especially, as she probed at her various lines of enquiry. Few of them panned out, but for me it was tremendous fun following her thought processes and then finding a way to prove or disprove each new idea she had. Locked room mysteries are a huge part of crime fiction, and I do hope you enjoyed the puzzle Fiona had to solve.

For the setting I used the magnificent Munro that is Beinn Bhuidhe and added a couple of authorial embellishments. To my knowledge there is no shelter on Beinn Bhuidhe, but I needed a 'safe haven' for the characters and somewhere they could congregate together. The shelter also gave me somewhere for Fiona to conduct the murder investigation. The old footbridge over the River Fyne is also fictitious, but I feel it added a vital edge to Fiona's pursuit of the killer. What wasn't made up was the Fyne Ales Brewery, which sits exactly where I said it is. There may be a vicious rumour circulating that it distracted me on my research trip. Don't believe that rumour, as it is not entirely false. What happened is I researched Beinn Bhuidhe first, and then got distracted as a newt. Which is kinda like my going off-piste with the outline, so I'm counting it as a successful research trip.

The more time I'm spending in Fiona's company, the more I'm discovering about her. She's a complex character and has way more than her fair share of demons, but she's a good person at heart, even if her role as a police officer, and my own influence on her, are giving her an ever more cynical and world-weary outlook. Her future holds light and shade, joy and misery, and I can't wait to see how she deals with it all.

I have many ideas for future cases to test Fiona, and I do hope my wonderful readers will follow Fiona through whatever I throw at her. Without readers I'm nothing more than a stenographer for the voices in my head.

www.grahamsmithauthor.co.uk

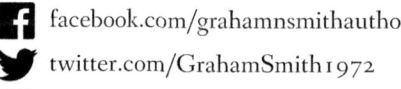 facebook.com/grahamnsmithauthor
twitter.com/GrahamSmith1972
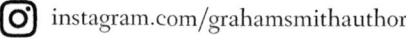 instagram.com/grahamsmithauthor

ACKNOWLEDGEMENTS

My first round of thanks goes to the most important people in this book's journey; the readers. Without readers, this story would never have been written. Or published. Nor would it have been given a classy cover, and it certainly wouldn't have been sent out into the wild to fend for itself. So thank you dear reader, your part in this story is as important as my own.

My friends and family have all been incredibly supportive of my writing and it is with humble gratitude that I thank them for leaving me in peace so I can write.

The crime writing community as a whole is a wonderful environment which supports, cajoles and champions authors of all stature. My Crime and Publishment gang are some of the finest examples of this trait and I thank the whole community, but especially the C&P lot.

The team at my publisher all deserve a huge thank you. From my editor Harriet Wade, who has to put up with the stupidest of ideas, and a lot of snarky comments from me, to the marketing and publicity teams, the guys in the back who do all manner of unseen, but vital, work in making my inane scribblings legible, marketing, and a whole host of other tasks that bring a book from my head to your hands. They're all stars, each and every one of them.

And finally, a wee shout out to Isobel Akenhead whose comment of 'put book three up a mountain in a snowstorm' really zeroed in on what the entire novel should be about.

Printed in Great Britain
by Amazon